Sweet T

She pointed a finger at him. "You'_ too_
charming for your own good."

"First, you said I was hot. Now you're
calling me charming. Are you sure *you're* not
the one trying to influence *me*?"

Her bark of genuine amusement warmed
him, and continued to thaw her, her posture
relaxing, her face open, her grin wide. He'd
been attracted to her from the moment he
laid eyes on her, but damn . . . she'd never
looked more beautiful.

She shoved his shoulder. "You wish."

He grabbed her retreating hand. "Yeah,
I do."

He stroked his thumb across her palm
and her eyes widened. So did his.

What was he doing?

This was a bad idea. He was tempting
fate. But on that quiet street, standing on the
porch, with the air and fall scents swirling
around them, they could've been the only
two people in the world. He felt like he was
back in high school, dropping his date off,
wondering if he dared try for a kiss.

He dared.

Also by Tracey Livesay

Sweet Talkin' Lover

A Girls Trip Novel

Tracey Livesay

AVONBOOKS

An Imprint of HarperCollins*Publishers*

SWEET TALKIN' LOVER. Copyright © 2020 by Tracey Livesay. All rights reserved. Printed in the United States of America. No part of this book may be used or reproduced in any manner whatsoever without written permission except in the case of brief quotations embodied in critical articles and reviews. For information, address HarperCollins Publishers, 195 Broadway, New York, NY 10007.

First Avon Books mass market printing: January 2020

Print Edition ISBN: 978-0-06-297954-4
Digital Edition ISBN: 978-0-06-297955-1

Cover design by Guido Caroti
Cover illustration by Reginald Polynice
Cover photographs © Alextov/iStock/Getty Images; © Dean_Fikar/iStock/Getty Images; © Shutterstock

Avon, Avon & logo, and Avon Books & logo are registered trademarks of HarperCollins Publishers in the United States of America and other countries.

HarperCollins is a registered trademark of HarperCollins Publishers in the United States of America and other countries.

FIRST EDITION

20 21 22 23 24   QGM   10 9 8 7 6 5 4 3 2 1

Acknowledgments

In my first year of college, I met four women who would change my life. Our friendship—the love, laughs, and loyalty—form the basis of this series. I've swapped, merged, and reshaped everything to protect the guilty (*wink*), but the bonding, affection, and major fun will still come through. I hope you enjoy *Sweet Talkin' Lover* and consider yourselves an honorary member of the #LadiesofLefevre as you follow the escapades of Caila, Nic, Lacey, and Ava.

And now, as the saying goes, it takes a village . . .

To my husband James, I say it every time, and it only grows truer: I adore you. You're my favorite person in the world and the best man I've ever known.

To my children, Trey, Graysie, and Will, I love being your mom. You're smart, funny, creative, and so damn amazing. I can't believe I birthed you, but I'm grateful that I did.

To Nalini Akolekar, agent extraordinaire, I appreciate your steady guidance, support, and advice. I'm so lucky that I get to go on this journey with you by my side.

To my editor, Tessa Woodward, thank you for advocating for me and for using your magic to always make my story better.

To the team at Avon publishing: Elle, Michelle, Kayleigh, Pam, Angela, Ellie, Guido (who designed my gorgeous cover), and everyone else who worked on this book. Thank you for your time and expertise and for helping me share my dream with readers.

To the talented, funny, and wise Mia Sosa, my Soul Train dance line partner. Thank you for your friendship, your advice, for talking me off the ledge more times than I can count, and for keeping me accountable and semi-sane.

To the #Thermostat crew, Mia, Tif Marcelo, Pris Oliveras, Nina Crespo, and Michelle Arris, you ladies inspire me. Thank you for being "open" travelers with me on this journey called Publishing.

To Alleyne Dickens, thank you for your friendship and honest critiques, even when the turnaround for said critique was brief and the request was a little manic.

To the LaLas, Sharon McGowan, Ashley Motley, Petra Spaulding, Leigh Florio, Chrissy Kuney, and Annette Carillo: We're not running as much these days, but our friendship is as enduring as our last marathon. (Which means forever!)

To Ann Rezelman, who, in October of 2017, told me an awesome line about two hands that I knew I had to use in my next story.

And finally, to my readers. In today's market, you have an infinite number of choices. Your continued support means the world to me. You guys are literally making my dreams come true.

Until the next one,

TL

Sweet Talkin' Lover

Chapter One

*M*istakes happen. You're lucky nothing leaves this department without my final once-over and approval. But there are no third chances. Fix it and have the revised version in my inbox by eight a.m."

Caila Harris ended the call and immediately made a note in her digital agenda to check for the report at 8:02 the following morning. What was that saying? If you wanted something done right, you had to do it yourself? She should get the words tattooed on her inner arm. A reminder that when all was said and done, relying on others was the surest path to disappointment. She couldn't afford to let a screwup, especially one not of her own making, mar her performance record in the eyes of the partners. Not when she was so close to getting everything she'd ever wanted. With one final tap on the screen, Caila glanced up and found three pairs of eyes focused on her.

"What?" Caila closed the cover of her iPad and opened her laptop.

"That's the third call you've taken in the past half hour," Ava Taylor said, stirring the mouth-watering lemon caper sauce.

Caila dragged a finger over the mouse pad and scrolled the list of files on her screen. She'd told her assistant to transfer the PowerPoint of the new digital marketing campaign for their anti-aging under-eye serum to her computer. Where did she put it? "It was work."

"So you're the only one with a demanding life?" Nicole Allen asked, pausing in the act of slicing cucumbers and gesturing with the blade. "I put off patients, Ava found another judge to temporarily take over her docket—"

"And I'm missing several performances," Lacey Scott added, gliding up behind Nic and removing the knife from her clenched fingers. "I'll just take this."

Caila rolled her eyes and continued searching for the file. "It was important."

Caila was a regional marketing manager at Endurance, the fastest growing manufacturer and marketer of organic skin care, cosmetics, hair care, and fragrance in the United States. Due to the success of her last assignment, her boss had suggested the possibility of entrusting her with the national rollout of the company's newest product.

She had to take those calls. This went beyond one employee's mistake in one report. Her entire future was on the line.

Ava snapped her fingers. "Hey!"

Startled, Caila jerked and shot a glance at her usually even-keeled best friend.

"Our careers mean just as much to us as yours does to you. But we shifted our schedules and pushed vital issues aside because we all agreed to make these days we spend together a priority."

Heat flushed Caila's body at Ava's censorious tone. The other woman was right.

The four of them had met their first year of college at the University of Virginia, when they'd all gathered at the same time in the dorm's TV lounge to watch *Oprah*. They'd become best friends—remained that way throughout all four years—and despite the exciting lives and successful careers that followed, they still managed to get together for one week every year. What began as a spur-of-the-moment invitation to join Caila on a work trip the year after they'd graduated had turned into cherished time they never missed. If a particular date didn't work for someone, they rescheduled. No one had to ask. These women were her sisters more than the two who shared her blood. They understood her in a way no one else did.

"I know, I know, but a national rollout is huge! The partners only assign them to senior marketing personnel, and I'm only a regional manager. But since our director of marketing for cosmetics recently left for one of our rivals, and if Kendra is considering me for the project . . ."

The conclusion was as obvious to her now as it had been when her boss first mentioned it. A promotion was in the offing.

One she deserved.

There was no way Caila could entrust her work to a coworker now. Would a coworker have caught the mistake in that report? Was she willing to take that risk?

"This promotion is the reward for all of my hard work."

"Didn't you say that after your last promotion to your current position?" Lacey arched a delicate brow while pouring a crisp sauvignon blanc into four stemless wineglasses.

So? It was still true. Caila motioned with a dismissive wave. "That was two years ago."

No one climbing the corporate ladder stopped mid-rung of his or her own accord. The goal was to reach the top. With this promotion she'd be one rung from the C-suite. Successful enough to be in control of her destiny, where the whims of others couldn't affect her life.

Caila narrowed her eyes. "Why are you guys acting like I'm the only ambitious one in this group?"

"We're not," Ava said, removing the large pan from the burner. "But it's the one night of vacay where we stay in, gorge ourselves on food and wine, and reminisce. And you're missing it all because of that phone fused to your hand."

Fine. She'd give them a few hours. Then she'd return calls and emails later tonight when the others went to bed.

"You win. I'll put my work away." Her phone rang and she looked at the display. "*After* this call."

She ignored the chorus of groans and a lone "You are so trifling" as she rose from the table and headed into the great room. A minute later, she ended the call, but instead of immediately returning to the others, she stood peering out of the sliding glass patio doors that extended the length of the far wall.

During the day the oceanfront view was stunning, with its cloudless blue Caribbean sky, idyllic rays of summer sun, and the foaming spray of ocean waves crashing upon the sand. But now that it was dark, all she could see was the sophisticated interior of their private luxurious villa reflected back at her, the nautical color scheme that brought their surroundings inside, the high rattan ceilings framed with dark wooden beams.

Caila leaned her forehead against the cool glass. She hated the idea that her preoccupation might be ruining their vacation. She valued her time with these women, looked forward to it with an eagerness rivaled only by children on Christmas morning.

But her friends hadn't been there when she was growing up. Her life had been perfect. She'd had friends, played sports, and been ranked as a top student to watch in the city. Because of her outstanding academic achievement, when she was thirteen, she'd been granted a scholarship to attend a prestigious prep school starting the following year. Her father had been overjoyed, but one month before she was to begin, he passed away.

She'd been devastated. Doubly so when her grandfather had come to their house in Baltimore and insisted that she, her mother, and her two sisters move to the small town in rural Maryland where he lived, claiming he was fulfilling a promise to his deceased son.

"Your father always told me if something happened to him, I needed to take care of his girls."

No one had asked Caila's opinion. They hadn't looked at options, like allowing her to stay with other relatives. In one fell swoop she'd lost it all: her father, the prep school, and her emotional stability.

Her mother had loved ceding control to a man. As did her sisters, who couldn't understand Caila's anger at the change. Pop-Pop somehow sensed Caila wasn't like her mother and sisters.

Rightly so.

She exhaled. She couldn't change her past, but she could focus on making sure history didn't repeat itself. When she returned to the kitchen, Nic was moving Caila's iPad to the counter and Ava was placing a steaming platter of chicken piccata in the middle of the table while Lacey handed out drinks.

"Are you done?" Ava asked.

"You'd better be," Nic said, a twist to her lips and a bowl of salad in her hands. A real-life version of a vintage housewife meme. "If you take another call tonight I'm going to toss that fucking phone into the ocean."

Lacey's exaggerated sigh seemed to spring from her soul. "Why don't you try not being a bitch for once, Nic?"

Nic shrugged a bare shoulder. "I did. It didn't take."

Ava sat down and placed a cloth napkin in her lap. "This promotion won't do anything for your love life. I can't imagine your mother was happy to hear about it, but Pop-Pop'll probably take out an ad in the local newspaper."

Caila's throat thickened at hearing the name she used for her beloved grandfather. She hadn't spoken to him in months, not since the argument they'd had when she'd missed her younger sister's baby shower because of a work trip. She was used to long periods of separation from her mother and sisters, but Pop-Pop . . . She absently rubbed at the spot over her heart. The estrangement was killing her, but she had a plan. Once she got the promotion, she'd head back to Maryland for a few days and surprise him.

"I haven't told them yet. Julie is still pissed about the shower. But, come on, it was her second one. In three years."

"But you're her sister," Ava said.

"She didn't need me there. She had her suburban mom squad. And I sent a gift!" But that hadn't been enough. "She called me 'frigid.' Said if I didn't hurry up and get married, I'd 'end up bitter, frustrated, and alone.'"

Nic's green eyes widened. "Damn!"

Caila hadn't been surprised by the sentiment. Both of her sisters had married young and their spouses were nice, if you liked the I'm-the-man-I'm-the-provider-I'll-take-care-of-you type.

Which Caila did not.

"You're always shading them for their choices," Lacey said, "but they seem happy. Maybe they just want the same for you."

"Being married isn't the sole destination of a woman's path to happiness," Caila said, her molars reuniting the way they did whenever this topic came up. She spooned some chicken onto her plate.

"Did you read that on a pillow?" Nic asked.

"No, smart ass . . . a calendar."

"It may not be the only one," Lacey agreed, a loopy grin illuminating her delicate features, "but you have to admit it would be nice."

Caila pursed her lips. She didn't *have* to do anything except stay black and die. "If married life is so great, why don't they focus on it and stop worrying about my social life."

"Or lack thereof . . ." Ava muttered.

Caila raised a sculpted brow. "*Et tu*, Ava?"

"C'mon, leave her alone."

"Thank you, Lacey," Caila said, reaching over to affectionately squeeze the other woman's arm.

Ava, Caila's mom, and Caila's two sisters all observed the same philosophy: Get Caila laid and mated, though her mother would gasp at the crude phrasing. But while their wording might differ, they employed similar methodology. If Ava wasn't sending Caila screenshots of eligible men from the various dating apps she subscribed to, her family was "casually" texting her about random Jims, Joes, and Bobs she went to high school with whom they ran into at the store. They were obsessed with her dating life.

They couldn't seem to grasp that she was content. Adding a man into the equation would change everything. What guy would put up with eighty-hour workweeks, constant travel, and dates when her phone constantly rang with incoming calls, texts, and emails? Not anyone who'd capture *her* interest. A man searching for a sugar momma held zero appeal. No, she loved her life the way it was, and she wasn't inclined to change any part of it because everyone thought she needed a boyfriend.

"Caila is a grown woman," Nic said, rising and grabbing another bottle of wine. "She knows what she wants. I know I wouldn't want to be tied to one man when there are so many to choose from."

"You never could," Caila murmured, taking a bite of salad.

Nic's caramel brown curls jiggled when she jerked her head back. "Really? I'm on *your* side."

"Remember that time Nic came home with one guy to find another one waiting on the couch for her?" Lacey asked, the corners of her mouth quivering.

"Don't even try it!" Nic yelled over their howls of laughter. "He was my organic chemistry lab partner."

Ava snorted. "Maybe, but from the look on his face, he'd had ideas for much more."

"It was *so* awkward," Lacey said. "She and her date were kissing like he'd been deployed and was heading off to war. They'd barely broken apart for her to open the door."

"And that poor boy was sitting there, his mouth open." Ava shook her head. "What was his name?"

Caila ticked the options off on her fingers. "Geoff? Jim?"

"Gordon!"

"Thank you, Lacey," Nic said, her voice lacking any gratitude. "If you could remember the important things, instead of twelve-year-old college gossip, we might let you plan a vacay."

Oh shit!

Grooves appeared in Lacey's forehead. "What do you mean 'let'?"

"Nic—" Caila warned.

The other woman ignored her. "You haven't noticed that you've never planned a vacation?"

Lacey's gaze landed briefly on each of them. "By the time I'd thought about it, someone else had sent the email. I assumed it was random, but . . . Wait a minute, this was a concerted effort?"

"I wouldn't say 'concerted'—" Ava began.

"Yup!" Nic interrupted with her trademark bluntness.

"Why?" Lacey's light brown eyes widened.

It wasn't the way Caila wanted to deliver the news, but . . . "Really? Do we have to spell it out?"

Lacey leaned back in her chair and crossed her arms over her chest. "Apparently, you do."

"You're allergic to planning. You're Ms. Spur of the Moment, which, for some mystical reason, always works for you. Just not for those in your orbit."

"That's not true!" Lacey said. "Ava, help me out!"

Ava grimaced. "I've got four words: What about Chase, tho'?"

That was all it took to make them roar with laughter and send their memories tumbling through time to their third year of college.

"It wasn't my fault!" Lacey protested.

"What happened was the very definition of your fault," Nic said.

Ava had been the first of their group to turn twenty-one and they'd wanted to do something more than the pedestrian barhop for their friend. When Caila got her first UTI, Ava was the one who'd taken her to student health, picked up her prescription, and stayed with her through the painful and frightening experience. When Lacey won the lead role in their college's spring dance recital, Ava had made her favorite dishes for an impromptu celebration. And when Nic caught her boyfriend making out with another girl in the library stacks, Ava had organized an early morning raid when they exposed his cheating by hanging a large sign in the lobby of his dorm. Ava was the mother hen of their group. She took care of them. So on this special and momentous occasion, they wanted to return the favor.

"We'd planned the surprise for months," Caila said.

Nic nodded. "Took double shifts at our jobs, saved up money . . ."

Lacey's gaze flicked upward. "Do you guys practice this little comedy routine during the year?"

"*Somebody* asked Caila for a task, promised she could handle the details." Nic jerked her thumb in Lacey's direction.

"Said booking him would be, and I quote, 'no big deal.'" Caila made quotation marks with her fingers.

Lacey pressed her glossed lips tight.

"We take Ava to dinner, keep her out for a while, and when we finally get home, expecting to walk in to the big surprise, we find . . . nothing." Nic deflated her posture in a dramatic fashion.

"It wasn't my job to pick him up and drive him to our apartment," Lacey grumbled.

"So we're trying to pretend it's all good, that everything's fine—" Caila said, grinning.

"And failing miserably," Ava said. "You guys were acting so weird and I didn't know why. Dinner had been perfect."

Caila continued. "Twenty minutes later—"

"—forty-five minutes *after* he was supposed to arrive—" Nic inserts.

"The doorbell rings and there's this five-foot-four white guy, with blond hair, wearing a double-breasted . . . tuxedo . . . suit."

Caila had difficulty getting the last few words out, she was laughing so hard.

"'I'm Chase, your stripper,'" Nic said in a perfect imitation of a stereotypical frat boy, before cackling and clutching Caila's arm.

"I was trying to figure out what's going on," Ava said.

"We were, too! He's *not* who we picked out," Nic said, using a napkin to wipe the tears from her cheeks. "We know your type. At least six-foot-three and chocolate brown."

"Chase was neither," Ava said, stating the obvious.

Lacey trotted out the same excuse she'd always given. "By the time I called, the guy you wanted was unavailable!"

"Because you waited until the week before her birthday to book him!" Caila cried, raising her hands in a ta-da motion.

"Chase did put on a show, though," Lacey murmured.

Caila pressed her palms against her aching cheeks. "He did his best, considering Nic and I were dying laughing, Lacey was huddled in the corner of the couch, and Ava kept offering him food."

"He was so little," Ava said. "I didn't want him to pass out from lack of energy."

"Then we took the picture at the end and Caila stooped down so he could look tall!" Nic laughed.

"I was seven inches taller than him in my heels. He came up to my titties."

Lacey covered her face with her hands. "It was so bad. I'm sorry, guys!"

The sounds of their hyperventilating laughter enveloped Caila in the warmth of their love and affection. She needed these vacations with her girls. They fed her spirit and rejuvenated her for the year to follow. She had her friends and she had her career. And when she needed sex, she had several male friends willing to ease the ache. It was enough.

"We made it work," Ava said, covering Lacey's hand with her own. "It's what we do."

"So I can plan vacay next year?" Lacey asked, fluttering her lashes for good measure.

Nic paused in the act of taking a drink. "Hell no! Were you listening to the story we just told?"

"It's actually Caila's turn," Ava said.

Perfect! Caila grinned. She'd been jotting down ideas since her last go-around. She preferred the vacays she organized. She knew what to expect and felt secure in the knowledge that everything would go according to her plan. "I'll send out the email in January, as usual."

"I hate you bitches," Lacey said, throwing her napkin across the table.

"No, you don't. You loooove us," Nic crooned.

"In your dreams," Lacey said, though the smile on her face belied her words.

"A toast." Caila reached for her glass and threw back her shoulders. "To the Ladies of Lefevre."

It was the name they'd given themselves based on the dorm where they'd met.

"To us!" They saluted each other.

Caila took a bite of chicken. "You'll never guess who I ran into last month. Rashad Jenkins."

Across from her, Ava stiffened.

"Big head Rashad! How's he doing?" Nic asked.

"Good, I think. I saw him at O'Hare when I was coming back from the WWD Beauty Summit in New York. He's in banking. Married. With four kids."

"Huh," Nic said. One corner of her mouth lifted. "I guess he still has issues with control."

Caila's shoulders shook as she struggled to contain her amusement.

Ava pointed her fork at them. "Don't start!"

"What? She was just making an observation." Caila exchanged a glance with Nic. "It's not like we were going to bring up that time—"

"Don't you *dare*!"

"—after the Q Ball when you and he were making out—"

"Caila, I swear before God—"

"—and you reached for his dick—"

"Caila!"

"—and he came all over your hand!"

Lacey shrieked and slapped the table.

Ava pouted. "I shouldn't have told you bitches anything!"

"But you did, so . . ." Caila shrugged.

The sound of ringing penetrated their laughter. Nic leaped from her seat and grabbed Caila's phone. "I told you what I was going to do!"

Caila blinked, stunned at the speed with which the other woman had moved. "Nicole Shavonne Allen, I'm warning you!"

Nic poked her tongue between her teeth, then glanced at the screen and answered it.

"Hello? Caila Harris's phone."

Caila lunged for her. "Nic!"

Nic danced away, a devilish smile on her beautiful face. "Hey, Ms. Mona, it's Nicole. We were just . . . Yes, ma'am. Hold on." She held the phone out to Caila, her expression serious. "It's your mom. She's crying."

Caila exhaled, her pleasure from seconds ago quickly diminishing. "Good Lord, what is it now?"

Nic bit her lip. "She sounds really bad."

"It's fine. Her hairstylist probably made her highlights too brassy before the junior league luncheon next week." She took the device. "Hi, Ma . . . Calm down . . . What's wrong?"

Her mother's words darted to her core and chilled her to the bone. "Caila, we need you to come home. It's Pop-Pop. He's dead."

Chapter Two

Caila straightened from the wall just as the elevator doors opened. She adjusted the sunglasses on her nose—visual protection from the bright lights illuminating the receptionist bay—and headed down the hallway on the left, barely acknowledging the "Good morning, Ms. Harris" from the young woman behind the desk.

Her stomach roiled and her taste buds carried the remnants of last night's folly, making each inhale, exhale, and swallow a potential trigger for the porcelain city blues. Add that to the clamor of a thriving business office and Caila was one minute away from executing a U-turn and heading back home to spend the day with her body huddled under her duvet and her head inches away from the nearest trashcan.

She tightened her fingers around the strap of her Goyard tote.

She'd never give them the satisfaction.

She was already irritated with herself for her unprecedented lapse of judgment the night before, but to not show up for work and have everyone believe that she'd finally lost it? That she couldn't handle the pressure and had gotten so bombed she couldn't be counted on to carry out her duties?

She'd make it, even if she had to drag her body the entire way. Which wasn't that far from reality. Still, while she'd wanted it known she hadn't shirked her responsibility, she wasn't keen on drawing the spotlight.

Unlike last night.

She kept her gaze forward, grateful when tile gave way to carpet, muffling the head-piercing tap of her heels on the floor. She pushed through the large etched glass door and strode into Endurance's main marketing department, where two large conference rooms and ten window-filled offices bordered dozens of cubicles.

"Ms. Harris?"

She flinched, then pressed a hand to the neckline of her kelly green shift dress, and stared at the marketing assistant who'd appeared out of thin air from the network of cubicles that often resembled a disorienting Halloween corn maze.

"Do you have a second?" he asked, scraping a hand through his short, dark hair.

No, I do not! My mouth tastes like stale ass, the pain in my head is so excruciating decapitation would be an improvement, and all I want is to get to my office so I can be alone and have some peace and quiet!

"Of course. What can I do for you?" she asked, proud that she'd managed her usual composed response.

"I've drafted the content you requested for the new social media campaigns featuring the skin care line."

"Perfect," she said, accepting the folder he offered while trying not to inhale the young man's offensive cologne. Good God! Did he bathe in it? "Which platforms did you target?"

He rubbed the back of his neck. "Excuse me?"

Great. She turned her head to the side, drew in three quick inhalations of air, offered a quick prayer to avoid passing out, and said, "Each platform appeals to a specific audience. Are you on Facebook?"

"God no!" His thin lip curled. "My *mother* has an account."

If she didn't feel like warmed-over scrapple, she would've laughed at the look of excessive horror that overtook his features. "Exactly. You're probably on Instagram or Snapchat or—"

He rolled his eyes. "Snapchat's my little sister and her friends."

Caila nodded. "So the content that would interest your mother on her favorite platform wouldn't work with your sister and her friends on theirs.

You need to tailor your content for each platform and the demographic we're trying to target."

"I understand." He winced. "Can I have a few more days to work on it?"

She handed him back the folder. "I'll have Diane call you and set up a meeting for next Wednesday."

"Thank you, Ms. Harris," he said, flashing her a grateful smile before disappearing back into the labyrinth of partially enclosed workspaces.

Pleased to resume breathing nontainted air, she rounded the corner—

—and almost dropped to her knees in gratitude when she saw her assistant standing next to her open office door, a steaming mug of coffee in her hand.

"Bless you," Caila said, handing Diane her bag in exchange for the cup. She cradled the warm porcelain and took a sip, not caring that the scalding liquid burned the roof of her mouth. Setting it on her desk, she sank into her office chair, tossed her glasses down, and leaned her head back against the headrest.

"You don't have time for that," Diane said.

"Why not?" Relief had finally made itself known, in all of its tension-releasing glory. Caila didn't open her eyes. "I don't have anything on my schedule for this morning."

"You didn't. But Ms. Mitchell called earlier and she wants to see you in her office in twenty minutes. I was starting to think you wouldn't make it in time."

Oh shit! Caila lifted her lashes and saw the worry she felt mirrored on her assistant's face. "Do you think she knows?"

"Everyone knows. Gerald Thorpe told his assistant, who couldn't wait to share with whoever would listen."

Fucking Gerald Thorpe! He couldn't keep his mouth shut even though he was constantly sticking his foot in it.

How many people could his assistant have told? She hadn't noticed any strange looks from people when she'd arrived. She glanced past Diane and encountered the curious stares of several assistants, analysts, and interns. At meeting her gaze, they scattered like a flock of skittish birds. Frowning, she pressed the button beneath her desk that frosted the glass windows facing the cubicles, affording them some privacy.

"What happened?" Diane asked, placing Caila's bag on the credenza, then propping herself up against the sturdy piece of furniture.

Caila put her elbows on the desk and let her forehead fall into her palms. "Other than making a complete ass of myself in front of the marketing department's entire executive lineup?"

When she'd been invited to join the team at the famed Coq d'Or restaurant at the Drake Hotel, she'd been ecstatic. This was it. For years she'd worked seven days a week, missed holidays— and baby showers!—with her family and had zero social life—neither a huge hardship—to show her dedication and commitment to this company. Add in her qualifications and proven track record, and it made her an ideal candidate for the recently vacated position of director of marketing for cosmetics. With the promotion, no one would dare question Kendra offering her the national rollout.

Had they invited her to dinner to see how she'd get along with the other department heads? Maybe they were going to announce she'd gotten the promotion.

"You've got this, baby girl. God would never give you more than you can handle. So handle your business."

Pop-Pop's words to her when she'd accepted the job offer from Endurance. He'd understood what having a successful career meant to her, knew she wanted the freedom to make her own decisions and wouldn't tolerate ceding that control to anyone else. He'd always encouraged her to follow her heart while the rest of her family implored her to follow a ring.

Pain squeezed her heart and threatened to rip it from her chest. It had been two months since the funeral. When would these feelings go away? She couldn't afford to fall apart every time stray memories of Pop-Pop floated to the forefront of her mind. Why couldn't they stay in the box where she'd stuffed them, tucked away until she was ready to deal?

Whenever that would be.

She still hadn't allowed herself a moment to weep for the man who'd become the most important person in her life. Who'd not only accepted her confident, take-charge attitude, but championed it. Who'd told her to never diminish herself to fit into anyone's mold, no matter what her family or the world might demand.

Whose last words to her had been uttered with such displeasure and disappointment that she hadn't spoken to him in months before his death.

Her friends had booked her on the next flight to Maryland and when she'd gotten there, she did what she'd always done: acknowledged the situation and devised her plan of attack. With her mother and sisters going into Prissy-from-*Gone-With-the-Wind* histrionics, there hadn't been time for her to indulge in her own emotional distress. She'd had to make all of the decisions.

Her mother had never remarried though she'd never lacked for "companionship." In fact, upon her mother's meltdown, her current "companion" had attempted to step in and make the arrangements, citing his own experience dealing with his parents' deaths and a desire to "remove the burden from Mona's shoulders."

Caila had nipped that in the bud with a quickness some might say bordered on rudeness. Well, actually, her mother *had* said it.

The memories of the days after Pop-Pop's death had left Caila unsettled and agitated. She didn't dare arrive to dinner in her current jittery state, so she'd had a shot of whiskey to calm her nerves before leaving home. When she'd shown up to the restaurant, she'd seen she wasn't the only guest of honor. They'd invited the other regional managers, including Gerald fucking Thorpe.

Her competition for the promotion and the new campaign.

She'd been unable to prevent the anger that charged through her. The chaotic emotion had been dogging her like a persistent bill collector, showing up when it was least expected or wanted. Its appearance in that moment had thrown her off her game, but some whispered words to herself and a drink from the bar had motivated her enough to wade into the fray and take advantage of the opportunity.

"I don't know what happened," she said now to Diane. "I planned to have my usual glass of white wine followed by club soda for the rest of the night. But one drink turned into two, which turned into three, and . . ."

Sometime in the wee hours of the morning, she'd torn herself away from bad eighties karaoke and stumbled out to the valet stand and hailed a cab home.

Diane made a sound in her throat and looked away from Caila.

She tensed at the uneasiness emanating from her assistant. "What?"

"It's just . . . that explains why Paul was humming 'I Wanna Dance with Somebody' when he saw me earlier."

Oh good God! What had she done?

"And that's not all." Although it was enough!

Caila massaged her temples. "I lost one of my shoes."

Diane gasped and splayed her fingers against the pearl necklace encircling her throat. "Not your boss bitch heels?"

"My boss bitch heels," Caila slowly repeated.

The moment she'd walked into the boutique and seen the nude and black ombre patent leather pumps with crystals covering the stiletto heels, she'd known she was meant to own them. They conveyed power and strength. The woman who wore those shoes would own a room the moment she stepped into it. The director of marketing for cosmetics would wear those shoes. She'd shelled out nearly a thousand dollars and placed them on the shelf in her walk-in closet, waiting for the perfect occasion to slip into them. Last night was supposed to be her moment before the ball.

Diane nodded. "I'll call the hotel and see if it turned up anywhere, but you need to pull yourself together. Ms. Mitchell wasn't there. You can't let her see anything that'll lend credence to what she might've heard."

TWENTY MINUTES LATER, Caila sat in a large corner office several floors above her own and resisted the urge to squirm as she stared across the wide cherrywood desk at her boss and mentor.

Some people might view Kendra Mitchell's light brown skin, delicate features, and petite frame and underestimate with whom they were dealing. It'd be the last time they'd make that mistake. Caila had watched her take down a junior executive with a raised brow and several choice words when he'd tried to mansplain basic online marketing concepts to her. Endurance's executive vice president of marketing didn't suffer fools lightly.

Kendra tapped a finger on the desk. "You're known for being cool under pressure. I've always admired that about you."

Caila pressed a hand against her belly in an attempt to disrupt the butterflies performing aerial feats. Hangover? Nervousness? "Thank you."

Kendra leaned back in her luxe leather chair. "But I can't let that deter me from what I have to do."

Caila's breath escaped her lungs.

"A few months ago we had a conversation about you taking on the new organic makeup line."

Caila scooted forward in her chair. "I'm honored you and the board have seen fit to entrust this campaign to—"

Kendra held up a hand, her palm facing outward. "I'm going to stop you there."

No! This couldn't be happening. She pushed on. "I've already come up with several ideas. I can do this, Kendra."

"I don't doubt you have the capabilities to successfully handle the job. I wouldn't have considered you for the position otherwise. But you're not in the right frame of mind to tackle a project of this magnitude."

What the hell did *that* mean?

"I disagree," Caila argued. "This year I developed and implemented strategic marketing plans for the new skin care line, ensured that the project milestones were met, and adhered to the approved budget, all while managing a staff of twenty."

"Which would be relevant if my concerns were work-based." Kendra shifted in her chair and cleared her throat. "I don't make it a practice to get involved in the personal lives of my employees, but . . . I know your grandfather died recently. I understand you were close."

Heat flashed through Caila's body. She dropped her hands into her lap, not flinching when her nails scored her palms. "I don't see what that has to do with anything."

Kendra's expression firmed. "In the past two months, you've been late to several meetings, failed to promptly turn in that final revised budget, and missed when one of your teams attached an old timeline to their client status report."

Ten years of near-flawless job performance were suddenly rendered irrelevant by a few oversights?

"With anyone else, these would be forgivable lapses. But you're not someone else. *We're* not anyone else," Kendra said, gesturing between the two of them. "We have to be better, and that has never been a hardship for you because you are. I knew it from the first time I interviewed you at your business school. It's the reason I offered you a position on the spot. And you've never made me regret that decision."

"I don't know what to say," Caila said, humbled by her boss's words, though disappointed to be hearing them in this context.

"But I can't continue to ignore what I'm seeing and I definitely can't risk screwing up the new rollout, especially in light of your behavior last night."

Crap. She *had* heard. Caila dipped her chin to her chest, not wanting to meet Kendra's dark brown gaze. "I'm so sorry. I've never acted like that before. I don't know what happened."

"Take some time and figure it out."

Cold fingers compressed Caila's lungs, making it difficult to breathe. Her head shot up. "Are you firing me?"

"No. But it's become clear that you need to process your feelings about your grandfather's death."

No offense to Kendra, but she didn't know dick-all about Caila's feelings. Caila had made a couple of mistakes. No one was perfect. Why did everyone persist in making a big deal about Pop-Pop? He'd died. End of story.

"Work's important, but it's not everything. Somewhere along the way, you seem to have forgotten that."

Caila hardened herself against the memory of Pop-Pop's dismayed words. "I can't sit around my condo and do nothing. I'll go insane."

"I know. And that's why I have a job for you."

She already had a job. Why couldn't she continue to execute that one?

"Endurance is in the process of acquiring Flair," Kendra announced.

Flair was one of the oldest cosmetics companies in the country, founded in 1855. Their classic ingredients and products were lauded by industry professionals, but their emphasis on old-fashioned customer interaction and brick-and-mortar stores over social media and selling on a website meant declining sales and a diminished market presence.

Caila straightened in her chair, interested in news that hadn't gone company-wide. "How quickly do you plan to integrate them into the Endurance brand?"

Kendra tilted her head to the side. "What's the case for not making that play? For reviving the company instead?"

Caila pursed her lips, considering her mentor's question. "Barriers to entry into the beauty industry have been lowered and brands are being created at the speed of light, and most leave just as quickly. This increase in independent brands shows consumer tastes are changing, creating a competitive threat to established brands. With a takeover of Flair, we have the opportunity to leverage their historical strength with the passion and creativity of a new independent brand."

Kendra's proud smile bloomed bright, and warmth expanded in Caila's chest. For the millionth time since she'd accepted her job offer,

Caila thanked God for the other woman's time and mentorship. Black women made up less than two percent of senior-level executives in the Fortune 500, so to find one in her chosen field willing to mentor her was a stroke of blessings she planned to make the most of.

And you almost destroyed it.

"We'd like to announce the acquisition soon, but there are some financial issues that must be cleared up to make this deal viable for us." Kendra swiveled her chair to face the large computer monitor on her right. She tapped some keys on her wireless keyboard, and the screen bloomed to life.

"Such as?"

"One of Flair's co-packers is a manufacturing plant called Chro-Make located in Bradleton, a small town in central Virginia."

Caila nodded. A co-packer was a company that packaged and labeled products for their clients. Some corporations handled packaging in-house, while others contracted the service out to private firms.

"Over the past few years, the costs associated with Chro-Make have skyrocketed almost twenty percent, making it financially undesirable for us to come to an agreement with the factory in that condition."

Caila held her breath as she sensed what was coming.

"We're sending you to Virginia."

No, no, no, no—

Caila exhaled an audible breath through her nose. "You're giving me an assignment that I'd normally delegate to an analyst right out of B-school?"

Kendra arched a brow. "Would you like entry-level work or no work?"

Valid point.

It'd been years since she'd been sent on one of these restructuring evaluations. She couldn't muster any excitement about a weeks-long hotel stay in an unfamiliar city where she'd spend countless days inside a small, windowless office, poring over reports and talking to members of each department, in order to decide how best to increase the company's viability.

But Kendra's next words doubled-down on Caila's unwillingness.

"Flair is adamant that we agree to continue using most of their factories, barring proof of financial hardship. We don't need to determine whether eliminating the relationship with Chro-Make will be a condition of the deal moving forward." She paused. "We've already come to that conclusion."

Caila winced. This wasn't an evaluation; it was a hatchet job. She wasn't being sent to find a way to make the factory more productive. They were sending her in to find the evidence they needed to justify their decision not to renew the contract. Damn. She was ride-or-die for Endurance, but interviewing people about their jobs when you knew they were soon to be unemployed? It left a sour taste in her mouth.

Worse than the one caused by her hangover.

"So it's a bit more delicate than something we'd assign to a marketing analyst right out of B-school," Kendra said, throwing Caila's words back at her. "But if you feel it's beneath you, I can give the assignment to Gerald Thorpe."

Fucking Gerald Thorpe. Heat rushed into Caila's cheeks. She knew when she was being given a choice that was no choice at all. "When do I leave?"

Kendra's lips curled in a knowing smirk. "As soon as possible, no later than the end of next week. I'll have my assistant email you the file and all of the relevant information. I can't stress enough how important your performance on this assignment is. I'm an important ally but I'm only one of five. If you do a good job with this, it'll go a long way toward showing them you've dealt with your recent . . . issues and you're back on track."

Caila's jaw tightened but she suppressed her annoyance, knowing the woman in front of her really had her best professional interests at heart. "Will that put the promotion and national rollout back on the table?"

Kendra's head jerked back. "How about you concentrate on successfully completing this assignment first?"

Caila shrugged her shoulder. "I had to ask."

Kendra winked. "I know. I'd have been disappointed if you hadn't."

Realizing the purpose of the meeting was over, Caila stood and made her way to the door.

"Oh, and Caila?"

She turned as Kendra produced a beautiful shoe from a drawer. The Swarovski crystals encasing the four-inch heel caught the sun reflecting off Lake Michigan and cast a spectrum of rainbow-colored lights across the desk.

"Workers at the hotel found this hooked into a light sconce next to a bank of elevators outside of the restaurant. Is it yours?"

Without hesitating, Caila looked her boss in the eye. "I've never seen that shoe before in my life."

Chapter Three

Wyatt Asher Bradley IV, mayor of Bradleton, leaned forward in his leather executive chair and studied his fellow council members seated around a U-shaped birchwood table on the platform beneath him.

"All those in favor of funding the expansion of West Main Street into Happy Creek Plaza, raise your hand. All those opposed?" He banged the gavel on the sound block. "Motion denied."

A smattering of applause from the audience in the gallery. *Ah, such appreciation for the workings of the council.* He winked at the older woman seated in the first row. Color bloomed in her cheeks and she returned his smile.

Wyatt glanced at the secretary. "Let the record reflect that Councilman Randall from Ward One was the only person who voted *in favor* of the motion."

Vince Randall curled his lip and crossed his arms over his striped polo–clad chest. Not much different from how he'd looked when he didn't get his way back in elementary school.

Shaking his head, Wyatt looked down at the paper in front of him, and excitement floated in his chest.

They were almost done.

Not that he didn't enjoy running town council sessions. They were fairly easy; sometimes they practically ran themselves. At agenda meetings, they finalized the agenda for the upcoming regular meeting. At work sessions, they informally reviewed materials for and discussed items on the agenda, though no official decisions or conclusions were made. Regular meetings, like tonight, were open to the public, and they formally discussed and decided upon those agenda items.

The following month, the process would start all over again.

There were times when the council needed to consult with the town's attorney regarding judicial action or administrative procedure. Or when they had a closed session to discuss which bids to accept on town contracts. On those rare occasions, Wyatt enjoyed being able to flex his mental skills, to utilize his Ivy League joint JD/ MBA degree.

But most of the time, it was the same. Simple and easy.

Every once in a while he wondered what would happen if he skipped a meeting. It wasn't as if the sessions wouldn't go forward. In his absence, the vice mayor could chair any town council sessions. And Wyatt could have some much-needed free time.

Take tonight, for example. The shipment of black walnut he'd been waiting for had come in that afternoon, and his palms itched to smooth along the lumber. He'd wanted to try his hand at making a serving buffet, but he couldn't get ahead of himself. The wood usually spoke to him, told him what it would allow him to create. Taking a chisel to a piece of wood, he entered an almost Zen-like state. He'd lose himself in the smell of the shavings, the intricacies of the details . . .

But he'd never shirk his responsibilities. He'd shown up tonight and presided over the session, just as he had each month before.

Like his family expected him to do.

Like the town required its mayor to do.

"Before we end this meeting of the town council, we'll open the floor for citizen comments," he announced.

He waited, exercising immense control to keep his leg from bouncing beneath the desk. A large part of him hoped no one would take him up on the offer to share their concerns with the council. The clock on the wall indicated he had half an hour until the hardware store closed. If he could make it out of here in the next fifteen minutes, he might have a chance.

But—

Something was going on. The mood had been slightly off-kilter from the beginning of the meeting. The air had been still, heavy, like the entire council chamber had been holding its breath. He'd initially chalked it up to his own eagerness for the meeting to be over, but now he wasn't sure.

He studied the assortment of people who'd assembled to watch the council spend the past ninety minutes discussing sewer connections, funding allocation, and development in Bradleton's historic downtown area. He realized that hum of restlessness he'd sensed hadn't been internal. It had emanated from *them*. People shifted in their seats, crossed and uncrossed their legs, whispered to their neighbors, fidgeted with their clothes.

He narrowed his eyes. The crowd was larger than normal, too. Some were regulars. Wyatt appreciated anyone interested in what the town was doing, but these meetings weren't exciting. He often wondered if some of them saw it as entertainment; a small-town dinner theater. There were times when discussions got heated. Last month, two council members got into a shouting match over whether they should increase the enforcement of jaywalking downtown. The week following the melee, the gallery had been filled, but attendance had dropped off again when another altercation hadn't been forthcoming.

When he saw Earl Creasey stand and make his way to the wooden podium, Wyatt understood the undercurrent of anticipation he'd discerned. He knew Earl's gripe; the old man wasn't shy about making his feelings on the subject known. At least here, versus at Turk's, there was a time limit.

Still, Wyatt knew there was no way he was getting out of here in time to get his shipment tonight.

"The floor is yours, Earl," Wyatt said.

"Thanks, Mayor. I want to talk about something important to me and most of us here in Bradleton." Earl brought his fist to his mouth and cleared his throat. "The football team hasn't made it onto the state playoff bracket in over fifteen years. Not since the team the mayor and Chief Dan played on. I don't know about y'all, but I'm sick of losing."

Wyatt glanced over to where Daniel Yates, his best friend and the town's chief of police, stood with his back propped against the wall, his arms crossed over his dark blue uniform shirt. Dan flicked his gaze upward and shook his head slightly.

"I don't think this new coach is gonna cut it," Earl said.

People seemed to lean in, their faces shining with excitement.

And there it was. The reason they were all here. Football.

He didn't blame them. Football was the most important religion in the South. More people watched games during the season than showed up at Bradleton Baptist Church on Sunday mornings. Finding out through the grapevine that there might be a discussion about firing the new high school coach? How could people resist? The drama imagined would be better than regular old dinner theater. They were anticipating *Hamilton*-level entertainment.

"I understand your frustration," Wyatt said, his voice holding no hint of his inner amusement, "but give the man a chance. He just started. He's doing the best he can considering the circumstances."

Vince spoke up from the council member's bench. "Y'all should be grateful we got someone with his pedigree and experience. His recommendations were impeccable."

"Or at least thank God his mother-in-law lives one county over and his wife wanted to move closer to her," Betty Lou Dannon said from the front row, over the rapid clicking of her knitting needles.

There was no such thing as gratitude and thankfulness in football . . . unless you were winning.

"I knew it!" Earl said, his Feed 'n' Seed trucker hat jostling on his head. "The only reason you hired him is because he came from up north and you were hoping he knew some magic techniques. The rules don't change north of the Mason-Dixon line!"

Wyatt steepled his fingers in front of him. "Don't rush to judgment. It's going to take time. It's not like he inherited the best-case scenario or that we had a lot of choices."

"Who's rushing? We're three games into the season, sitting at oh and three, and Coach had the nerve to bring his family into Luciano's on

Tuesday night. Laughing." Earl almost spat the word. "Can you believe that?"

"If he has time to whoop it up, how 'bout he get some extra practices in to shore up that O-line," Clyde Roberston added. Clyde had been sitting next to Earl, partners in trouble-making ever since Wyatt could remember. "I know the parents won't mind. I saw Rondale Jackson's father at the bank last week and he said he was surprised the team wasn't doing two-a-days."

"If they keep playing like this, we'll never make the state championship," Earl said, smacking a hand against the podium.

"Time," the secretary called out.

Wyatt straightened in his chair. "Earl, I appreciate your comments. However, the time allocated for citizen comments is over."

The older man squinted his faded eyes. "What're you gonna do about Coach Alvin?"

Asked as if he'd just successfully argued his point before the Supreme Court.

Wyatt spread his hands. "I'm going to continue to show up to the games and show my support for the coach and for the team."

"Is that it? You're not going to fire him?"

"Of course not. We didn't hire him. That's between you and the school's athletic director."

Earl's mouth dropped open. "You mean I sat here for two hours for nothin'?"

Wyatt raised a corner of his mouth. "Afraid so."

"Son of a bitch! C'mon, Clyde."

The two moseyed down the aisle, grumbling under their breaths about the "damn bureaucracy" and getting a mayor who was poor and would listen because their "tax dollars pay his salary."

"And with that, ladies and gentlemen, this meeting is adjourned."

Wyatt banged the gavel again and pushed back from the desk. If he left immediately and hustled, he might make it to the shop and pick up his package before they closed.

"Mayor Bradley?" The feminine voice was Northern and a tad nasal.

Dammit.

Reining in his frustration, he turned and conjured a smile for the pretty woman before him. "Holly, how many times have I told you to call me Wyatt?"

"I know." Holly Martin, Bradleton's newest resident, laughed and shrugged one shoulder. "But I like calling you mayor. There's something so . . . authoritative about it."

Hey now.

He leaned a hip against the back of his chair and crossed his arms. "You settling in okay?"

Her blue eyes followed his movements and she bit her bottom lip. "It's a great little town. Way . . . different from where I come from."

"Pretty soon, it'll feel like home," he said, giving her his standard tourist bureau line. "You're already attending council meetings. Are you interested in getting involved?"

"With local government? No." She tilted her head and tugged on one of her blond curls. "Do you remember when I was here visiting my aunt back in July? You promised to show me around."

"Of course."

He didn't, but she wouldn't care for that admission. If he had mentioned showing her around, he'd meant it casually. The town was nine and a half square miles; he was pretty sure Holly had already seen everything Bradleton had to offer.

Still, she was cute and he wasn't busy, so . . .

"How's your Saturday afternoon?"

"I'd prefer Saturday evening," she countered.

Wyatt raised his brows. Kinda hard to see the town at night. "How's seven?"

Holly reached out and squeezed his biceps. "It's a date." She gave him one last slow smile and sauntered away.

He allowed himself a moment to appreciate the sway of her denim-clad hips before his gaze hurried back to the clock. Shit! It'd be impossible for him to make it to the store in time. The shipment would have to wait until tomorrow.

Dan sidled up next to him. "You live a charmed life, my friend."

"What do you mean?"

"You think everyone is a young, handsome, rich man who gets approached by beautiful women during boring council meetings?" Dan sighed dramatically. "Everything always seems to go your way. I know a hundred men who would trade places with you in a heartbeat."

Wyatt knew it was what everyone thought of him. Because he didn't allow them to see anything else.

"Are you one of them?" Wyatt teased. "You're a good-looking guy. Women would ask you out, too. First, you'd have to take off your wedding ring and stop parading around town with Laura, holding hands, kissing, and looking blissfully happy . . ."

"Oh! So you got jokes?"

"I've got more than that according to—what the—"

Vince bumped into Wyatt, his backward capped, blond head turned at an awkward angle. "It must be jelly cuz jam don't shake like that!"

Dan shook his head. "It usually helps when you watch where you're walking."

"Dude," Vince said, ignoring Dan and zeroing in on Wyatt, "you were talking to the new dental hygienist from Dr. Saunders's office."

"Very observant."

"Well?" Vince asked. "What did she want? She was asking about me, right?"

Vince was such a douchebag. If Wyatt had met the other man today, he could guarantee they wouldn't be friends, but they'd grown up together, both scions of prominent Bradleton families. It was a relationship cemented by proximity and familiarity, not by affection.

"You're right," Wyatt said, clapping Vince on the shoulder. "She did ask about you. She wanted to know about the prick who voted to fund the road extension."

Vince's arrogant expression soured and he shrugged off Wyatt's hand. "You're an asshole."

"What are you doing?" Wyatt asked. "That extension would destroy a good chunk of Happy Creek Plaza. I thought the park was important to your family? They owned the land before selling it to the town for that specific purpose. They even donated the picnic shelters and the children's play area."

Vince snorted. "Why should I care what my family did almost forty years ago? Things have changed. Expanding the road will make it easier to get from one side of town to the other. It's good for my constituents."

"And it has nothing to do with the fact that the new road would run past your car dealership?" Wyatt asked.

"I mean, if that's true, that's a definite bonus, but my concern is strictly for the people of Bradleton." Vince's innocent tone didn't pass the smell test, but it didn't matter.

The motion hadn't passed.

This time.

"Speaking of new things." Vince pressed his hands against his middle. "If I told Holly Martin she had a beautiful body, do you think she'd hold it against me?"

"Is that my phone ringing?" Dan pulled out his cell. "Hello."

Vince looked around. "I didn't hear anything."

Dan held out the phone. "The seventies called. They want their pickup lines back."

"Screw you, Dan." Vince looked at Wyatt. "We done here? Let's head across the street to Turk's."

Since the opportunity to pick up his lumber order had slipped away and he still needed to eat, Wyatt said, "Sure."

They said good-bye to the other council members and the few people who still remained and headed out of the municipal building, starting the block-long trek to their favorite local diner.

Vince shoved his fists into the pockets of his pleated khakis. "You know she moved here from New Jersey last month and is staying in her aunt's house on the outskirts of town."

"Who?" Dan asked, his head swiveling as they walked.

Not that Bradleton was the crime capital of the commonwealth. But Dan was never off duty. Being a cop was embedded in his DNA. He'd often said he couldn't imagine doing anything else.

Wyatt envied his freedom to choose the life and career he wanted.

"Holly Martin, the dental hygienist!" Vince said, his voice threaded with exasperation. "I heard she lost her job. Or was it that she caught her fiancé in bed with her cousin? No, I think she wanted to leave the city for the charm and slow pace of a small town."

Dan frowned. "Do you hear yourself? You sound like a stalker."

"I wasn't stalking her. My mom stopped by the car dealership to bring me lunch. She told me."

Wyatt smirked at Dan. "Likely story."

Once inside the diner, they called a greeting to Shirley and headed to the booths in the back, passing Earl and Clyde hunched over mugs of draft beer at the bar.

Wyatt removed his phone from the back pocket of his jeans, then slid into the red upholstered booth, smiling and nodding to the customers seated nearby.

Vince flicked the laminated menus with a finger. "I don't know why they keep these on the table. The last time Turk's offered anything new was the Swedish meatballs in 2012."

"When he was part of the Recipes from Around the World Club." Wyatt exhaled. "Those meatballs made me sick."

"You and half the town," Dan said.

"So long, recipe club!" Vince sang, waving.

"Thank God," came a voice from the table behind them.

"I'm going to ask Holly Martin out," Vince said. "Early bird gets the worm and all that."

Dan smirked. "Save your energy. And your dignity."

"Why?" Vince asked. "Is she a lesbian?"

"Really?" Wyatt's tone was scornful. *"That's* what you're going with? If she's not interested, she must be into women?"

Vince jutted his chin. "I'm good-looking, I own my house, and I run a successful business. I'm a catch. The women in this town know it—"

"—and don't care—" Dan interrupted.

"—Holly Martin will, too," Vince concluded.

"Evening, Mayor. Chief." Shirley placed three fresh bottles of beer and a basket of pretzels on the table. "Give it up, Vincent. She was in here at lunch talking 'bout Wyatt. Y'all want the usual?"

Dan's eyes widened and he lifted his beer, a wide smile splitting his face.

"Unbelievable!" Vince threw his hands up in the air.

"The usual it is," Shirley said, walking away.

Wyatt's skin prickled from the interested stares of the other customers, and he knew this situation had the potential to add to the imagined lore of "Mayor McHottie." He hated that nickname, but it was beyond his control to suppress it. The town sopped up his supposed escapades faster than Turk's legendary biscuits and sausage gravy.

Vince curled his lip. "When I think about it, it's truly amazing you haven't run through the entire female under-thirty population."

"That's an ageist thing to say," Dan said. "I know for a fact that Wyatt has dated older women."

Ha-ha.

"You're a dick," he told Dan, launching a pretzel across the table. Dan caught it, his grin spreading.

"You don't even try," Vince grumbled. "You just stand there and they come to you. Like metal shavings to a magnet."

Wyatt shrugged, not willing to be swept along on Vince's emotional tide. "I like to have fun. I show women a good time. I'm honest about my intentions from the beginning, and they appreciate that."

"Until they want to get serious and you don't," Dan pointed out.

Wyatt's phone buzzed and he checked the screen. A text from the owner of the hardware store. Since Wyatt hadn't made it in before they'd closed, he'd dropped the shipment off on Wyatt's porch.

Perfect!

"Let me guess, another woman asking you out on a date?" Vince accused.

"Bitter much?" Wyatt asked, before tilting his bottle of beer and taking a lengthy swig.

Maybe he seemed different because everyone else in Bradleton started coupling from young ages. It wasn't uncommon for people to marry their high school sweethearts. What was wrong with having a good time? Keeping things light and easy?

Besides, marrying into his family carried a lot of . . . baggage. If his mother and grandfather ever got a hint that he was serious about someone, they'd book the reception venue and begin planning the rest of his life before he'd even popped the question. With practice, he'd mastered the delicate balance of doing what he wanted and still managing to satisfy his family and fulfill his duties. His life was great exactly the way it was.

And he'd keep it that way for as long as possible.

"Look, my feelings about commitment are not a secret."

The gossip mill in Bradleton made sure of that.

Vince shook his head. "Of course they aren't. It's part of your allure."

Wyatt choked on his beer. "Allure? You think I have allure, Vince?"

"Not my word. They see you as a challenge. They all believe they'll be the one to get you to settle down even though you treat them the same. First date, is always dinner—"

"At the fanciest place in town, La Petite Maison," Amos Jackson, seated in the booth in front of them, pointed out.

"Is everyone keeping track of my schedule?" Wyatt asked, grabbing a napkin from the silver dispenser and wiping up the hoppy spray he'd caused.

"Don't forget dancing at the Watering Hole," Eunice Hollis called from her table, where she sat with the other members of the senior center's bridge club.

"Not you too, Miss Eunice!" Wyatt said.

A smile broke across her brown, lined face. She wiggled her fingers and blew him a kiss.

Vince rapped his knuckles against the table. "And you'll end the night back at her place."

"Because the world would have to end before he lets a date darken the doorstep of his house," Dan said, popping a pretzel into his mouth.

"Are you having fun?" Wyatt asked through gritted teeth.

"Absolutely," Dan said.

The bell over the front door jingled and an older woman hurried in wearing Chro-Make's unofficial uniform of jeans, a flannel shirt, and boots, her thin, graying hair pulled up into a ponytail.

"Hey, Fran!" Shirley called out. "You want a beer?"

Fran braced an arm against the bar and inhaled gulps of air. "They're closing it down!"

"You're damn right," Vince said grumpily. "I'm gonna need several drinks tonight!"

"Not here. The plant!" Fran's words pierced the crowd's laughter. "They're closing it down."

Wyatt frowned. "Hold up, guys! Fran, what's going on?"

"Chro-Make. I just heard from someone who heard from Nate that Flair was bought by another company and that the new company wants to pull their contract!"

Unease coiled low in Wyatt's belly, ready to slither up to his chest. He wasn't the only one who recognized the import of Fran's news. The restaurant's previous mirth had been vacuum-sucked from the air, leaving everyone crumpled and deflated.

Clyde straightened from the bar. "They can't do that!"

Eunice shook her head. "I worked at that plant. My husband worked there. My daughter works there now."

Dan nodded. "That's true for a lot of families around here."

"That plant employs half the town!" Vince exclaimed, glancing around.

"A third," Wyatt corrected absently, his mind racing.

Losing the cosmetics contract would essentially close the plant and devastate their local economy. Hundreds of families depended on the income provided by those jobs. He'd seen the devastating effect that losing a manufacturer can have on a small town. Five years ago, the nearby town of Grange imploded when a major shoe company moved its factory overseas to take advantage of lower production costs. The loss decimated their downtown area, with several banks, two supermarkets, and a shopping center closing down.

They never recovered. It was like a modern-day ghost town.

Earl exploded. "We can't stand by and let this happen! What are you going to do about it, Mayor?"

Every head in Turk's swung in his direction, their expressions of panic, fear, and anxiety a palpable, suffocating wave.

Sometimes the burden of being Wyatt Asher Bradley IV weighed on him like a thousand-pound bag of shifting sand.

What would he do? The only thing he could.

"I'll take care of it," he said.

And he would.

It's what the town expected its mayor to do.

It's what his family expected him to do.

It's what his father, Wyatt Asher Bradley III, failed to do.

Chapter Four

Three hours from the nearest commercial service airport. Ninety minutes since she'd seen a Starbucks. Every third automobile was a pickup truck.

Welcome to Small Town, USA.

When she'd begun her journey—after picking up her rental car in D.C.—her view had consisted of concrete and steel, loads of people and traffic congestion. But when she'd left the major southbound interstate for state roads, the tableau blossomed into a beautiful bounty of nature, with colorful foliage and charming roadside businesses.

Even though she'd attended college in Virginia, she hadn't had the opportunity to explore the commonwealth beyond the university's borders. Which was a shame. There was an appeal to the area, one she couldn't deny. As she'd driven past the town limits and onto the tree-lined streets of the historic downtown, with their fall-decorated vintage light posts and people strolling along with baby carriages or friends, she couldn't repress the upward tilt of her lips.

I've cruised onto the set of a cable channel movie or sitcom.

Flexing her fingers, she gripped the steering wheel tightly and followed the automated voice of her GPS, past signs that touted stores selling authentic Amish quilts and Confederate battle-field tours only twenty miles away. Making the final turn, she pulled into the gravel parking lot of a gray brick building on the edge of town. The drab green awning read "Chro-Make Manufac-turing." A few cars were parked haphazardly in the lot.

What the hell?

Caila checked her watch. It was five-thirty in the afternoon. She'd purposely timed her arrival to coincide with the shift change. People were usually very talkative at the end of their shifts, milling around, catching up with coworkers and recounting their days. She could learn a lot just by listening to what they said. She'd also thought to maybe peek inside the plant and see what she was dealing with before her meeting with the plant manager the following day. It was the reason she'd decided to arrive a day earlier than she'd origi-nally anticipated. There was no such thing as too much information in these situations.

But instead of hordes of people entering and exiting the plant, the parking lot was almost bare. She grabbed her tote bag and headed toward the building.

She pulled on the glass door, surprised when the handle slid from her grasp and she almost chipped a nail. The door didn't open. She tried again. It didn't budge. What was going on? She cupped hands on either side of her face and peered in. No one was seated in the vestibule, and instead of the usual hum of a working factory, the place was eerily silent.

This is what happens when you veer off your initial plan.

She stepped back from the building—cursing as she stumbled when her high heel caught in the gravel—and surveyed the large warehouse. A closed factory? She'd never known a manufacturing plant to keep nine-to-five hours. Didn't they run in shifts?

She twisted her lips. No wonder this place was having problems. They ran on limited hours and they had no security. How did they expect to produce the amount of inventory necessary and to safeguard it once it was created?

Frustration constricted her chest and she glanced up at a sky gone violet with the setting sun. She'd endured a two-hour layover in Boston, a middle seat in coach on *both* flights, and long hours on the road with no bathroom break, all so she could get here a day early . . . and stand outside a closed chemical plant.

On cue, her stomach grumbled, a salty reminder that in her urgency, she'd consumed only a cup of coffee all day. She remembered passing a restaurant on Main Street that looked well populated. If the locals ate there, the food must be good. She'd grab a quick dinner before getting settled for the night. She'd come back in the morning.

Fifteen minutes later Caila raised a perfectly sculpted brow at the scene before her inside Turk's Good Times & Good Eats. A large U-shaped counter with red leather stools was the main focal point of the restaurant. Upholstered booths and single tables filled the left side of the space, while several old-school video arcade games and a pinball machine inhabited a small alcove off to the right. Even though it was early in the evening, the entire place seemed filled to capacity. She stood at the hostess station and stared at the occupied booths and counter, wondering if she'd be able to get a table.

Although . . .

Maybe it wasn't a good idea to eat at an establishment that boasted the food as the *second*-best thing it was known for?

Before she could back out of the door as unobtrusively as she'd entered, a stocky older woman in jeans, a red T-shirt, and a short black waist apron hurried over. "Just you?"

Since she was alone . . . "I guess so."

The waitress glanced around, then pointed to a spot in the middle of a crush on the right side of the counter. "Grab that seat."

Caila hefted her bag on her shoulder and made her way to the indicated stool, sliding in between two guys wearing flannel shirts.

Another waitress placed a glass of water down in front of Caila. "What can I get for you?"

"Do you have a menu?"

The woman frowned. "You must be visiting."

Caila nodded. "I am."

"Please tell me you're not staying at the motel on the edge of town? It's not a safe place for a young woman traveling alone."

"I'm not."

The woman stared at her expectantly. She wanted Caila to tell her where she was staying? Caila almost laughed. A tourist would never do that in Chicago.

But you're not in Chicago, remember? You drank too much and thought you were Whitney Houston reincarnated.

Caila winced, then leaned forward and lowered her voice. "I'm staying at one of the B&Bs. Sinclair House."

"Oh, that's only ten minutes from here," the waitress said, loud enough to neutralize any sort of privacy Caila had tried to retain. "You'll love it. Gwen is a treasure. Unlike this menu! It's about as useful as a handbrake on a canoe! Everyone loves Turk's fried chicken platter. It comes with mashed red potatoes, green beans, and cornbread."

Caila would have to run ten miles to account for all of those calories! But her empty belly and watering mouth overrode any "healthy food" protests her mind tried to put forth. "That sounds delicious. I'll have that."

"No problem. You want something to drink or is water enough?"

Was water enough?

After the day she'd had? "Do you have a house red?"

"We do."

"I'll take a glass of that, please."

The waitress scribbled her order down on a notepad, then stuck the pencil in the hair above her ear. "My name is Shirley. Holler if you need anything."

Caila hung her purse on the hook beneath the counter, bumping into the guy seated on her left. "Sorry."

His hard glare sliced through her, and heat suffused her body.

Calm down, dude, it was an accident. We're sitting elbow to elbow. It's not like I was trying to hit you.

But while her comeback would've been automatic in Chicago, she was in a small town in the South where she didn't know a single soul. And while there were *some* black people in here, she could count their number on both hands, with a finger or two to spare.

Swallowing her angry retort, she shifted away from the asshole and thumbed on her phone, intending to check her emails. She'd missed an entire day of work, completely unheard of before today. She wouldn't be surprised to find her inbox loaded with several hundred new messages.

"Don't tell me not to worry! If that plant closes down, the entire town is screwed!"

She blinked and turned toward the source of the apprehensive statement. A group of men and women stood in the small space next to the video games.

"So am I! I've got three kids to support. I can't afford to lose my job," a woman said, running a shaky hand through her short red hair.

"The plant isn't closing, Carrie. You will not lose your job."

The deep voice with a slight drawl cut through the steady din of the restaurant, stealing her breath with its ability to soothe and arouse. Drawn by an intangible force, she leaned forward to peer around the man seated on her right, attempting to see its owner.

"What about the Harvest Festival? How are we supposed to celebrate when we're faced with unemployment?"

"We celebrate because you still have your jobs and we have each other. This is our town. Our home. I promise you I will get to the bottom of this."

There was that voice again!

When a few people shifted positions, Caila caught a flash of white teeth against a square stubbled jaw and dark tousled hair.

Moisture flooded her mouth.

"I recognize that look," Shirley said, placing the glass of wine down in front of Caila. "I see you've noticed Mayor McHottie, Wyatt Bradley."

She froze. *That* was Wyatt Bradley, the man who'd been calling Flair requesting a meeting about the Bradleton plant?

"Wyatt Bradley is the mayor?"

D'uh! That's what Shirley said.

The odd look Shirley gave her seemed to suggest she concurred with Caila's thought. "Yes."

His messages had been forwarded to her, but she'd set them aside, assuming he was a concerned citizen looking to influence her decision. Had the messages mentioned he was the mayor? She honestly couldn't remember. Taking into account what she'd seen only half an hour earlier, however, she now understood his attempts to get in front of the problem.

And she'd ignored him.

He was probably pissed, which would make him adversarial, but his cooperation could be useful. He knew all the players, could make the introductions. Fuck! She'd screwed up. Big time. How had she missed that detail? Was this what Kendra had meant when she'd questioned the quality of Caila's frame of mind?

No! She squashed that doubt before it could take root. She didn't recall a note that he was the mayor and no one in her position would ever think to connect a caller's complaint to the one person whose assistance would make her assignment easier.

Even so, she needed to rectify the situation and there was no time like the present. She took a hefty swallow of wine and swung off her stool.

A man had started playing one of the video games and several people had gathered around to watch. The mayor joined them, standing with his back to her.

And what a back it was . . .

He wore a midnight blue long-sleeved T-shirt that hugged his broad shoulders and biceps like reunited lovers. The material stretched across a muscled expanse that tapered to slim hips and a very fine ass. He'd rolled the sleeves up to reveal forearms sprinkled with dark hair; one draped along the top of the machine, the other hanging down by his side, long fingers clutching the neck of a sweating bottle of beer.

Caila swallowed. She identified with that bottle. If those big hands had been holding her, she'd be wet, too.

Wait, what? She shook her head. Was she losing her mind? She couldn't have *these* thoughts about *this* man!

Members of the group caught sight of her before he did, their laughter fading as she approached. Inhaling, she shored up her defenses. "Mayor Bradley?"

His posture stiffened.

He turned and their eyes met, the intense hazel gaze searing through her. She was a tall woman, and even despite her three-inch heels, he still topped her by several inches. Damn!

Why couldn't this have been a Monet situation? He'd look good from far away, but the closer she got, the more the lines and angles of his face would merge into an unappealing mess.

Ah, the blissful naiveté of wishful thinking.

In close proximity, his features were carved into a masculine beauty that seemed unreal.

High round cheekbones, long straight nose, dimpled chin. Hell, even his lashes were amazing. Cosmetics companies used computer graphics to falsely convince women that using their product would give them *his* lashes. His dark hair was cut short, the wavy strands enticing her fingers to have a go.

She struggled to find a reason to resist.

He was doing some scoping of his own. His eyes traveled southward from the top of her head to the points of her shoes, pausing long moments at certain rest stops in between. She groaned inwardly. Why hadn't she taken the time to freshen up after her flight and the long drive? Put on some lip gloss? Mist her face? Something. She buried the urge to smooth her loose hair back into a bun and adjust her clothes. She would not give him the satisfaction of a reaction.

Unfortunately, her body didn't feel the need to live up to that declaration. Her heart slammed against her chest, and her nipples hardened against her bra. Thank God for the blazer that covered her thin blouse.

What in the hell are you doing, Caila?

This couldn't be happening. She wasn't here to insert the hot mayor's Tab A into her Slot B. She was here to complete her assignment and get back to her life and career in Chicago.

You're a very efficient woman. Who says you can't do it all?

Oh, shut up!

At the edges of her vision, a handsome man wearing a law enforcement uniform smiled. "Here we go again."

A blond bro-dude, cheeks flushed with either alcohol or excitement, elbowed him. "I wonder if there's some kind of spell on this town? As soon as an attractive woman crosses the border, she immediately searches out Wyatt."

The idea that she was acting like some mayoral groupie was enough to yank her from the sensual trance she'd descended into. She inhaled, willing the action to expel the weird lethargy his presence had caused until she once again felt like herself.

"I'm Caila Harris. From Endurance Cosmetics."

The shiny gloss of interest vanished from his expression. His gaze sharpened, his mouth tightened. A muscle ticked in his jaw.

And so it begins.

"Miss Harris. Welcome to Bradleton."

That voice . . . The audible equivalent of warm caramel.

The mayor wasn't the only one who now knew who she was. The information spread through the diner's crowd until most of them openly stared at her with varying degrees of curiosity and hostility.

Nope. Not uncomfortable at all.

"It's Ms. And thank you," she said, feeling as popular as a telemarketer calling during dinner. She moved several feet back and shifted her body so she could address the group, since it was clear the conversation had grown to include more than just the two of them.

Which was probably a good thing.

"I'd appreciate any cooperation you can give me. Once I get the information I need, I'll be out of your hair."

"Why would we do that?" asked the man she'd sat next to at the counter, his words barely hiding his animus. "Everyone knows you're here to shut down the plant."

"I'm here to *evaluate* the plant. The company decides what to do. Trust me, this isn't personal."

She recognized her blunder the moment the words left her mouth.

"Trust you? That'll be the day!"

"What do you mean it's 'not personal'? How are we supposed to support ourselves and our families?"

A prickle of unease darted through her and she glanced around, disturbed by the menacing stares directed her way. Caila eyed the door and took a cautious step toward it.

"Everyone, please! Give her a chance to speak."

And like a magician waving a wand, Wyatt's words calmed the crowd's growing animosity.

That type of strength and leadership was impressive . . . and sexy as hell.

"Thank you," she said, unable to stem the intensity of her attraction to his display of influence.

"You're welcome. But—"

Ugh! Her bud of interest withered on the vine.

"—they do have a point. What *is* the plan for Chro-Make?"

Awe pebbled along her skin. Oh, he was good. Get her on his side with a charming smile and a heroic gesture, then go in for the kill, with swift, surgical precision. *Well played, Mr. Mayor.* He'd executed the move with an ease that suggested he'd implemented the tactic often. And it had always worked for him.

Not this time.

"I can't answer that."

His smile faded and twin lines appeared between his brows. "Why not?"

"Because she's already made up her mind!" An angry voice from the crowd.

A chorus of agreement sounded from the horde.

Caila winced. Had she made a mistake approaching the mayor in this informal setting? Another miscalculation on her part?

Wyatt raised his hand. "Calm down. This isn't helping. Mi—Ms. Harris isn't our enemy."

"Says you."

He shot the utterer of that retort a sharp look before turning to face her. "I apologize. Please understand that we're a small community. We take care of each other. And having someone from the city come down here and threaten the livelihood of a third of us is, well, quite upsetting."

"I haven't made up my mind or made any decisions."

And *she* hadn't. She was only getting information for Endurance. Any decision they made based on that information had nothing to do with her.

But if it did, would this behavior help their cause? Maybe if the town spent more time working and less time hanging at the neighborhood hot spot being rude to visitors, she wouldn't be here "threatening their livelihood." Nevertheless—

"I apologize as well. The local diner isn't the best place to have this discussion. I only wanted to introduce myself."

And alleviate any damage she might have caused by not returning Wyatt Bradley's phone calls. But now she could see that coming over was an even bigger mistake.

And a rookie move.

Swallowing, but determined not to give away any of her inner turmoil, she fortified her posture. "Anyway, I'm sorry for interrupting your discussion. Have a good evening."

There was no way she could eat here now. She'd tell Shirley to bag it for her and—

"Wait!"

The mayor's exclamation, verging on desperation, delayed her retreat. He drew closer and lowered his voice. "That wasn't our best look, but, as you can see, we're feeling a little powerless here. Maybe there's a way you can help us to gain a little control? Feel like we have a hand in our own fate?"

What? No! That wasn't part of her agenda. She needed to stick to the business at hand. She didn't have time for this.

"It might help with the cooperation," he added.

"I can't stress enough how important your performance on this assignment is."

Kendra's words. This task was do-or-die.

"What did you have in mind?"

He smiled wryly, slid a quick look at the crowd, then stepped back and raised his voice. "How about a game of pinball?"

She frowned. That was the last thing she'd expected. "Pinball?"

His half shrug was easy and confident. "A quick, friendly game. Highest score after . . . three minutes wins."

Looking around, she was surprised at the nodding heads and bright looks suddenly gracing the faces in the crowd.

Were they all nuts?

"And the point of this would be?"

"If I win, you stay and enjoy a few days of Bradleton's Southern hospitality. Then when you go back to Endurance, you'll have no problem recommending they keep the plant open."

He'd said "if," but his tone dripped with "when."

Smug bastard.

It didn't matter, but she was curious. "And if I win?"

He spread his arms wide, his expression magnanimous. "Full cooperation."

Her brows flew northward.

During her time at Endurance, she'd been privy to some unusual negotiation suggestions. There was the Nashville music executive who'd wanted to hold their brand pitch meeting in his private hotel suite, wearing onesie pajamas he'd provide . . . at eleven o'clock at night. Then there was the regional sales distributor for a major chemical company who'd suggested they meet at a flea market beforehand to strengthen their haggling skills as a way to ensure a "top-notch round of bargaining."

But she'd never participated in a transaction where someone bet something so important on the outcome of something so trivial.

She narrowed her eyes. "You really think it's in your town's best interests to rest their fate on the outcome of a game?"

"It's not a game of chance. It's a game of skill. And I have complete confidence in mine."

His tone was innocuous, but his eyes burned with the unspoken message—

He had complete confidence in *ALL* of his skills.

Heat pulsed between her thighs.

Caila pursed her lips. "Why would I agree to those terms? Do I look like some young coed who'll be mesmerized by your smile?"

"You think I'm mesmerizing?" he asked, his honeyed, husky drawl sending shivers down her spine.

She ignored his question. "This is between my company and the people who run the factory. I can do my job with or without your cooperation."

"I beg to differ, Ms. Harris. We're a small, intimate town and we don't have the amenities you may find in the big city," he said, adding extra syllables to "amenities" as his delicious drawl morphed into a cartoonish Southern accent that was a cross between Foghorn Leghorn and Kyra Sedgwick from *The Closer*. "Sometimes, things happen. Keys are lost and you can't get inside the building."

She rolled her eyes. "That's what locksmiths are for."

"Sometimes they're booked and can't get there."

"Then I'll call the police."

"Oh, you mean like Dan?" Wyatt tipped his head toward the man in the uniform she'd noticed earlier. "Let me introduce you to Bradleton's chief of police and my best friend since we were boys."

Dan tapped two fingers to his forehead in a salute.

"And I'm Vince Randall," said the blond guy who'd been talking to Dan earlier. He grabbed her hand and cradled it between his moist palms. "I'm the councilman from Ward One and the owner of the car dealership on the southern edge of town."

Wyatt's mouth firmed into a thin line. He glared at Vince and pulled her hand free but remained silent.

Grateful for the save, though she was more than able to take care of herself, she wiped her hands down her thighs before crossing her arms over her chest. "Let me guess. If I agree to this fun little game of pinball and win, those small-town deficiencies will go away?"

His gaze followed her movement and lingered, before he lifted his eyes to meet hers, one corner of his mouth elevating. "We can be a very friendly people."

She snorted and motioned to the mass surrounding them. "Yes, I've been feeling the amicable vibes."

His bark of laughter appeared to shock them both, and for a split second she saw genuine amusement gleaming in his beautiful eyes.

She tapped a finger against her chin, as if pretending to contemplate his proposal. "How about this: If you win, I'll make all *close* decisions in your favor. And if I win, everyone cooperates fully and there's no issue with missing keys, unavailable workers, or anything else that might happen."

"Sounds good to me," he said, as if a decision had been reached.

"No, wait—"

This was ridiculous. Conducting business via a pinball game was the epitome of unprofessional behavior. In fact, acting in such a lax and improper manner was the reason she was in Bradleton carrying out a task that was way beneath her pay grade. She'd indulged him long enough.

She held up her hand, palm out. "This is cute, but it isn't the appropriate way to handle—"

A chorus of jeers and dismissive gestures interrupted her. Seriously? She set her jaw. Why was she trying to play nice? If they didn't see the absurdity in allowing their mayor to behave this way on their behalf, why should she educate them? They thought they had the upper hand. That she couldn't possibly know how to play this game.

He had no idea what he'd gotten them into.

"So, do we have a deal?"

He held out his hand and she hesitated, momentarily heeding some sense of self-preservation. Time slowed and the background noise faded until he filled all corners of her vision. Unsure of where to look, she landed on his mouth. Good God! Those lips should be outlawed! Wide, wicked and—next to his lashes—the lushest feature on his face. Heat surged through her as she imagined them pressed against hers.

Both sets . . .

She blew out a breath and his nostrils flared. The fingers flexed on his outstretched hand. Right. She swallowed and placed her palm against his, watching as it was engulfed by his long fingers. A thunderbolt of electricity skittered up her arm. His eyes darkened and he swayed toward her.

This was not good.

She pulled away, and the sounds of the diner came roaring back, bursting the intimate cocoon they'd briefly created.

"You're on." Dammit! Did she have to sound so breathy?

Why don't you just brace against the pinball machine and stick your ass in the air, Caila? It'd be way less obvious.

He cleared his throat and gestured to the machine. "Ladies first."

She started. Had he read her mind? *Don't be silly.*

She strode past him, attempting—and failing miserably!—to ignore the ache of awareness his proximity caused. She finally glanced at the game she'd agreed to play.

Ooh, classic Star Wars!

She gestured to the other arcade games nearby. "Are you sure you don't want to play Pac-Man or Space Invaders?"

"You're the big corporation and we're just the small town." He splayed both hands on his broad chest, that hackneyed accent reemerging and pouring from him like thick marmalade. "You have all the power. I should at least get a chance to pick the game. Give me all the advantages I can get."

"Very well. But since you picked the game, I should decide playing order. I'll go second."

A cacophony of objections and opinions met her declaration. Wyatt raised both hands in the air and gestured to the bystanders, confidence saturating his aura. "Settle down, settle down. I don't have a problem with her request at all."

He slid in front of the machine and inserted a quarter. Synthesized music blared and multi-colored lights flickered to life. A stainless steel ball rolled down the right-side shooter alley and he pressed the button on the side to engage the flippers.

He was good. His style of play was more than competent, and like most players, he jiggled and jostled the machine. She studied those moves, because it was important to see how much give a machine had. The fact that the digital display never flashed "tilt," and that he never lost his ball meant they must've loosened the tilt bob inside the machine to make it less sensitive to movement and allow a rougher mode of play.

At one point she noticed the police chief studying her, his brow furrowed, and she worried she'd given away her familiarity. So she stepped back, bit her lip, and shook her head, hoping her "anxiety" would ease his concerns. For good measure, she added several looks of longing.

Although that part wasn't a hardship. The man was an orgasm generator in motion, the muscles in his back and triceps flexing as he played the game. He twisted his hips and thrust his pelvis and she had to quickly look away, redirecting her gaze and her mind before images of those same movements in a more private location were permanently seared on her brain.

Her attraction was dampened slightly by the lack of aggression in his play. He didn't take advantage of multiple ball plays or fight to save balls that landed in the alley, all clues that seemed to suggest he believed she wasn't a match for him. He'd never leave those points on the table unless he thought she'd never get close to his score.

"Time!" Dan called.

Twenty-nine million, seven hundred and fifty thousand, one hundred forty.

"That's how you do it!" A voice in the crowd.

The mayor stepped away from the machine and handed her a quarter, his fingers grazing her palm. "Your turn."

The hairs on her arm stood at attention. She shivered.

Shake it off, Caila!

She approached the machine and stared at the back glass showing the classic Star Wars image, where Leia isn't portrayed as the capable person she is, but rather as a sexpot, in the gold, metal Jedi bikini.

And of course, no people of color.

Not even Lando? C'mon!

She squared her shoulders and tested the flipper buttons. The crowd still buzzed with sounds of excitement and anticipation, but in her periphery she noticed the police chief whisper to the mayor and nod in her direction.

So he *hadn't* bought her besotted act? Too late now.

She straightened and kicked off her shoes, lowering her height by several inches, but, more importantly, giving her a stable base to work from.

"Don't know why you're getting comfortable, honey. This won't take long," that same inebriated male voice from earlier said.

She flipped a smile in the direction of the condescending words as she slid the quarter into the slot. "You're absolutely right."

And she proceeded to kick ass. At first, the crowd was jovial, high on their presumed win and her humiliation. She could tell when people figured out it wasn't going the way they'd anticipated.

It got quieter.

She knew the mayor had picked pinball because he thought she wouldn't know how to play. He'd assumed, based on her gender, her race, or both, that the closest she'd ever gotten to a pinball machine was seeing one in a movie. And honestly, that probably wasn't an unfair expectation to have.

What he *didn't* know, and what she didn't feel inclined to tell him, was she knew pinball games very well. She didn't have a lot of experience on this particular game; she'd played it only once before. But she'd had thousands of hours on the pinball machine at the Sav-Mart while Pop-Pop shot the breeze and played cards with his friends.

Pop-Pop . . .

Unshed tears stung her eyes, blurred the flashing lights before her.

No! No! You will not do this! Not here. Not in front of these people!

The grief was still too raw to acknowledge, let alone accept, so she welcomed the anger instead. Let it rush through her, burning any gossamer-thin threads of attraction starting to form. Reminding her of her purpose here. What she was sent to do.

Mayor McHottie thought he'd had the upper hand. That he'd make her look like a fool in front of the community, teach her a lesson, and send her cowed city ass home.

Well, fuck him!

He'd made a mistake, as sure as cornbread goes with greens or the sun rises over the meadow or whatever down-home, Southern-spun platitude they said here.

And he'd pay.

Seconds later, she passed his score. The mood had shifted by then, the whistles, laughter, and clapping having given way to lowered heads and even lower grumbles, though she did notice more feminine voices calling out encouragement and support. Her last shot had rebounded weakly and her ball was trending straight down the middle. She could've been a good sport and let the ball die.

Game over.

But she needed to make her point. She nudged the machine with her hip, causing the ball to hit a rubber post, ricochet off another post, and head back into the main area.

"Yeah, baby!" she crooned.

That move earned her a special three-ball bonus round, which she proceeded to play out until a voice called, "Time!"

Thirty-five million, forty thousand, one hundred points.

Yes! She shimmied her shoulders and hips, her heart beating faster than a sprinting cheetah. She shot a triumphant look over her shoulder, expecting to find him irritated and annoyed, his bruised ego on display. Instead, admiration and respect beamed from the mayor's gaze, and then his handsome features froze into an inscrutable mask.

Before she could take a moment to decipher that look—and the way it made her feel—a hand landed on her shoulder and spun her around.

Shirley smiled. "Good for you, sweetie! I love Wyatt, but it never hurts for that boy to be taken down a peg or two." She held Caila's purse in one hand and her dinner in a to-go container in the other. "Thought you'd probably enjoy it better once you got settled in at Gwen's."

Judging by the hostile undercurrent she was sensing, Shirley had a point. Caila may have been prideful, but she wasn't stupid.

"Thanks." Caila slid her feet into her heels and took the items the other woman held out to her.

The mayor's face was still devoid of expression. "You played me."

His voice was low and dark, and it made her wish he'd insert the preposition "with" into that sentence and make it a question.

"Don't even try it. This 'quick and friendly' game was rigged from the beginning." She took a deep breath and let it out in a huff. "Now, if you'll excuse me, I've had a long day of travel. I'll be at the plant bright and early in the morning. Please tell the manager I'll expect total cooperation from everyone."

She took several steps and, still riding the high of her victory, added, "And thanks for the trip down memory lane."

Chapter Five

Of all the idiotic, foolhardy, and undisciplined things she could've done! What was *wrong* with her?

Caila braced her arms against the roof of her car and dropped her head, trying to calm her racing heart after her mad dash from the diner.

All she'd wanted to do was introduce herself to the mayor, apologize for not returning his calls and suggest a time for a brief meeting when she could get the information she needed. Communicate clearly, build trust, and maintain professionalism, some of the first skills she'd learned about project management.

Instead she'd visually undressed him, bet the success of her assignment on the outcome of a pinball game, and then embarrassed him at said game in front of his friends and constituents.

Maybe she needed a refresher course on what those core skills actually meant.

She supposed she could blame it on exhaustion . . . and shock at meeting Wyatt Bradley. She never would've expected to find a man who looked like that living in a place like this. Not that she'd thought about what the men who lived here looked like, just that she'd expect to find someone like him living—Ugh, he was even affecting her thought processes!

She straightened from the car. Shake it off, she told herself, literally moving her limbs like a rag doll. Anyone who happened by would think she was possessed. Religiously. Demonically. Pharmaceutically.

Her reaction to him was a complication she couldn't afford. Despite her earlier bravado inside the restaurant, she thanked her lucky stars the wager ended in her favor. Nothing like that could happen again. Not if she wanted to save her professional career.

And there was nothing she wanted more.

She'd stumbled slightly in her climb to the top. She could've been facing a terrifying free fall, each rung she'd already attained flying past in an uncontrolled descent. Instead, she'd been offered a lifeline. A second chance. She intended to take full advantage of it. She'd get the information she needed for Endurance to justify pulling the contract, draft her report to the board, and get the hell out of Dodge.

In the meantime, with the plant closed and her eat-in dining plans scrapped, there was nothing left to do but check in at Sinclair House. While Bradleton might possess a lot of aesthetic charm and a gorgeous mayor, it did *not* have a Four Seasons or a Ritz-Carlton. Hell, she would've taken a Holiday Inn Express! But unless she'd planned to drive two hours back and forth to Richmond each day or spend the next few days in the no-tell motel off the highway that Shirley had mentioned, she'd had to make do with one of the town's many bed-and-breakfasts.

Her original reservation began tomorrow at three, but when she'd decided to arrive a day early, she'd had Diane call and change the booking. Her assistant had been assured they'd have no problems accommodating her tonight, and being here, she now understood why.

Bradleton wasn't the tourist capital of Virginia.

With the wind kicking up, the temperature dropping, and the adrenaline wearing off, Caila couldn't think of anything in that moment she'd prefer more than a soft, warm bed. She'd be lucky if she managed to eat her dinner before passing out.

Sinclair House turned out to be a large white colonial with black shutters, four columns, and a wide front porch. A beautiful home that wouldn't have been out of place plopped down in the middle of several acres of land.

In fact, from what she'd seen so far, Bradleton appeared to revel in their town's antiquated style. And though the trees had been lovely and the local shops looked charming, she hadn't missed the small touches that proclaimed the town's pride in its Southern heritage. The Battlefield Cafe, the Blue and Gray Truck Depot, the Rebel Brewery.

Her skin tightened over her bones, and a
prickle of disquiet inched up her spine. That unease was one of the reasons she'd left her own
small town in Maryland and had never looked
back. She didn't like living in a place that showcased its role in an event that caused the suffering
of so many.

Never mind the constant concerns about her
safety.

Brushing the dark—paranoid?—thoughts aside,
she exited the car, grabbing her dinner, purse, and
luggage, and hurried up the sidewalk. Golden
yellow and vibrant red leaves littered the pathway and fluttered in the breeze, providing an
autumnal welcome mat. As she stepped onto
the porch, the warm, spiced scents of cinnamon,
maple, and apples enveloped her, unconsciously
sweeping away her concerns.

Large ceramic planters and rocking chairs with
colorful blankets draped over their backs decorated the wide porch. Caila's heels clicked on the
wooden planks as she passed the rippling Virginia state flag and a white wicker porch swing
on her way to the front door.

Inside, it was as if she'd stepped back in time.
She'd have appreciated the dark oak floors, warm
sunny walls, and period furnishings even more
if it weren't for the loud music and shrieks of
laughter that immediately assaulted her ears.

What the hell . . .

"Hello?" she called out.

Could they even hear her over the commotion? Apparently not, because no one responded. Pursing her lips, she followed the trail of audible breadcrumbs. No one was in the first room she encountered, but, with the exception of the large flat-screen TV on the wall, the receiver, and several speakers, the decor stayed true to the home's vintage feel. An iPhone sat on top of one of the speakers, connected to it by a cord. This must've been the origin of the music.

She left her briefcase on top of her luggage and went farther down the hall. The second room she stumbled upon revealed the source of the laughter. Two groups of four white women wearing neon feather boas, sparkly top hats, and face masks sat at either end of a long dining room table. In the middle of the table, between each group, sat large serving dishes with salad and pasta, platters filled with cheese, crackers, and desserts and more than half a dozen bottles of wine.

The women rolled dice, pumped their fists in the air, and high-fived each other. Some made notations on small pieces of paper in front of them. Others sang along to the music and drank liberally from their cups. They were having such a good time, they never noticed her standing in the doorway.

Was she in the correct place? This was Sinclair House, right? Or—good Lord!—had she walked into a complete stranger's house? They shot people down here for that type of trespass, didn't they?

Caila pressed two fingers to her temples. Exhaustion had given way to a pounding headache that wasn't helped by the sudden piercing blast of an air horn followed by one woman yelling, "That's bunco, bitches!" Caila started backing out of the room, intending to recheck her email and compare the address she'd been given with the one on the house, when she bumped into the sideboard by the entryway.

Her heart stopped and she froze as she found herself the sole recipient of eight confused stares.

Shit.

"Can we help you, honey?" asked the woman still holding the air horn aloft.

"I'm looking for Gwendolyn Sinclair," Caila said, raising her voice to be heard over Carrie Underwood crooning about a cowboy Casanova.

A petite woman in her mid- to late forties sporting a blond pixie cut, a navy boat-necked top, and a purple boa stood, her forehead wrinkled. "I'm Gwen."

Thank you, Jesus! "I have a reservation. Caila Harris."

Dawning horror crept over Gwen's features. She blinked twice rapidly. "From Endurance."

With those two words, the expressions on the other women's faces began to change, an assorted mix of embarrassment, hostility, and drunken amusement. One woman said, "Well, damn!" and yanked the silver glitter top hat off her head. Another, wearing a brightly colored feathered face mask, stood and scooted past Caila. A few seconds later, the music stopped in the middle of Carrie exhorting them to "run for your life." The sudden, shocking absence caused a temporary ringing in her ears.

"So that's how you pronounce it. Kay-lah," Gwen said. She grimaced. "I kinda wasn't expecting you until tomorrow."

Really? Such a warm welcome. They should put it on their website: *Welcome to Sinclair House. We weren't expecting you.*

"We'll see ourselves out," said a voice behind Caila.

She turned and saw the woman who'd left to turn off the music, sans her mask and multi-colored Mardi Gras beads. She motioned for the other women to follow her. There was some giggling, some grumbling, but the remaining six women filed past Caila, though none met her gaze. In the music-free quiet, the sounds of stumbling steps and the front door closing were apparent.

"It's our monthly bunco event." Gwen twisted her fingers in front of her. "Do you play?"

Caila stared at her. "I have no idea what that is."

"Right." Gwen bit her lip. "You know, the fact that the Endurance rep showed up in the middle of our bunco game will be all over town by morning."

That's what passed for news here? Although Caila shouldn't be surprised. That was one of the main characteristics of a small town: Gossip spread like a forest fire during a drought. If that held true to form, it would take less than twenty-four hours for everyone to hear about her little performance at the diner, too.

But right now, none of that mattered.

"Do you have a room available for tonight or do I need to come back tomorrow?"

"We have the rooms. It's not a busy time. In fact, you're my only guest."

"Tha—"

"Now, if this were during the Civil War re-enactment tour or the holiday parade of historic homes, it would've been a different story. We get people from all over during those times. Can't throw a rock without hitting a visitor. But nothing much happens in October. Although maybe that would've been a better time for you to see Bradleton. When we're at our best." Gwen's brown eyes widened, as if she realized she was babbling but she couldn't make herself stop. "We *do* have the Harvest Festival starting this weekend, which draws a nice local crowd. You'd enjoy it if you're still around . . ."

Her words petered off and an awkward silence settled between the two of them.

Jesus.

Gwen rubbed her hands down the sides of her jeans, her fingers fidgeting with the scalloped edge of her shirt. "Come on, I'll show you where to sign in."

Caila almost dropped to her knees as gratitude surged through her. Between the long day, meeting the too-sexy-for-his-own-good mayor, and the fear of being in the wrong house, the adrenaline roller-coaster ride was playing havoc with her equanimity. She didn't care what happened next. She'd accept it with a smile on her face and a spring in her step. Despite what she'd said, there's no way she would've been able to drive the hour back to Richmond. She'd been spared the privilege of paying for a sleepless night at the no-tell motel.

Gwen led her out of the dining room and into an open area in the center of the house. Against the wall stood a beautiful cherry credenza that held a sign-in book and a bell.

Caila added her name to the list of visitors who apparently enjoyed their stay in the "charming" and "welcoming" B&B.

That remained to be seen.

"I'm really sorry about this," Gwen said, flicking her hand in the air, "but I thought your reservation started tomorrow."

Caila wanted to roll her eyes, but she squashed her instinctive annoyance.

Smile on your face. Spring in your step.

"My assistant called yesterday with my change of plans and one of your employees assured her it was okay for me to arrive early."

Gwen shook her head. "I don't have any employees that would answer the phone and I'm pretty sure I didn't talk to anyone from your company."

Caila thought back on her conversation with Diane. "She said she spoke with a young man who—"

"A young man?" Gwen's features hardened. "Kevin!"

Caila jumped, startled to hear such loudness come from the tiny woman. Plus she hadn't known anyone else was there.

A voice from somewhere above them. "Ma'am?"

"Did someone call and tell you they'd be coming tonight instead of tomorrow?"

Silence. Then . . . "Crap."

Footsteps thundered down the wooden staircase facing them.

"Sorry, Mom. I was going to tell you but then I—"

A tall, blond, strapping boy wearing jeans and a dark green Bradleton High sweatshirt skidded to a stop on the landing.

Gwen's gaze bored into him. "We'll talk about it later. Kevin, this is Caila Harris. She'll be staying with us through the weekend."

The young boy's lashes flickered and a flush crept up his neck, turning his already ruddy cheeks so crimson, he resembled a blond-topped tomato.

Caila forced a smile. "It's nice to meet you, Kevin."

Her voice pulled him from his suspended animation. He walked toward her, his movements jerky, his body appearing to act of its own accord. Unfortunately, he forgot the final few steps that led from the landing to the main level. He tripped but caught himself before he fell into a clumsy pile at her feet. He crossed his arms, uncrossed them, then stretched a hand out and leaned against the wooden banister. "Hey."

Gwen shot a look at her son, her delicate brows furrowed. "Kevin graduated from Bradleton High in the spring. He's taking the semester off and working for me to make some money. He'll start classes at the community college in January."

Caila nodded, growing increasingly more uncomfortable with his wide-eyed, unblinking stare. "That's . . . wonderful."

Can I go to my room now? Caila knew what she'd just promised herself, but she'd dare anyone to endure another moment as an unwilling participant in this painful vignette from a Woody Allen movie.

"Did you leave your luggage in your car? I can send Kevin out to get it."

"It's okay," Caila said. "I left it near the room with the TV and speakers."

Gwen nodded. "Kevin, grab Ms. Harris's bags."

"On it," he said, his eyes bright.

Uhhh . . . . "Thank you."

He nodded and ducked his head before loping off.

"This way," Gwen said, as she started walking. "Most of our bedrooms are on the second floor, but we have a larger suite on the main level. I thought you'd be more comfortable there, since it has a small seating area you can use as a workstation."

Caila followed Gwen out of the large antique-appointed parlor—finally!—and down a hallway on the other side of the house. Kevin caught up to them as they stopped at a wooden door.

"Welcome to the Tulip Room." Gwen turned the antique brass handle and opened the door.

All five people gasped in unison.

The walls were painted a luminous butter yellow, the color pairing delightfully with the bright green that adorned the curtains and the matching duvet. Across the room a round table and a yellow and green patterned armless chair comprised the work area Gwen had mentioned. It was a lovely, well-lit space.

But that wasn't why everyone stood motionless, eyes bulging, jaws on the floor.

"Shit!" Gwen's hands flew to her mouth. "I forgot you were in here."

"Mom!" Kevin resembled a large fish gasping for air on land, his gaze glued to the queen-sized bed.

Gwen moved like she'd recently acquired the power of super speed. "Go back to your room. Now!" She pushed her son out the door and closed it firmly in his stunned face.

"I'll be around if you need anything, Ms. Harris," Kevin called through the door.

Caila didn't respond, unable to look away from the unexpected scene. A large white box labeled "Intimate Treasures" sat open on the bed. Scattered around it were dildos, vibrators, and anal plugs of all different sizes, shapes, and colors, along with fuzzy handcuffs, the occasional scrap of red and black lace, tubes of lotion, and jars of cream.

Two women sat at the small table.

Or, rather, they had been sitting.

The redhead scrambled to her feet. "Oh God, oh God," she moaned. Her shoulders curled forward so much Caila thought they'd meet in the middle.

The other woman, a brunette with long curly hair, rose more nonchalantly. "Is everything okay? I thought I had another two hours."

Caila wished she could take a picture of the room at that moment, without being noticed. It would've made a wonderful visual for when she recounted this story to Ava, Nic, and Lacey.

"You did, but my guest showed up early," Gwen said. She grabbed the box, put it on the table, and began dumping the wide assortment of sex toys and lingerie into it. "Caila Harris. From Endurance."

The brunette's brows rose. "Got it."

"When it's slow, I let Evelyn use one of the bedrooms to hold a trunk show," Gwen said, a whirling dervish in motion. "I get a small percentage of everything she sells."

"We did pretty good tonight," Evelyn said.

"This is supposed to be private," the redhead cried.

"Calm down, Daisy." Evelyn ushered her to the door, rubbing soothing circles on her upper back. "I already have your order. I'll call you tomorrow to get your credit card."

Once they left, Caila and Gwen stood there. Alone.

Again.

Caila closed her eyes and pinched the bridge of her nose. Was this uncomfortable silence number three or four?

Gwen sighed and shoveled a hand through her short blond strands. "Do you want another room? You can pick whichever one you want. Or . . . I'll . . . I'll understand if you want to stay someplace else. I can make a few calls. Jenna has a nice place over on Somerset. It's a ten-minute drive from here. The Newell Inn, on the other side of town, has a pretty good breakfast buffet."

The thought of getting back in her car and driving to another B&B with no guarantee of what she'd find?

No thank you. She might not be as lucky next time. She could walk right in on a séance. Or an exorcism. This was the situation she knew, and she only planned to be here about five days. A week at the most. "This is fine."

And it was. It wasn't the sleek modern furniture she was accustomed to—in both the hotels she frequented and her own apartment—but it possessed a comfortable, relaxed feel that suddenly reminded her of Pop-Pop's house. Especially the cushioned window seat on the far wall that recalled the reading nook he'd made for her.

Impending tears stung the backs of her eyes. She exhaled through pursed lips, lowering her lashes and busying herself with wheeling her suitcase into the room and placing her items on the bed.

"That door leads to your en suite bathroom," Gwen said. "The library is down the hallway on the other side of the kitchen. And the wifi passcode is 'sinclairhouse,' one word, all lowercase. We provide breakfast and lunch, but I don't offer a dinner service."

Caila nodded. Speaking of dinner . . .

"Can I use the kitchen to microwave my takeout?"

"Of course." Gwen held out her hand. "Here, I can do it for you."

Caila gave her the bag. "Thanks."

"Feel free to use the kitchen whenever you need." Gwen shook the bag. "Turk's is the best but there are some fast-food places if you head back out of town, and a couple of cafes, too."

"Sounds good."

"And here's a key to the front door. You shouldn't need it unless you get back after eleven."

Caila almost laughed and took the key she was offered. She couldn't remember the last time she'd used an actual key to gain entrance into a place. Her own apartment had upgraded to key fobs several years ago.

"Is there anything else I can do for you?"

Leave me alone so I can pass out? "Not at this time."

Gwen smiled. "I'll bring your food as soon as it's heated. Thank you for staying. I promise I'll make your stay as nice as possible."

She strode briskly to the door and closed it behind her.

Peace at last! Peace at last! Thank God almighty, peace and quiet at last!

Caila exhaled, spread her arms wide, and fell spread-eagle back onto the bed.

She sneezed.

Great. The mattress was more comfy than she'd anticipated but it was a good bet the sheets, blankets, and fabrics weren't hypoallergenic. A field day for the dust mites.

She stared up at the wooden slats of the ceiling fan. How had she gotten here? A few weeks ago she'd been on her way to a partnership and now she was in bum fuck nowhere with buncos and dildos, doing a task that was levels beneath her. And why? Because one night she'd had a little too much to drink at dinner?

It was more than that and you know it.

There was a knock on the door.

"Come in," Caila said, expecting Gwen with her reheated dinner.

Evelyn stuck her head in. "I'm so sorry, but I forgot my box . . ."

Caila couldn't help it. Amusement bubbled up and exploded from her. She laughed until her cheeks hurt and tears were streaming down her face.

She waved the other woman into the room and wiped her eyes with the back of her hand, attempting to catch her breath. "I haven't laughed like that since I heard about . . . in a long time."

"Well, you're welcome," Evelyn said, smiling as she lifted the box.

Caila eyed her. "And the orders are confidential?"

"Absolutely. It's a small town. I wouldn't make any money if people thought I'd blab to their neighbors about their purchases."

"Good." Caila reached for her wallet. "I won't be here long enough to place an order. Which of those vibrators do you have in stock?"

Chapter Six

Wyatt knew lots of women and had dated his share. So why couldn't he banish the memories of Caila Harris that had monopolized his thoughts since last night?

The muscles in his shoulders stretched as he carefully smoothed the planing sled over the thick slab of wood contained between its rails, flattening the surface to use as a coffee table. The jig vibrated in his hands and kicked up a dense cloud of sawdust.

Of course you're thinking about her. She's the representative from Endurance who holds the fate of the plant in her hands. The plant that's vital to your town's economic survival. She's all you should be thinking about.

That would make him feel much better if his musings were relegated to the business implications of her presence in Bradleton and coming up with strategies to defeat her plan. Instead, he couldn't help entertaining all sorts of inappropriate thoughts about her.

Thoughts where they stood so close he could see each individual strand of her lashes and breathe in her warm, enticing scent.

Where he brushed his thumb across her plump lower lip and discovered it was as soft as it looked.

Where they were alone in Turk's, under the flickering fluorescent lights, and she'd agreed to his suggestion of an additional use for that pinball machine . . .

Wyatt shook his head in another futile attempt to eliminate her from his mind and began another pass over the wide, textured slab. The tool's muffled whine provided a familiar and soothing ambient sound.

He'd noticed her the moment she'd first entered the diner. He'd been listening to what felt like the millionth conversation about the plant closing when he'd observed a sexy feminine form in his peripheral vision. He'd instinctively turned to see who it was; his first thought was that he didn't recognize her.

His second thought was now that he'd seen her, he'd never forget her.

Dark, wavy hair fell around her shoulders and framed a face with skin the color of dark gingerbread, round cheekbones, and a sharp chin. She was tall, with a body that made his palms itch to discover all its dips and curves, hills and valleys. When she took her seat at the counter, she moved with a long-limbed grace that couldn't help drawing gazes.

Her clothes and handbag screamed city money. Not that Bradleton didn't have wealthy women; some were in his family. But they dressed differently. Bright colors instead of slick, sharp neutrals. Pearl necklaces instead of diamond studs.

He'd stared at her strong profile, willing her to look in his direction. He wanted to see her eyes, heeding some nascent whimsical notion that her eyes would tell him . . . everything. She never glanced his way, and since he didn't want to act like the stalker they'd accused Vince of being, he'd returned his full attention to the conversation. But it wasn't long before the hair on the nape of his neck stirred.

"Don't look now, but someone is staring at you," Dan had murmured.

Considering it was what he'd craved only minutes before, Wyatt longed to ignore his friend's directive. But he didn't. "Does anyone know who she is?"

"I never said it was a woman, let alone a particular one," Dan countered, sliding him a sidelong glance.

Wyatt winced. Busted!

Dan shook his head, his mouth screwed into a mocking twist. "No idea, although I heard her say she was staying at Gwen's."

So she wasn't just passing through. She was specifically visiting their town. Why? Sure, Bradleton was situated close to both Washington, D.C., and Richmond, but most people traveling between the two cities or doing business in either usually stuck to places along the Interstate 95 corridor, not venturing miles west to find their small town.

Did she have family here?

"She's coming this way," Dan whispered theatrically, like they were characters in a scene from a high school comedy.

Accordingly, his heart rate slipped his control and pounded in his chest.

"Mayor Bradley?"

His skin had tingled at the honey-on-gravel huskiness of her voice. And when he'd turned around . . . her eyes. Velvety brown, they were thickly lashed and slightly downturned at the outer corners, giving her a sultry, slightly sad look that did something he'd never experienced to his insides. His reaction to her unsettled him and he blamed that agitation for his lack of judgment that followed.

The router jerked in his hand. Dammit! He released it and blew out a frustrated breath. He'd cut a level deeper than he'd intended. All because his mind had been on Caila Harris and not on what he'd been doing. Unless he wanted to ruin the entire slab, he needed to quit while he was ahead and come back to it when he was far less distracted.

Wyatt powered the tool off. He removed his safety glasses and hearing protection earmuffs and laid them on the workbench against the far wall. He'd do well to hold on to that goal. To avoid distractions. Stay focused. Keep his thoughts of Ms. Harris as professional as possible. She didn't know it, but he planned to crash her meeting with the plant manager this morning. He'd promised the town he'd do everything in his power to save their jobs, and he always kept his promises.

Even if that meant staying close to the only woman who caused him to think and act in ways he didn't recognize.

Forty minutes later, Wyatt shut his car door and strode across the driveway to the palatial home where he had daily breakfast with his family.

Twelve thousand square feet on over twenty acres of land, it was an impressive estate. He knew it well, having grown up playing in the twenty-five rooms in the house, plus the caretaker's cottage, and throwing parties around the swimming pool and in their manicured gardens. Although he had a key, he didn't need to use it. He rarely entered through the imposing front door, preferring to head along the brick pathway that ran along the side of the house and use the informal entrance near the kitchen that remained unlocked during the day.

"Mother," he called out, closing the glass-paneled door behind him. He knew where she was, just as he knew she'd reprimand him when she finally saw him.

He strode down the long hallway, his footsteps muffled by the carpet runner, and turned into the room on the right. Renee Bradley sat at the far end of the long, lacquered wood dining room table, a fine bone china teacup raised in one delicate hand.

"Good morning, Wyatt. And please stop yelling. It isn't necessary."

He hid a grin as he crossed to her and grazed her cheek with a kiss, the familiar smell of her perfume wafting up to greet him.

"Just announcing my presence, like you taught me."

She waved him away. "That's not what I meant, and you know it."

It was barely eight in the morning, and his mother was impeccably dressed, her light brown hair pulled away from her artfully made-up face. Neat and well-groomed. He'd never seen her any other way.

Not even when his father left.

Renee wrinkled her nose. "Why are you dressed like an auto mechanic? You're the mayor of this town!"

Wyatt looked down at his olive green chinos and dark jean shirt. That comment was uncalled for. His clothes were of a good quality and fit him well. "Things are a bit more casual now. No one wears a suit and tie anymore."

"More's the pity," she murmured.

He'd settled into the cream upholstered chair on her left when the door in the far corner swung open and their housekeeper walked in, carrying a teapot.

"Good morning, Violet."

"Morning, baby." Violet's voice rose in surprise. She topped off his mother's cup. "You're here early. You hungry?"

"For your food? Always."

Violet had worked for his family for the past twenty years. He loved the other woman, having fond memories of spending afternoons in the kitchen watching her bake and being the lucky beneficiary of her sweet treats.

Violet grabbed a stainless steel carafe from the sideboard and poured him a cup of coffee, patting his shoulder before heading back into the kitchen. After taking a blissful sip of the hot, bracing brew, he opened his eyes to find his mother watching him.

"I received a call from Eloise Langford."

Wyatt sighed and set his cup down in its saucer. "Why do you indulge her? You know I can't wave a magic wand and make a Miller & Rhoads appear in Bradleton. One, I'm not a wizard, and two, that department store went out of business almost thirty years ago."

"I've explained that to her. But she's ninety-two and her memory isn't what it used to be. She still thinks your father is the mayor. He would allow people to contact him directly with their complaints."

His chest tightened. "I may share his name, but our styles of governing are quite different."

I actually stuck around to do the job I was elected to do.

The words clamored to be free, but he reined them in, not wanting to hurt his mother or ruin her illusions about his father.

"And Bradleton is the better for it," Wyatt Asher Bradley II said, clearly not concerned about sparing Renee's feelings.

Wyatt straightened in his chair, as his grand-father strolled into the room. Asher Bradley was a distinguished man in his eighties, and though he'd slowed considerably over the years, he still retained the tall, erect bearing that led many to correctly guess he'd served in the military.

"Good morning, Wyatt."

"Morning, sir."

Violet reappeared and placed a steaming plate of food before Wyatt. She gave his grandfather a tall glass of orange juice and took Renee's empty bowl, disappearing again behind the swinging door. Asher took his place at the other end of the table.

"You don't have time to entertain the whims of lonely old women," Asher said. "You have a town to run."

"Yes, sir."

"A Bradley has been involved in running this town since its inception. And save a few rare lapses, we've done well."

His mother's features tightened, but she didn't respond.

Asher removed a newspaper from the stack at his elbow, opened it with a brisk snap, and began reading it. His grandfather was a firm believer in staying informed. Every morning he read through the *Washington Post*, the *New York Times*, and the *Bradleton Herald*.

"Are you the one responsible for single-handedly destroying the rainforests?" Wyatt teased. "Why don't you use the iPad I bought you two years ago?"

Asher eyed him over a folded-down corner. "I prefer the feel of paper. If it was good enough for my father and grandfather, it's good enough for me."

That was Asher's personal life philosophy, considering how often he used that same statement to justify his decisions.

Wyatt took a bite of eggs. "You could save time and just watch MSNBC."

Asher scoffed. Actually scoffed! "I don't want my news filtered through liberal talking heads or conservative conspiracy theorists. I still believe in facts and I'll take mine straight from the source."

It was the answer he'd expected. The same one his grandfather gave each time Wyatt asked. In spite of the current chaos happening in his town, it was good to see that some things never changed.

Violet entered the room, placed a bowl of oatmeal in front of Asher, and refilled Wyatt's coffee.

"I heard the Endurance rep breezed into town a day early," Asher said, his steel blue gaze sharp.

Wyatt choked on his food. He dropped his fork and coughed, shooting a teary smile at Violet as she handed him a glass of water.

When Asher hadn't immediately mentioned Caila, Wyatt had gotten complacent.

Big mistake.

"Yes, sir," he managed.

How much should he admit to? How much did Asher know? Shown by his daily perusal of newspapers, his grandfather was keen on gathering as much information as possible. Wyatt swore the man had spies everywhere.

Which was confirmed when Asher said, "Since when do mayors conduct critical town business over pinball machine contests?"

Similar to the sentiment Caila Harris had expressed.

Wyatt wiped his eyes with a napkin and drank some water, forcing himself to swallow carefully. The food he'd already eaten had hardened into stone in his belly. "I've never given you any reason to doubt my abilities to do my job."

"What do you call that scene last night at Turk's?" Asher crisply folded his newspaper closed. "This woman is here to essentially fire a third of this town's workforce. Do you understand what the consequences of such an action will do to Bradleton?"

"Woman?" Renee leaned forward.

Wyatt bristled. "I don't need to be lectured about the town's economic future. I know exactly what's at stake."

His mother raised her voice. "They sent a woman?"

Both men looked at her.

"Yes," Wyatt said, confused why she'd locked on to that particular detail.

"What is she like?" Renee asked.

Beautiful.

Intelligent.

Competitive.

Sexy.

Wyatt shrugged and looked away. "How should I know? I just met her."

"Don't you find it interesting that they sent a woman? I wonder why?" she mused, her index finger tapping against the side of the teacup she held in her hands.

Was she serious? "Because it's her job. Women have been participating in the workforce, Mother. For centuries."

Renee ignored his sarcasm. "Do you think they've heard about you?"

She could be relentless when it mattered to her. She'd missed her calling as a federal prosecutor or an investigative reporter.

"What does that mean?"

"You know, your reputation? Maybe they sent her here as some sort of Trojan horse?"

He wanted to laugh at his mother's suggestion, but he couldn't discount his strong reaction to Caila Harris. That reaction had caused him to act out of character. Was Renee on to something? Had Caila been sent here to let them down easy? Not that any cosmetics company would know or care about his reputation—and seriously, *what* reputation? He went on dates. Big deal!—but maybe they believed a beautiful woman would make a better bearer of bad news.

Wyatt rubbed his brow. "I'm pretty sure that's not it."

Asher jumped in. "How do you know? Big corporations are ruthless when it comes to their business and making money. I wouldn't put anything past them. And if you're smart, you won't, either. If this was their plan, it appears to be succeeding."

"That's not true."

"Did you think showing her you were better at pinball was going to be a powerful opening gambit?"

Wyatt tightened his fist on the table. He didn't like what Asher was saying, mainly because he knew his grandfather was right. He could've handled last night better. But from the moment he'd seen her, he'd been unable to resist the longing for her to see him as more than just the mayor. He could imagine his friends' obnoxious amusement if they'd known what he'd been thinking. For once, Wyatt had wanted to further a personal interaction.

Something *was* going on with him.

But he'd be damned if he'd let his grandfather know that.

"I don't need to be debriefed by you," he said.

Asher wasn't deterred. "Obviously you do."

"You weren't there. It was a playful atmosphere, but it won't interfere with business."

"It already has. You lost any home court advantage you had. You are the next generation of Bradleys in Bradleton. That's a huge responsibility. You don't have time for playing."

"I'm well aware of my commitment to this town. You've drilled little else into me since I was a child!"

"Someone had to. Your father didn't stay around to do it."

"And it's conversations like these that cause me to wonder if he didn't make a wise decision!"

His chest rose and fell with the force of his enraged breath.

"Darling, please. Sit down," Renee pleaded, placing a cool hand on his forearm.

Until his mother spoke he hadn't been aware that he was standing. He forced himself to calm down as the red haze loitering on the edge of his vision receded. He settled back in his chair and stared across the table at his grandfather. The older man's displeasure was evident.

"That outburst wouldn't have happened if we'd sent him to VMI for college as I'd wanted to."

Another Bradley male tradition: attending the prestigious military institute a couple of hours away. Because what had been good for Asher's grandfather and father . . .

"You bring that up every time Wyatt disagrees with you," Renee said. "He didn't want to go there. I know how much you treasure the discipline your alma mater instilled in you, but attending the Virginia Military Institute doesn't cure all ills. It didn't prevent his father from leaving."

"Now, don't you blame—"

"Enough!" Wyatt swiped the air in a violent motion. "Stop discussing me as if I was an absent, disobedient child."

A muscle ticked in Asher's jaw but he didn't complete his statement. He shared a look with

Renee. "If Chro-Make closes it'll be catastrophic for this town, but the possibility of a shutdown has forced me to accelerate certain plans."

Asher had been president of the local community bank for the past twenty years. Was he finally going to retire? Take the opportunity to travel?

"What plans?" Wyatt asked.

"The state representative for our district isn't seeking reelection next year."

His grandfather had been mayor of Bradleton years before, but he'd never expressed any other political aspirations.

"I can't imagine you not working at First Commonwealth."

"I'm not leaving the bank," Asher corrected, his brow furrowed. "You're going to run, not me."

Wyatt's bark of laughter surprised everyone. "I don't want to be a Virginia state delegate!"

Why would he? His life was just the way he wanted it. As mayor of Bradleton, he worked normal hours and was still able to have a life outside of his family obligations.

Being a Bradley was more than just being a member of the family. It was about duty and responsibility. To the family name and to the town. It could be a soul-crushing experience to learn that your wants and needs came second to what was best for the family. Most of them accepted it. Others couldn't. Like his father. In the end, Tripp Bradley had chosen himself over the family.

And his grandfather had never let *Wyatt* forget it.

Wyatt would never do what his father did. He was smarter and stronger. He'd crafted a situation where he could fulfill his family obligations and still find a way to be happy. And he wasn't interested in giving that up.

"Good. Because the state delegate position is only temporary. It's to give you some experience. The real goal is the governorship in four years."

Wyatt blinked. The governorship? When they'd mentioned it in the past, he hadn't taken them seriously. The Bradleys usually ran Bradleton for a while and then settled locally into their roles as pillars of the community. They'd never run for statewide office. But his mother and grandfather hadn't been joking. They'd planned his entire life, all without granting him the respect of a consultation.

He shook his head. "I think my focus should be here."

"I know you do. Which is why it's my job as head of this family to carry the responsibility of thinking ahead. And why I've been planning to announce your run at the Harvest Ball. It'll be the perfect end to the festival." Asher's thin lips firmed into an imperceptible line. "I had this dream for your father and he did everything right . . . until he didn't. I took my eye off the ball. I won't make that mistake with you."

So this was in *his* best interests?

"We can discuss this later," Asher continued. "Right now, you need to focus on figuring out how to prevent the plant from closing. What are you going to do?"

Like he would tell Asher? So he could control that, too?

"I'll handle it." Wyatt wiped his mouth with his napkin and pushed back from the table. "I have to go."

"Wait a minute! Do you have a plan of action for dealing with this?"

"I do."

"Because I'd be more than willing to make a few phone calls and—"

"Let me be clear," Wyatt said, ignoring the wide eyes and raised brow invoked by his sharp tone. "I'm not interested in reflecting on your failures from the past or your political aspirations for me in the future. I have a job to do *now*. So"—he stood—"if you'll both excuse me, I have a meeting with Ms. Harris at the plant."

And to think it was only an hour ago that managing his unexpected attraction to the Endurance rep had seemed like his most challenging predicament.

Chapter Seven

A full night's sleep could do wonders.

Caila stood outside the plant, in the same place she'd been sixteen hours earlier, and smoothed her hands down the sides of her navy and white pinstriped dress. Yesterday's events had been farcical. As she looked back on them now, with a clear head and well-rested eyes, it was apparent her unusual behavior and reactions could be explained by her extreme fatigue.

It wouldn't happen again.

She'd been sent here on a simple assignment. A couple of days working at the plant, a day or two around town, and she'd have everything she needed. She could be on her way back to Chicago before she even had time to unpack. The prospect of being in this town any longer than necessary made her skin crawl. Even with her brief exposure, the near-intimate knowledge people had about their neighbors made her feel slightly claustrophobic. It was difficult to be invisible when everyone knew who you were. So for the remainder of her time in Bradleton, she would focus on her work and avoid all distractions.

And that included the town's sexy mayor.

She opened the door, strode into the lobby, and skittered to a halt, surprised to find the vestibule empty. Where was everyone? There was no excuse this time. It was a weekday during business hours.

She looked around. The once-bright blue walls were dingy and stained, and the linoleum flooring had seen better days. Where were the displays of the various products they manufactured? Where did they exhibit the products they sold? Save for a counter where a receptionist should sit and another door that probably led into the factory, the space was empty.

As if on cue, the door opened and Wyatt stood there. Her breath seized in her throat. It should be a cardinal sin for a man to be that attractive, especially standing in a building that manufactured products to enhance a woman's looks. He needed no improvements. She bit her bottom lip and took in the view: dark denim shirt, olive khaki pants, sharp, stubbled jaw. Even the white nylon hairnet he wore, which should've looked silly on him, added to his dark appeal. He looked rugged, stylish, and sexy as hell.

That's the last time, Caila. Stop noticing he's sexy.

"So glad you could join us, Ms. Harris," he said, his hazel eyes sparkling and a smug smile twisting his kissable lips.

She clutched the strap of her tote bag with both hands. "What are you doing here?"

"Where else would I be? Your assessment of this plant is the most important item on my agenda. As long as you're in town, your . . . exploits are my top priority."

Great! So much for avoiding distractions.

He leaned a hip against the counter. "I guess 'bright and early' means something different in the city?"

"I blame your lackadaisical roosters. I didn't hear them crowing and I was counting on them to get me up."

His heated gaze captured hers. "It'd be my pleasure to get you up anytime you need me."

Her knees actually wobbled. She locked them in place and swallowed. "No thanks. Now that I know they're unreliable, I'll use the alarm on my phone."

Good Lord, the man was potent. Did this mean her reaction to him couldn't be explained away by exhaustion?

It didn't matter. She was stronger than some unwanted attraction.

She straightened her shoulders. "While this witty back-and-forth has been charming, I have a long day ahead of me. Can you direct me to Nate Olshansky's office?"

The sooner she could get away from this man and meet with the plant manager, the closer she'd be to her goal of leaving. Olshansky would be able to give her access to the reports she required and introduce her to other members of management she'd need to interview.

"Sure. But he asked me to give you a tour of the facilities first."

She shook her head. "That isn't necessary."

Especially if he was her tour guide. What she really wanted was to get the paperwork in her hands. Something concrete and definite that would center her and help her get back on track. Spending time with Wyatt had the danger to do the exact opposite: scatter her focus and derail her progress.

"No, it isn't. But Nate's on an important phone call at the moment. The tour won't take long, and by the time we're finished, he should be done."

So taking that call was more important than promptly meeting with the person who held the future of your company in her hands?

Good to know.

But in the meantime, what was she going to do? Stand around for fifteen or twenty minutes looking like an idiot? Especially when she'd need a tour of the plant at some point anyway?

"Fine." She took the hairnet he offered and placed it over her hair.

He reached behind him and opened the door to the inner portion of the factory, motioning for her to precede him. When she passed . . . God, he smelled amazing! His intoxicating fragrance was a mixture of cologne, fabric softener, and him. It made her want to grab him by his open collar, pull him close, and nuzzle his neck to see if that deliciousness clung to him everywhere.

Yeah, she needed to get away from him as soon as possible.

The drone of the machines on the main floor startled her at first, coming as she had from the quiet vestibule, but it didn't take long before she grew accustomed to it, relegating it to white noise. The air actually smelled nice. Not Wyatt-nice. More sweet, like vanilla and cream.

He directed her to an area where blue and white barrels, shrink-wrapped shipping containers, and large brown sacks were piled high on wooden pallets.

"Here's where we keep inventory for the products we make."

She almost snorted. "Is that the royal 'we'?"

As if Wyatt had ever worked a day in this manufacturing plant.

"Bradleton is a small town. *We* are like family. We're very proud of the work done here. We all feel like we have a hand in its success."

If they were that successful, she wouldn't be here.

Wyatt was popular. He stopped to speak to everyone and shake hands with many of the workers. They all seemed genuinely happy to be in his presence.

"Hey, Mayor, are you coming to the game on Friday? Henry might actually get some playing time."

"Are you doing the color run?"

"Looking forward to seeing you lead the parade."

"We can count on you at the bake sale, right?"

She followed him across the large main floor, observing the mixing vats of colorful creams and powders and the enormous metal shelving stands with trays of product racked on them. Though the place was immaculate, the machinery was old, at least a generation behind, and almost half of the machines weren't in use. At that realization, she noticed there were less than half the number of people working that she'd expected, based on their annual output. What was going on here? How did they expect to make any money when they didn't work at full capacity?

"The offices are up there," Wyatt said, indicating a set of stairs visible through a half-glass steel door.

The space on the other side was tight, as she learned when Wyatt closed the door behind them. He stood so close, the heat from his body threatened to singe the hairs at the nape of her neck.

She didn't move, feeling it begin to form again. That cocoon that wove around them until they were the only two people in the world and nothing else mattered. It had happened last night at the diner. And as her heart raced and her lids inched lower, she knew it was happening again. She'd broken the spell the last time. What would happen if she just did nothing? If she let it be?

Would they eventually emerge as something new and beautiful?

"After you," he finally said, his voice a deep rumble from his chest.

Guess they'd never find out. Which was for the best.

But by waiting and getting caught in her feelings, she'd now have the indignity of walking up the steps with her ass practically in his face.

Hefting her bag higher on her shoulder, she said a prayer that her skirt wouldn't hike up and climbed the metal staircase.

"Fuck. Me." A barely audible hiss.

Her toe caught on the tread of the ascending step and she stumbled. She reached out and grabbed the railing. Had she imagined the tortured utterance or had he actually said it?

There was another entrance at the top of the steps. Having learned her lesson, and not wanting another close encounter, she didn't wait for him.

Instead of the wall she expected, a pane of glass stretched the entire corridor, showcasing the main factory floor beneath them.

For a brief second she thought she was stepping into air.

A swell of instability and anxiety nearly overwhelmed her. Startled, she stumbled backward— into Wyatt's broad chest. His hands came up to grab her arms, his touch searing through the thin cashmere of her gray sweater.

"Whoa. I got you."

And he did. Have her. He felt warm, solid, safe. And he smelled So. Damn. Good.

But it wouldn't last. It never did.

Despite still feeling light-headed, she pulled away from his embrace. "Thank you for the tour, but after you take me to Mr. Olshansky's office, you can go."

"Trying to get rid of me?"

Yes! "Of course not," she said, flustered, feeling heat pool in her cheeks. Her gaze bounced around like a trapped insect: off the glass, off his gorgeous face, eventually landing on the concrete floor. "I don't want to keep you from your duties."

"I appreciate your concern, but as I told you before, there's nothing on my agenda more important than securing the solvency of this factory."

As they started down the long walkway, Caila tried not to focus on the panoramic glass meant to provide an unobstructed view of the work area.

Or the thirty-foot drop to the cement floor below.

"Are you okay?" Wyatt asked from behind her.

Before she could stop herself, she flicked a quick gaze to the vista of bright lights and air on her right . . . then wished she hadn't. Beads of sweat popped out on her upper lip.

If this messed up her flawless makeup application . . . "I'm fine."

You are not fine.

She stopped and squeezed her eyes tight. She took several long, deep breaths, claiming a moment to compose herself. She wasn't afraid of heights; she could stand on a chair, drive over bridges, fly in a plane. It was the fear of falling that scared her. The risk of impact, the loss of control. The last time she'd felt this way was five years ago when she'd taken Ava to Willis Tower in Chicago and had refused to get off the elevator onto the building's all-glass observation deck on the 103rd floor.

She sensed movement in her vicinity and opened her eyes. Wyatt stood next to her, his tall, broad body essentially blocking her view of the open space. Her chin trembled but she pressed her lips tight to stop it. She nodded briskly, unable to meet his gaze, and they continued on in silence until they reached a door at the end and Wyatt knocked on it.

A short, reed-thin man, wearing a colored smock with "Chro-Make Manufacturing" stitched on the right pocket and his name on the left, came to greet them.

"Miss Harris, I'm Nate Olshansky. I'm sorry I couldn't give you the tour myself but I had to take that call." He bared his teeth in what Caila assumed was a smile. "But I'm sure the mayor here did a great job."

Olshansky wiped his hand on the side of his faded jeans before holding it out to her.

Back on emotional terra firma, she accepted his handshake.

"It's Ms. And I understand when business calls. Mayor Bradley was an adequate tour guide."

She saw Wyatt smile slightly and shake his head at her statement but Olshansky reclaimed her attention.

"Let's go into my office."

His boots echoed on the floor as she slid her hairnet off and followed him into a small, cramped room where a large round table with six metal folding chairs competed for space with two desks and several filing cabinets.

Olshansky must've noticed her expression. "We don't have a lot of available enclosed space, so our office doubles as a conference room."

Caila placed her bag on the table and looked at Wyatt. "I think we'll be fine now."

"Nice try." He pulled out a chair and sat down, tossing his hairnet on the table and crossing his arms over his chest. "I think I'll stay around. In case Nate needs my help. Remember, I've seen you in action."

Great! She forced a smile and sat down, doing her best to ignore Wyatt's distracting presence and focus on the plant manager.

"Mr. Olshansky—"

"Nate," he supplied.

She tipped her head in acknowledgment. "Nate. Has anyone from Flair talked to you about why I'm here?"

Nate nodded. "They sent me a letter saying they were in the process of selling the company to Endurance."

Caila pulled a monogrammed leather folio from her bag. "As part of our due diligence in acquiring

Flair, we're looking at their assets and inventory, including their contracts with vendors. When analyzing your financial reports we noticed your costs have skyrocketed twenty percent in the last four years."

"Well," Nate began, shifting in his seat, "it's been a tough economy and we employ a lot of people. We've done our best to work within the limits of both."

"I appreciate that, but your expenses have increased, your profits have decreased, and you're not working to your full potential. I stopped by here yesterday when I first arrived and the entire plant was closed. How can you meet your orders if you're not running around the clock shifts?"

Nate's brows dipped and he shot a look at Wyatt before responding. "We're not running full shifts because we're in turnaround."

What the fuck? Had Endurance known this when they'd sent her here? Why hadn't she been informed?

During turnaround, plants either closed down or worked with an extremely reduced staff while they inspected, tested, and revamped their machinery and procedures. The extensive undertaking could take several weeks or drag on for several months, but it was conducted as quickly as possible because the lost revenue, as well as the direct costs associated with its execution, made turnarounds an expensive process.

This wasn't an ideal time for her visit. How

was she supposed to assess the plant if it was shut down for all intents and purposes?

But you're not here for a true evaluation, are you, Caila? This may work in your favor.

"The rise in costs can be explained by the increase in price of raw materials. We also had to get creative when Flair cut orders. Our choices were to lay off people or reduce shifts so everyone could keep their jobs. Unlike some, we value our people," Wyatt said.

Caila tilted her head. "I'm sorry, Mayor Bradley, but do you have a position in this plant that I'm not aware of?"

"My job involves managing the day-to-day operations of this town as it relates to its long-term planning."

"Doesn't that have to do with infrastructure and real estate development?"

"The viability of a major employer in my town plays a large role in our long-term planning. I'm here to lend any help I can to Nate and the entire Chro-Make team. It could be seen as a breach of my duties to not keep up with this. And I take my responsibilities seriously."

"I do as well, and it's my job to figure out the reason behind the increasing costs and determine a way to bring those costs down."

"And if there's not?" Wyatt asked, in a tone that made her clench her teeth.

"All I do is provide Endurance with the information. They'll make the final decision."

"And that would be?" he pressed.

She pursed her lips. "They may decide to pull their contract and look for a co-packer that can function within the budget allotted."

Nate leaned back and ran a hand over his balding head. "Shit. I was afraid you were going to say that."

Caila braced her elbows on the table. She hadn't been a part of discussions like this for a long time and they had never been her favorite part of the job. What she wouldn't give to be back in her office in Chicago coming up with plans for the new organic makeup line.

It won't be long. Just do your job.

Right.

She inhaled. Based on the preliminary numbers she'd seen, Chro-Make was a liability. Saying so in her report would just be telling the truth. Whatever Endurance did with that information wasn't her fault. Just a few days in town to give the appearance of propriety, a week on the report when she got home to show her thoroughness, and then life could get back to normal.

"What should we have done?" Nate asked, distress ravaging his already haggard features. "Flair may have cut its orders, but we were still responsible for the people who work here."

Wyatt scooted forward in his chair, his palms flat on the table, his hazel eyes beseeching. "A third of this town depends on this plant for their livelihoods. Do you know what losing their jobs will do to those families? To this town?"

Caila hardened her heart. Their choice to

run the plant as a charity and not a business had led to these problems. It wasn't her job to help them figure out the consequences of their decisions.

Opening the folio, she pulled out a sheet of paper and slid it across the table to Nate. "Here's a list of the reports I'll need. I've also noted the department heads I'll need to speak to."

The muscle in Wyatt's jaw twitched at her avoidance but he didn't comment on it.

The ensuing seconds passed in a heavy and uncomfortable silence. Nate scratched his cheek. "I can't help you with this."

Caila frowned. "I'm not asking you to prepare anything special. These would've already been done in your normal course of business."

"I understand, but—"

"May I?" Wyatt interrupted. At Nate's nod, he pulled the paper closer and scrutinized the details. "Ah, I see what the problem is."

He didn't elaborate, and his slow smile suggested he knew she'd rather chew glass than ask.

She flicked her gaze upward. *Lord, save me from sexy, incorrigible men.* Dammit! She was supposed to stop noticing his sexiness!

"And?" She made sure her voice advertised her annoyance.

"This is accounting information."

Was the click of her upper and lower molars meeting audible?

"Yes. I need to see the financial records, including the profit and loss statements beyond the four years I already have. This is about the profitability of Chro-Make. It's the reason I'm here."

"But you requested a meeting with the manager of the plant."

"Of course I did. I wanted to speak to the person with the sole responsibility of running the day-to-day operations."

"Nate is responsible for the day-to-day operations with regards to production quality and shipping orders out on time. He deals with manufacturing, not accounting."

Manufacturing, not accounting . . .

Was she being *Punk'd*? Other shows were coming back and it was the only thing that made sense. How else to explain this forced semi-demotion and exile to a small town, where normal words meant something different, than that she was on a revival of the hidden-camera practical joke reality TV show?

"Then who deals with the financial side of the business?" she forced out.

"That would be Joe Keslar," Nate said.

She crossed one hand over the other on the table. "Is he here?"

It was a long shot, considering the plant was in turnaround, but she was due some good luck.

"No."

"Can you call him in?"

Worst-case scenario, she'd lose a couple of hours, although the idea of waiting made her insides scream in frustration.

"That's going to be a problem," Nate said, sliding an uneasy look in Wyatt's direction.

She tightened her lips. Guess the universe disagreed about owing her some good luck. "Why?"

"Because he isn't here," Nate said.

"I know. You already said that."

"He didn't mean Joe isn't here at the plant," Wyatt said. "He meant he's not here in Bradleton."

Both of these men were in the process of doing a Texas two-step all over her last nerve. "Are you kidding me? You knew I was coming, right?"

"Well, yes, but we weren't informed of your intentions until a few days ago."

Wyatt drummed his fingers against the table. "If someone would've asked, I'm sure Nate would've told you this wasn't the best time for your evaluation."

He was so smug. That's what every company would've said. No one likes when an analyst comes in.

"Turnaround is scheduled months in advance," Nate said, "and Joe isn't needed for it, so . . ."

"'So,' what? Where is he?"

"Joe takes his family on a hunting and fishing retreat every year and he usually coordinates it with turnaround," Nate said.

The hits just kept on coming. Why was this happening to her? She was a good person, she gave to charities, she didn't kick cats or dogs. She was practically a saint!

"Call him and tell him we need him back here."

"I couldn't do that! It's the highlight of his year. It would take an act of God to get him to cancel it."

Then call her Athena, goddess of war, wisdom, and strategy. She'd figure out a way to get what she needed.

"Where does he go?"

Virginia was large, bordered by the ocean on the east and mountains on the west. If he left now to drive back, he'd be here by—

"Appleton, Wisconsin."

Son of a bitch!

Okay, breathe, Caila. Just breathe. "What are we talking, two days? Three?"

"Two weeks."

Why did Wyatt look like the cat who ate the goddamn canary?

"That's unacceptable. I need his reports! I can't even tell what areas I need to focus on without that information. Look, I don't need him for the reports. Can't you find the files? I can interpret them myself."

Nate shook his head. "I can't access his files. I don't know his password."

This was un-fucking-believable! "So what are you saying?"

"I think it's pretty obvious," Wyatt said, not bothering to hide the grin spreading across his handsome face. "I guess you're stuck here for the foreseeable future."

Chapter Eight

The moment the factory door closed behind Caila, Wyatt threw his head back and blew out a long breath.

Nate braced both arms against the counter in the vestibule and dropped his head. "I can't believe I let you talk me into doing that."

"We did what we needed to do."

"But if she ever finds out—"

Wyatt walked over to the glass door that looked out on the parking lot. "How would she? We have no reason to tell her and Joe definitely won't."

"But what if she does find out and that impacts her decision?"

Outside, Caila headed to her car, the sun gleaming on her dark, thick hair. Wyatt could practically feel the earth shake from the forceful anger of her steps. A few seconds later, she drove away and he turned back. "Then that's the chance we're taking. But doing nothing wasn't an option."

"Why not?" Nate asked, pacing in the tight space. "Maybe going along with her and giving her what she wanted was the right move. We're a good, solid co-packer. Our quality is amazing, we've never been late with an order, and we value our employees and treat them well. That should be enough!"

"It *was* with Flair. But Endurance is a large corporation. They only care about the bottom line. I wouldn't be surprised if she'd already made her mind up before she got here. Like she said, the plant's expenses have increased by twenty percent."

"What were we supposed to do? Flair is our only customer. We can only fulfill the orders they give us. When they cut back, we have less work. But we still had to take care of our people."

"Hey!" Wyatt cupped Nate's shoulder. "You're preaching to the choir. I understand and think what you did is admirable. But you're costing them money. And she doesn't seem like the type of woman who'd overlook that sort of thing."

He wished he could stop fantasizing about the type of woman she was.

"I don't see how lying to her will change anything," Nate said. "What you're saying will be just as true in two weeks as it is right now. What's the point of lying to her and making her stay here longer?"

Wyatt knew he'd have no chance of saving the contract if Caila stayed in Bradleton for only a few days and he knew from Gwen that she planned to check out on Monday. He couldn't stand by and watch her perfunctory evaluation, knowing the harm her casual words could cause.

Joe did take his family on vacation every year, but they usually stayed in Virginia in the Smith Mountain Lake area. And they were never gone for more than a week. In fact, they were due home on Monday. But Wyatt had needed more time. He'd called Joe and explained the situation. Convinced him to extend his vacation an extra couple of weeks.

At Wyatt's expense.

"She needs to see us as more than just numbers on a spreadsheet. She needs to understand what the plant means to this town and she can't do that in a day or two. I've given us two weeks to fill her with the Bradleton spirit. If we do our part and get her on our side, she'll give a good recommendation to Endurance and they'll keep you on as their co-packer."

He hoped.

It might not be the most ethical plan, but it was the only shot he had to save jobs and prevent the utter decimation of the town he loved.

WYATT ROLLED THE highball glass of whiskey between his hands and watched as Bubba Woodson tried to pick up Caila Harris. The other man leaned down and said something to her that Wyatt couldn't hear over the jukebox. Caila barely glanced his way, uttering some words and giving a swift shake of her head. Bubba looked annoyed as he stalked away, his posture tense with annoyance.

Of all the bars, in all the small towns, in all the world, she walks into mine.

It had been a hell of a day. Between the bombshell his grandfather dropped on him, the meeting with Caila at the plant, and reviewing solicitations for bids for several town projects, he'd had enough of duty and responsibility. He'd stopped for a drink at his favorite bar before heading home to work on his coffee table, when the hairs on the back of his neck stirred and he'd looked into the mirror over the bar to see Caila stride into the place, looking as cool and confident as she had this morning.

His body had kicked into eager-puppy mode and he'd been annoyed by the reaction. Why this particular woman? He doubted there was a more unsuitable choice for the object of his powerful, single-minded desire.

He'd sat, nursed his drink, and watched as five guys had approached her in the past forty minutes, all with the same result as Bubba. Two of the guys had let it go. A couple of them appeared to still be stewing about it, standing at the corner of the bar, sending dark looks her way as they nursed the beers they'd ordered to soothe their egos.

Not liking where this might go, he finally got up from his seat and approached her.

She was staring into her glass of wine.

"Seriously?" she protested, without looking up. "Does anyone in this place understand the meaning of the word no?"

He slid in across from her and rested an arm along the back of the booth. "They better. And if they don't, I'll make sure it sticks."

She stiffened, then raised her head to look at him. Her eyes widened for a brief second and he held back his smile, used to that reaction from most women. He liked knowing that she wasn't immune to his charm.

Before he could dislocate his shoulder patting himself on the back, her lips tightened and she returned her attention to her drink.

"It's going to be a long couple of weeks if I can't enjoy a drink by myself without getting hit on."

"Probably. But come on, don't tell me you're not used to it."

That got her full head-up-posture-straight-eyes-on-him attention. "I'm used to it so I have to accept it?"

"That's not what I said. But look at you. You're gorgeous. You know it's going to happen, so give the guys a break."

"You're right, it's all my fault. I should change my behavior instead of telling them to not bother me." She shook her head.

He folded his arms on the table. "It's a small town, one where most of us know each other. We don't know you. You'll have to forgive us if we want to get to know the beautiful stranger in our midst."

She stared at him, and one corner of her full mouth ascended. "Oh, I see. The obnoxious approaches don't work, so they send in Mayor McHottie?"

"You think I'm hot?"

She winced. "No, but I think that line is old."

He laughed, charmed against his will.

Don't fall for it! You're here because she's threatening the livelihood of people in your town and you can't allow that to happen. This isn't personal.

Yeah, he wasn't the first man to lie to himself when it came to a woman.

He was captivated by her intelligence and sharp wit. She energized him, kept him on his toes. What would it be like to order another drink and spend the next hour getting to know her? Not as mayor and corporate representative, but as a man and the woman he found irresistibly attractive?

The fact that he seriously considered finding out was the very reason he wouldn't.

"Look, can I buy you a drink just to say there's no hard feelings?"

She shrugged her shoulders. "I'm not going to stop you."

At least that was something.

He signaled to the bartender. "Hey Donnie, can you put her next drink on my tab?"

Donnie lifted a hand in acknowledgment. "Sure thing, Mayor."

He sighed and moved to the end of the bench. "Have a good night and be careful."

She looked at him, her forehead furrowed. "You're not staying?"

"Is that an invitation?"

"No!" she said, too quickly. Then, "More like a relieved observation."

He smiled. "As welcoming as that sounds, I have . . . plans for this evening."

"Of course you do." She lifted a brow. "I mean, what else is there to do in small towns but . . . plan?"

"There's a lot you don't know about small towns."

"Oh, I know plenty," she said, with a wry twist of her mouth.

He made a pointed show of looking her up and down. "Nothing about you screams small town."

"Good. Then the big-city fairy godmother did her job."

And on that note, he should go. Except—

He didn't want to.

He propped his elbow on the table and dropped his chin into his palm. "What big city saw fit to lend you to us?"

Her grin was reluctant. "Chicago."

"Chi-Town! Great city."

She gave him a dubious look. "You've been to Chicago?"

"You look surprised. What, small-town people can't travel?"

She had the grace to look embarrassed. Her chin dipped down.

"You're right. I'm sorry. I'm being a raving bitch."
She inhaled deeply. "Thank you for the drink. I
don't want to keep you from your . . . plans," she
said, once again mimicking his hesitation.

She held out her hand and he took it, braced for
the impact this time around. Were they destined
to generate sparks every time they touched?

She pulled away from him, flexing her fingers.
"I'll see you around."

He tapped a finger against the table. "Yeah, you
will."

He went back to his table to collect his belong-
ings. Bubba sidled over.

"What a bitch."

The slur chafed. "Why? Because she's not interested?"

"Well, yeah. And it's the way she said it. Like
she thought she was better than me."

"She *is* better than you, Bubba. It doesn't take
much."

"Fuck you, Wyatt."

Caila laid a bill on the table and gracefully
slid to her feet. Several men shifted to watch
her leave, including Bubba, who still stood next
to him. Heeding the unease stirring in his gut,
Wyatt followed her out of the bar. He found her
just outside the door, looking at her phone.

"Can I walk you to your car?"

"A drink doesn't entitle you to anything more
than a thank-you. Actually, not even that when
said drink was given in apology. Your apology
was accepted. Transaction completed."

He ignored that. "While you're here, you may want to reconsider going to a bar by yourself."

She stared at him. "You're not a six-foot-four black man with a mustache and full beard?"

He looked at his hands and patted his face. "Last time I checked."

"And your name isn't Lawrence Harris?"

"Nope."

"Then you're not the ghost of my deceased father issuing advice from the great beyond and I don't have to listen to you."

Challenging women had never been his thing but Caila Harris fascinated him. He wished he understood why. "True. But it's late, you're in a strange town, and some of the men you rejected are acting like babies. I don't want—"

"I get it! But I didn't drive."

"Then can I see you back to Gwen's? Please?"

She glanced up and down the darkened street and then pressed a button on her phone. "Okay."

He couldn't remember ever working this hard for an opportunity to take a woman home.

The mood inside the car was somber, and the close, intimate confines of his BMW convertible fucked with his head. He couldn't escape her. He was aware each time she shifted in her seat and smoothed back a strand of her hair. His eyes were drawn to the bare patch of skin above her knee that glowed in the light from the streetlamps shining through the windows. And with each inhalation, he took in faint traces of her perfume until he was damn near dizzy with desire for her.

Why hadn't he driven his roomier, more rugged Land Rover?

As he turned onto the main road that led out of the historic downtown area to the surrounding neighborhoods, a gust of wind rustled the large vinyl banner strung between two light posts that announced the town's upcoming sporting event.

"The homecoming game is tomorrow night. We usually get an impressive turnout."

There was nothing like a high school football game. In the crisp autumn air, beneath the bright Friday night lights, the community came together to celebrate and support its local athletes.

She stared straight ahead but frowned. "I'd forgotten how important football is in a small town."

Forgotten. Not *imagined*, which was what someone might say when they assumed a fact. She'd said *forgotten.* As if she'd once known. This was the second time she'd made a comment about understanding life in small towns.

He drummed his fingers on the steering wheel. "Were you born in Chicago?"

She hesitated, then shook her head. "No."

That was it. She didn't elaborate with additional words or invite more questions with her tone. He should respect her wish to not discuss it any further, but he couldn't deny the yearning within him to know more about her. To know *all* about her.

Strictly for business purposes.

"Where?" he pressed. "East Coast? West Coast? The South?"

She finally turned to face him, the street-lights casting frustrating shadows over her face. "Maryland."

Surprise disoriented him for a moment, and he almost missed his turn. Out of all the places he thought she'd say, he hadn't expected to learn she'd been so close.

"Where in Maryland?"

She was doing her best to twist her fingers into pretzel-like shapes. "Baltimore."

Well, he'd gotten that completely wrong! Had he been so eager to believe that she could relate to Bradleton that he'd picked up on cues where there were none? He needed to get back on track.

"In addition to the game, there's also a parade. And I'll be there to help crown the homecoming court."

She lifted her hands and let them fall back in her lap. "A mayor's duties never end."

They never did. Some might say what he was contemplating with regard to Caila went above and beyond his duties, but he believed his job included doing what was in the best interests of his community. Most of the town would show up for the game. It would be the perfect opportunity for her to see Bradleton's strong sense of community firsthand.

"You want to come to the game with me?"

She jerked and touched her throat. "Oh no, I couldn't."

Not the response he usually received to his invitations. "Come on. It'll be fun."

"I don't think so. And I don't have anything to wear. I only packed for work."

"Is everything you have with you like that?" he asked, motioning to her outfit.

Not that he was complaining. She looked classy and elegant in her navy and white pin-striped sheath dress and her gray cardigan, but her clothes clearly marked her as an outsider. He wanted her to blend in, to feel comfortable while she was here.

"If you mean business attire, then yes. I don't think my bosses at Endurance would approve of me showing up to work in yoga pants and a tank top."

He almost groaned aloud at the picture she presented. He'd approve.

Very much so.

"Since it turns out you'll be here for longer than you anticipated, you may want to pick up some other clothes. You won't be comfortable walking around like you're expected in the board room any second."

Since she'd yet to easily agree to anything he said, he was surprised when she said, "That's not a bad idea. I'll talk to Gwen."

"No need. I'd be happy to take you."

"Does this town run itself? Don't you have other things you need to attend to?"

"You can keep saying it, but I'm not going any-where. As long as you're here, you're the most important person in my world."

The levity with which he intended the words were lost when they hit the air. His statement hovered weighty and sentimental between them, and a large part of him feared their import and prescience. He rushed to save their previous camaraderie.

"Plus, if you're with the mayor, you get the mayor discount," he said.

She treated him to some side eye. "That's not a real thing."

No, it wasn't. "Of course it is."

He pulled up in front of Sinclair House and before he could shift the gear into park, she tossed a "Thanks for the ride" over her shoulder and hurried from the car.

Damn, she was fast.

The house practically glowed in the moonlight, the surrounding trees and shadows adding to its old-world appeal. He'd always loved it. When he was younger, and before Gwen had turned it into a bed-and-breakfast, he remembered walk-ing through most of the public rooms during the town's holiday candlelight tour.

He caught up with Caila on the porch. "So, will you go with me?"

She exhaled and released her hold on the screen door, letting it shut. "I'm not sure what game you're playing, but let me save you the effort. You can't influence my evaluation. If that's your plan, you can keep your invitations. My report will be unbiased and based only on the facts."

Wyatt knew there was no such thing as an unbiased report, and he planned to do everything in his power to ensure his town and the plant were seen in the best light possible.

"Just what are you accusing me of, Ms. Harris?" he asked, pressing a hand to his chest and laying it on thick with his Southern drawl. "I'm talkin' about a lil' shopping and enjoyin' a wholesome football game. Spendin' some time together. Any improper presumptions you've made says more about your intentions than mine."

She studied him, her face a blank mask, before her lips began to twitch, her eyes flashing beneath the porch lights. She pointed a finger at him. "You're too charming for your own good."

"First, you said I was hot. Now you're calling me charming. Are you sure *you're* not the one trying to influence *me*?"

Her bark of genuine amusement warmed him, and continued to thaw her, her posture relaxing, her face open, her grin wide. He'd been attracted to her from the moment he laid eyes on her, but damn . . . she'd never looked more beautiful.

She shoved his shoulder. "You wish."

He grabbed her retreating hand. "Yeah, I do."

He stroked his thumb across her palm and her eyes widened. So did his.

What was he doing?

This was a bad idea. He was tempting fate. But on that quiet street, standing on the porch, with the air and fall scents swirling around them, they could've been the only two people in the world. He felt like he was back in high school, dropping his date off, wondering if he dared try for a kiss.

He dared.

He tugged gently on her hand, prepared to stop if he felt any resistance.

There was none.

She gazed up at him, her dark eyes soft, and his heart began to pound a frenzied beat in his chest. He knew all the reasons he shouldn't do this, but none of them mattered. He wanted her with a blind irrationality that wasn't helped by the blood in his brain conducting a mass exodus southward.

"Wyatt," she whispered and heat flooded him at the way she said his name. He yearned to hear it in all iterations: in a sigh as he feathered kisses along her jaw, on a gasp as he flicked and teased her nipples to hard buds, in a yell as she trembled and came apart in his arms.

Her fingers squeezed his and he inhaled sharply, breathing in more of her heady scent. Mesmerized, he stared at her mouth. Watched as her tongue darted out to wet her lips. Shivered as he imagined his tongue doing the same—

The screen door screeched open.

"I was just hanging out and I thought I heard—" Kevin Sinclair broke off, his eyes narrowing, a flush blooming on his round cheeks.

Goddammit!

One minute they were sharing personal body spaces and the next she'd practically long-jumped away from him. Frustration coiled in his belly, and he turned angry eyes on the intruder, who swallowed and took a step back.

"Sorry, Mayor. I didn't mean to disturb your conversation."

Fuck! Wyatt raked a hand through his hair. Now he was scaring his younger constituents. He took a deep breath and let it out slowly. This was not the boy's fault. If anything, Kevin had probably done him a favor.

"No worries, Kevin," he said, forcing a smile. "I haven't seen you since this summer. You excited about starting classes in January?"

"Yes, sir," Kevin said, his eyes bouncing back and forth between Wyatt and Caila, who stood with her back to them on the other side of the porch. "Is everything okay?"

"Kevin, what are you doing? Who are you talking to? Oh! Mayor Bradley. Ms. Harris," Gwen said, appearing behind her son.

Wyatt was amazed at the sudden shift in mood. The desire that had threatened to overwhelm him only moments before had abruptly vanished in the strained silence. Well, that wasn't entirely true. The desire was still there, hidden under layers and layers of awkwardness.

Caila was the first to breach the uncomfortable moment. She nodded in his general direction as she made her way to the door. "Yes, well. Thank you, Mayor Bradley, for the ride home."

It had been Wyatt. Now they were back to Mayor Bradley.

He shoved his hands into the pockets of his pants. "I'll pick you up tomorrow after lunch and take you downtown."

She paused, and for the first time since their near kiss, she looked at him. "I told you, it's not necessary."

"I know. Sooo . . . one?"

Caila shook her head and looked skyward. "You know what? You win. One o'clock is fine. Can I go in now? There's a hot shower calling my name. Good night, everyone."

She slipped into the house.

Kevin looked like he'd been punched in the stomach.

Wyatt coughed and hid a smile behind his fist. Poor sap. But he didn't stand a chance. Caila. In a hot shower. Hell, he was having the same reaction. The only difference was he had the experience of more years to appear cool.

Kevin blinked rapidly, then cleared his throat. He jerked a thumb over his shoulder. "I was playing Fortnite with Gary and Sean, so . . ."

He disappeared, leaving Wyatt and Gwen staring at each other in amusement.

"I'm looking forward to the big game tomorrow night," Gwen said. "We should beat Highland Point. They've sucked for years."

"You never want to lose your homecoming game, that's why they always schedule a team they know they can beat."

"I see you've met Ms. Harris. She seems like a nice lady." Gwen clasped her hands in front of her. "If only she wasn't here to shut down the plant."

He felt an unexpected churning in his stomach. "Is that what she said?"

"No, but everyone in town is buzzing."

"That they are." He bounced a curled knuckle against his lower lip.

"Chro-Make has been a vibrant part of Bradleton for decades," Gwen said, pressing her thumb and middle finger against her temple. "I never imagined a time when it wouldn't be here."

Maybe that was the problem. They should have. For lots of reasons, they shouldn't have expected the manufacturing plant to always be the backbone of their town's economy. Businesses downsized or closed. Until now, they'd been mercifully spared. Shouldn't his family have been looking ahead to the future? To find another way to ensure Bradleton's fiscal health?

"Was there anything else?"

"I'm sure you have a lot to do, Mayor, so I won't keep you. Good night."

Gwen waved and headed into the house, leaving Wyatt to wonder if he'd be able to get through the night without visions of Caila's wet body running wild through his head.

Chapter Nine

The sun shone through the curtains in Caila's room and spilled onto the window seat where she sat. She drew her bare legs to her chest, wrapped her arms around them, and rested her cheek on the tops of her knees.

How had she allowed *that* to happen?

Oh. Right.

It had started when she'd called her boss after that disastrous meeting at the factory.

"What is it?" Kendra's tone had been brisk, as if she'd only had a second to deal with this issue before moving on to the numerous others on her itinerary.

"Chro-Make is in turnaround."

Silence. Then—

"Shit."

"Exactly. And the man who deals with the financial side of the business is on vacation."

"This is unbelievable!"

"They're working with a sparse staff and I don't have access to the information I need."

"Of course." Kendra sighed. "And anything helpful you did gather during turnaround could be attributed to the low attendance."

"Right."

"How much longer will this take?"

"Two weeks."

"Two weeks? That's a hell of a complication!"

"I know. The timing is extremely inconvenient. I have a call in to the travel office. I told them I can fly out this evening, so I should be back in the office no later than tomorrow afternoon."

"The office? You're not coming back here."

"But there's nothing for me to do in Bradleton until the finance guy returns."

"Well, there's nothing for you here, either."

An icy blast of dread rendered her immobile. "Kendra, I thought you said—"

"I haven't changed my mind. You're not fired. But the only thing you can do to help your cause is to return with a report that will give us the ammunition we need to break Flair's contract with Chro-Make."

"It's two weeks! What do I do in the meantime?"

"Something is going on with you. Take this time to figure out what it is."

She tried to laugh it off. "Kendra, I'm fine."

"You may be, but there are people doing their level best to make it look as if you aren't."

Caila frowned. "Who?"

"I don't know. They're careful to exclude my people. But they're talking. You're on the board's radar for the promotion. Don't give them any reasons to vote against you."

"This is crazy! I had a few drinks at an event and participated in an impromptu karaoke concert. I haven't acted more out of line than any other executive! Two years ago, Colin McHugh got drunk at the holiday party and ended up pissing on everyone's coat in the coat check closet because he mistakenly thought it was the bathroom. And he's still here."

"You're right. He's still here. In his same job. He didn't get fired, but he hasn't been promoted. And he never will. Is that what you want?"

"No."

"Then take my advice. Work on your issues. Because if you do manage to get back on track, you've cashed in your second chance card. I won't tolerate another lapse in your job performance. I can't. No matter how much I personally wish otherwise."

Appalled by the turn her life had taken, and not sure what to do next, she'd walked aimlessly around the town before ending up at a bar. Looking back on it now, it probably wasn't her best idea, considering a few too many drinks contributed to how she'd ended up in Bradleton.

She hadn't gotten drunk. Thankfully. But what was her excuse? How did she explain her behavior?

She'd almost kissed the mayor of Bradleton. Almost. And yet her body still strummed as if they had actually done it . . . and more. She couldn't seem to block out the memory of the heat from his hard body so close to hers, the brush of his thumb against her skin, the dark shadow of his lashes on his cheekbones as his eyes closed and he leaned forward—

She shook her head. Nothing had gone right since Pop-Pop's death. She'd lost her focus at work and had almost lost her job. She'd been sent to Bradleton with one goal: Gather information for a report.

That's it.

And now, because of that same lack of discipline, she was on the verge of ruining the second chance she'd been given. What was she doing? There were too many entries in the "con" column for her to justify getting involved with this man or even daydreaming about doing it. No matter how much she wanted to. The smart move was to keep her distance.

She was here to do her job.

At least she was trying.

She picked up her phone to call Ava for some advice, the ringback tone trilling twice before she remembered the three-hour time difference instead of the usual two. She hung up immediately, deciding not to leave a message. She should be able to figure this out on her own.

Wyatt and Nate Olshansky had made it clear she wouldn't get the reports she needed for a couple of weeks. Kendra hadn't said *where* Caila needed to work on these so-called issues.

Caila didn't need to stay in Bradleton the entire time. It was probably best if she didn't. Then she wouldn't have to worry about constantly testing her faulty willpower against her strong attraction to Wyatt. She should cancel their plans for later in the day and leave. Nothing was keeping her here.

The fact that she experienced a pang of disappointment was strong evidence in favor of putting some distance between them.

No matter what she decided, she would go crazy if she remained in this room. Exiting, she headed to the kitchen, a beautiful mixture of old-fashioned appeal and modern conveniences. The golden yellow walls, gleaming hardwood floors, and warm incandescent lighting created an atmosphere that invited people to relax and stay for a while. She wandered over to the refrigerator—cleverly refaced with a wooden surround that matched the floors—intending to retrieve a bottled water.

There, sitting on the shelf, was a platter loaded with an assortment of cheesecake bars. Her mouth watered.

"Good morning! Or rather, good afternoon," Gwen said, coming into the kitchen. "Have you eaten?"

Caila spun around. "You scared me."

Gwen's gaze fell to Caila's hand. Caila looked down, shocked to see a pumpkin cheesecake brownie bar clutched in her fingers.

Heat rushed into her cheeks. "I'm sorry. I didn't intend . . . it looked good, but I swear I wasn't—"

"Don't worry about it. Everything I make is for our guests." Gwen gingerly removed the treat from Caila's grasp. "Let me get you a plate."

"I really shouldn't."

Gwen didn't even bother with a response, a hint of a smile curving her lips. She went to the antique glazed cabinet and began getting out dishes and utensils.

Caila shuffled over to the center island and sank onto the country-style wooden barstool, placing her cell phone facedown beside her on the granite countertop.

I really shouldn't.

Who was she kidding? Considering her frame of mind, that dessert had been destined to meet her belly from the moment she'd seen it in the refrigerator. She'd need to get her ass in gear and run several miles soon to counteract the effects.

Gwen handed her a napkin and plate with the pumpkin treat she'd initially tried to abscond with, then placed the entire platter on the counter. Caramel dripped off the apple crisp bars, and the cheesecake swirling on top of the pumpkin brownies was an appetizingly visual feast.

"Can I join you?" Gwen asked.

"Please do."

Gwen sat next to her and selected the apple bar. Caila took a bite of the pumpkin dessert and the flavors exploded on her tongue. The sweetness of the pumpkin and chocolate were tempered by the tartness of the cream cheese.

Caila rolled her eyes in ecstasy. "This is amazing! You made this?"

"I did. It's an old family recipe."

"You do the recipe and your family proud. It's delicious."

"Thank you." Gwen exhaled heavily and wiped her fingers on a napkin. "I want to apologize for my behavior on Wednesday."

Caila licked cream cheese from her thumb, still engrossed in the dessert. "What do you mean?"

"When you first got here. I was surprised and I handled it badly. I wasn't very professional."

True. But from Gwen's perspective, Caila had arrived a day early, with no notice.

"I was nervous. Everyone in town knows your recommendation could effectively close the plant. It's all anyone talks about. We depend on that plant. Generations of families have worked there. Almost everybody who lives here is directly affected by it. Hell, I worked there for a while after Kevin was born."

"I imagine that brings a town together," Caila said.

"It does. And for that reason, I'd wanted to do my part to make a good impression." Gwen slid a lock of blond hair behind her ear. "It sounds stupid, but I thought if I made a wrong move or angered you somehow, you'd take it out on the town."

The woman's candidness and obvious apprehension worked to unfurl the knots in Caila's belly, and she smiled her first real smile of the day. "Don't worry about it. If anything, this dessert totally makes up for it!"

"I wasn't worried about me. I mean, I am concerned about what will happen to Bradleton if Chro-Make closes, but it occurred to me that this must be difficult for you, too. It probably feels like the whole town is against you. And while I can't say that isn't true, I want you to know I understand that you're only doing your job."

Humbled by Gwen's kindness and generosity of spirit, Caila dropped her chin to her chest as an acidic sweep of guilt burned through her gut and unshed tears stung the backs of her eyes.

"Have you found Mayor Bradley helpful?" Gwen's words were benign enough, but Caila detected more behind the woman's innocent expression.

It didn't matter. Mentioning the mayor was the jolt she needed. Caila straightened. "Helpful" wasn't the word she would've used to describe Wyatt.

Sexy. Infuriating. Tempting.

She casually took another bite of her dessert and managed a noncommittal, affirmative sound.

"He's like our crown prince, a perfect mixture of Will's sense of responsibility and Harry's charisma. Smart as a whip, too, but he barely has to show it."

Caila believed her. Wyatt definitely worked his easygoing persona, but there wasn't a moment during their interactions where she wasn't aware of the intelligence brewing behind the pretty exterior.

"Did you know Bradleton is named after the Bradleys? They're one of the town's founding families. Every generation of Bradley has been mayor and part of the town's politics for as long as I can remember."

Sounded very incestuous.

Maybe that was the problem. The town didn't have the opportunity for fresh ideas or new growth because one family kept a chokehold on the seat of power.

But Caila was confused. Why was Gwen telling her this? Never mind that she was gobbling up the information almost as much as she'd devoured the pumpkin bar. Why did Gwen think she would want to know more about Wyatt?

What had she seen?

Caila's phone rang.

"Excuse me." She flipped it over and saw Ava's face on the screen. "I need to take this. Thanks for the snack and the chat. I'll come back and clean up my—"

Gwen waved her away with a hand. "I'll take care of it. Part of the service here at Sinclair House. Go on and take your call."

Caila slid from the barstool while accepting the FaceTime call. "Hey! Give me one moment to get to my room."

"Sure." Ava's sharp cheekbones lifted with her smile. She sat at her desk in her chambers, her black robe open over a royal blue shirt.

Caila settled on the window seat and pulled her knees to her chest. "Tell me to get my head in the game."

"Get your head in the game," Ava immediately parroted. "Why am I giving advice from a Disney teen movie? Is that why you called?"

Caila smoothed her free hand over her hair. "It's this project from work. You'd think no one else at that company had ever made a mistake."

Ava nodded. "You know how that goes."

Kendra's words came back to her. *"We have to be better than everyone else . . ."*

"I've given that company close to ten years of my life." She'd worked to the exclusion of almost everything else. "It's all I have."

"Did you hear what you said? *That's* why I'm concerned about your personal life. Because I don't want work to be all you have."

Warmth spread within Caila's chest. "I appreciate that, girl, I do. But I'm not willing to give up my life for a relationship."

"No one is saying you have to."

"In every relationship I've seen up close, the woman has given up her identity to participate. I won't do that."

Ava frowned. "Caila—"

"I didn't call to talk about my personal life, or lack thereof."

Well, not exactly.

Ava held her hands up, palms out. "Okay, okay, I'll let it go. For now. So, are you still planning on heading back home on Monday?"

She and Ava had an agreement. Any time Caila traveled for work, she informed her friend of her travel dates and her destination. Just in case anything happened.

"It's possible I may be here longer than anticipated."

"Why?" Ava flicked locks of her long black hair over her shoulder. "You said this would be a simple assignment. An evaluation of a factory in a small town. Similar to projects you were assigned as a marketing analyst when you first started working at Endurance. A slap on the wrist for what happened at the Drake."

Caila hadn't told Ava the full extent of what she'd been tasked to do because she knew her friend wouldn't approve. As much as she loved Ava, the other woman could be judgmental about the choices people made. It was the former prosecutor, current superior court judge in her.

Caila could feel the familiar twist of frustration tightening her chest. "From the moment I got to this place, nothing has gone according to plan. The plant is in turnaround, which means it's not running at full capacity, and the main person I need to talk to is on vacation. For two weeks."

"Shit," Ava breathed. "Are you going to stay there the entire time? You up for that?"

Ava understood how difficult it was for Caila to be back in a small town that was so much like the one to which she'd been forced to move as a child.

"No. I don't know. I should leave, but . . ." Caila pulled on loose threads on the window seat cushion's cover.

"What's going on? I can hear your mind working from here." Ava narrowed her eyes. "Is it being there? Does it remind you of Pop-Pop?"

Caila's throat thickened, making it difficult for her to speak. "Of course not. I'm fine."

Ava eyed her for a tense moment. "So you essentially have two weeks off?"

Caila wasn't viewing the situation as a supplemental vacay. "I guess."

"Have you seen any hunky cowboys in . . . where are you again?"

Caila rolled her eyes. "Bradleton, Virginia. And you went to school here, too. When did we ever see any cowboys?"

"I went to college there. I didn't conduct a county by county tour of the state. What about gorgeous men? See any of those?"

Wyatt's image flashed in her mind. "Not at all," she murmured, biting her lip.

Ava perked up. "You've noticed the men where you are?" she asked, interest in her voice. "That's progress. Who is he?"

Damn. She'd let down her guard. "It doesn't matter."

"Ooh, you're equivocating. That means there *is* someone. You better tell me. You know I won't let it go."

And she wouldn't.

Caila sighed. "Nothing can come of it."

"Why?" Ava raised an elegant brow. "Is he married?"

"Of course not."

"Gay?"

"No."

"Felon?"

"Ava!"

"Then what's the problem?"

"He's the mayor."

Ava's head jerked back in surprise. She blinked several times. "And? That just means he's employed. Bonus points!"

"It's not that simple. He's trying to save the plant and I'm . . . doing the evaluation."

"Okay. I can see how that might make things difficult."

"Exactly. And the fact that I find him extremely attractive doesn't help."

"How attractive?"

"Like, if I met him in another time or circumstance I'd want to jump his bones attractive."

"Wow," Ava breathed.

"I know. But I can't. We're on opposite sides of this situation. My career is on the line and I won't jeopardize that. I'm not sure what I want to do."

"It doesn't have to be a big deal. I'm just thrilled you've met someone who's piqued your interest. Is it mutual?"

Caila remembered the way he'd pulled her to him, the evident need in his gaze when it dropped to her mouth, the flush upon his cheeks.

"Yes. He asked me to go to the homecoming game with him."

"Oh, honey, that's wonderful. Is he getting you a corsage and taking you to the dance afterwards?"

"I'm gonna call Netflix and have them cancel your comedy special. You're not funny."

"Sorry, but you said it so earnestly. 'He asked me to homecoming!'" Ava's eyes brimmed with laughter and she exhaled a shaky breath. "Are you going to go?"

She wanted to, but—"I don't think it's a good idea."

Ava looked offscreen and Caila heard a voice informing her the docket was about to start. Ava nodded and refocused on Caila. "I have to go. But I don't see a problem. He's not your client or the owner of the factory, so there's no ethical dilemma. If you're both in agreement, up front with what you want, and you can remain impartial, what's the harm in getting to know each other and enjoying yourselves?"

SHE SHOULD'VE LEFT.

In fact, when Wyatt had called Sinclair House about picking her up, it'd been on the tip of her tongue to cancel their plans for him to take her shopping. But Ava's words had stopped her. Maybe Wyatt Bradley was an itch she needed to scratch. They both seemed to want it and she had no qualms at all about her objectivity when it came to work, so was there any harm in pursuing a physical relationship?

Still, she'd declined Wyatt's offer to pick her up at the B&B. She didn't want to be dependent on him for her comings and goings. Besides, being in his car evoked feelings and sensations she wasn't ready to explore. When she'd explained that she'd prefer to meet him, he'd reluctantly given her the address. She'd followed up with Gwen, who'd confirmed that she'd like the place, as it was one of the nicer boutiques in town.

But when Caila walked into the store, her presence announced by a cowbell over the door, she wondered how Wyatt and Gwen could have ever thought this store was in line with her style, even though it was indeed nice inside.

Gleaming planks of light-colored knotted wood covered every surface except the back wall, which had been painted a bright orange. Track lighting shone down on various racks of shirts, sweatshirts, and camouflage gear. She walked farther into the space, past tables displaying hiking boots, trucker hats, and a small selection of camping gear.

A large wooden spool table showcasing a selection of colorful T-shirts caught her eye.

"Proud to Be a GRITS (Girl Raised in the South)."

"Diamonds Are Made Under Pressure."

"What Part of Redneck Don't You Understand?"

Was this some kind of joke?

A middle-aged, bespectacled white woman with short dark hair came over to Caila, looking as if her presence in the store was confusing.

"Can I help you find something?" she asked.

"I don't think so," Caila said.

"Are you looking for a gift? We don't carry a lot of, um . . . urban-type clothes."

Caila glanced down at her camel-colored trousers, crisp white dress shirt, and brown crocodile-embossed leather pumps.

The very epitome of street wear, she thought sarcastically.

Her fingers tightened around the straps of her purse. "I'm waiting for someone."

"Oh. Okay." The shop owner nodded, as if Caila's explanation finally cleared up her confusion. "Holler if you need anything."

The cowbell clattered and Wyatt strode in looking annoyingly handsome in a white T-shirt, dark-wash jeans, and a stone-colored cardigan. Her heart demonstrated its approval by threatening to leap from her chest, and for the millionth time she cursed the effect he had on her.

The older woman hurried to the front of the store. "Mayor Bradley! What are you doing here?"

"Mrs. Anderson," he said, sounding surprised. He took her outstretched hand. "How have you been?"

"Just fine." She eyed him over the rims of her glasses. "Are you picking up something for your grandfather? Or has he finally convinced you to go hunting with him?"

"No, no, I'm just . . ." His voice trailed off, and rubbing his jaw, he scanned the place, his brows drawn together. When he spotted Caila, partially hidden by a double rack of puffy coats, his eyes brightened and he smiled. "Never mind, I found her."

"No worries, and I'll see you tonight at the game."

He shoved his hands in his pockets as he approached. "Hey."

"Hello."

"I wasn't sure—" He exhaled and shook his head. "I see you found the place."

Damn him. It would've been easy to remember it was only physical if he'd come in with his usual winning smile and seductive words. But that one hint of shy uncertainty . . . It cracked a hole in the shield she'd erected to separate her heart from her desire.

"I used this thing called a GPS," she teased, "but I think your sense of direction must be broken. No offense, but this place isn't for me."

He looked around and frowned, before pulling out his phone. "My friend's wife suggested this store." He slid his thumb up the screen several times, then he laughed. "I thought she'd said 460 Maple Street, but it was 640." He slid the device back into his pocket. "Come on, it's only a block and a half down."

Twenty minutes later, having found the correct place, she ran her fingers over the cute floral-print maxi dress she'd added to the jeans, V-neck tees, and sweaters Wyatt held.

"What am I doing?" she asked.

He shifted the load in his arms. "You're going to be here longer than you intended. You needed more things to wear."

He thought she was talking about the clothes when she'd actually been questioning if she'd made the right decision to stay. People who hit it and quit it didn't go shopping or attend football games together. She was beginning to enjoy herself a little too much. But she went along with his assumption.

"You have dry cleaners here, right? I would've been fine."

"You want to be fine or do you want to fit in?"

"What's wrong with what I'm wearing?"

His gaze seared a leisurely path down her body, and butterflies executed flights of fancy in her belly. She mentally ordered them to calm the fuck down.

"Nothing," he said, his voice husky. He cleared his throat. "But you don't have meetings the entire time you're here. There's the football game and the Harvest Festival. You don't want to be walking around in a business suit and heels."

"Wait a minute! I didn't say I was going to the game, let alone the Harvest Festival."

"We can discuss it later. Go try these on."

"You're so bossy," she said, grabbing the stack from him and making her way to the dressing rooms in the back.

It was a nice setup. A chandelier hung from the ceiling, lighting the common space that contained a three-panel mirror and a large green velvet bench. On the far wall were three curtained stalls. She went into the first one and placed the clothes on the chair provided.

She hated shopping for clothes. It was torture and an experience, if not invented by a man, then made worse by his "improvements." It didn't matter how smart or accomplished you were; in the dressing room, under the harsh overhead lighting and image-distorting mirrors, every woman was made to feel inferior.

She slid out of her slacks and pulled on the first pair of jeans. The boyfriend cut was relaxed through her hips and thighs and cropped at her ankles. She turned and checked out all angles. Not bad, although she didn't like the light wash.

"Come on out. Let me see."

She started. He'd followed her? She peered around the curtain and discovered him sitting on the bench, staring at his phone.

"I'm not doing an impromptu fashion show for you."

He looked up, almost managing a sincere expression. "Strictly business. I have expertise on how the women dress in Bradleton."

Total bull, but his quick comeback amused her. "I bet you do."

She pushed the curtain aside and walked out. He hid his triumphant grin by cupping his chin in consideration.

"Nice, but they're a little high around the ankle."

"That's the style. I thought you were an expert in women's fashion?"

He smiled and shrugged sheepishly. "Do you like them?"

"They're fine."

"You don't sound excited, which means you need to try on another pair."

"These'll work."

"I thought women were supposed to like shopping?"

"I love clothes. I hate shopping."

Which was why she employed a personal shopper.

"What kind of jeans do you normally wear? Do they have those here?"

"I don't wear jeans."

His eyes widened. "That's crazy. Everyone wears jeans."

She put her hands on her hips. "I. Don't."

"You're joking, right?"

Jeans were for people who lived normal, relaxing lives and did fun things on the weekend. They weren't for women trying to make partner at a prestigious firm where very few people looked like her.

"I work for a Fortune 100 company. We don't do casual Fridays."

Or any other day of the week, for that matter.

"And when you get off work?"

"I'm at the office between twelve and fourteen hours a day. I'm not kicking it with the girls when I'm done. I usually go home. That's if I don't have a dinner meeting or professional function to attend."

He stared at her, wide-eyed. "Weekends?"

"Work."

"You wear business suits to the office on the weekends?"

"No, but I wouldn't wear jeans, either."

And in the few hours when she wasn't working or sleeping, she wore running gear.

His incredulity annoyed her. She motioned to his outfit. "What about how you dress?"

He stood and held his arms out to the side. "What's wrong with my clothes?"

Nothing. You look good enough to eat.

"Shouldn't you wear something a bit more professional? That befits a man of your station?"

"My station?" He snorted. "You should meet my mother, you two would probably get along."

She could tell from his tone that it wasn't meant as a compliment.

"You're the highest-ranking official in your town, but you dress like the lead in a teen drama. Haven't you ever heard the saying 'Clothes make the man'?"

"And have you heard 'The measure of man lies in the content of his mind, not in the clothes on his back'?"

She frowned. "No."

"That's because I just made it up," he said, grinning.

The next pair she tried on were a standard straight leg cut with fraying on the right thigh and left knee. They were actually pretty comfortable. She stepped out of the changing room and pushed her hands into the front pockets.

Wyatt smiled. "Those look good."

She hated the pleasure his words gave her. His opinion on whether the jeans suited her shouldn't matter. It was up to her if she liked them or not.

"I know."

"Are there more?"

"A couple, but I'm definitely getting these."

"Nice choice," he said, returning his attention to his cell phone.

She stared at his bent head. "You know, I appreciate you bringing me here, but I'm fine now. So if there's somewhere else you need to be or someone else you need to focus on, I'll be okay."

His head shot up and she shivered from the heat in his gaze, before he blinked. Had she imagined the look? "There's no place else I want to be. Now quit stalling and go back in."

She shimmied into the super skinny third pair and studied herself in the mirror. The dark fabric looked like it had been poured on her body. The jeans showcased her hips and legs and made her ass look amazing. They ended in a snug fit at her ankle. She couldn't wear these in public. They were practically indecent.

"If you don't come out, I'm coming in." There was amusement in his tone, but his intent was clear.

She hurried out.

"I thought that would get you mov—" Wyatt broke off and stared at her, like she was a prime piece of steak and he hadn't eaten in a very long time.

She licked her lips. "What do you think?"

As if he couldn't help himself, he stood and walked over to her. Her feet were rooted to the floor. She couldn't move, couldn't look away from his burning hazel gaze. What was that sound? Was that her heartbeat? Was it really that loud? Could he hear it?

Without her heels, he towered over her. "I think you look amazing."

"Will these make me fit in?" she whispered, attempting to get things back on safer ground.

"No."

She started, surprised by his answer. "Why not?"

He cupped her cheek and trailed his thumb along her jawline. "Because I was wrong. You could never blend in, Caila. A woman like you will always stand out."

His lips tentatively brushed hers, and the touch sparked a delicious heaviness in her core. He didn't attempt to deepen the kiss, and she curled her fingers into fists to refrain from hauling him closer. Instead, she gave herself up to the erotic thrill in the slight pressure of his lips against hers.

When he pulled away, her eyes flickered open. He stared down at her, a flush on his cheekbones, a muscle ticking in his jaw. He resembled a dark, hot, avenging angel.

She swallowed thickly. "So these are good?"

"Absolutely." He cleared his throat. "I'll wait for you out front."

Only after he left, did she press a hand to her chest and sink down onto the bench as if her knees could no longer support her.

Holy hell!

That kiss had been as innocent as her first one in middle school, but her pulse was racing and her nipples were as tight as if he'd tongued her down. If she was this shook over such a brief peck, how would she react when their real kiss happened?

And was she still sure she could keep her emotions out of it?

Chapter Ten

Crisp cool air.

Clear, cloudless night sky.

Bright lights shining on the well-tended and manicured field.

It was the perfect night for the homecoming football game.

And for once Wyatt, and the closing of the plant, weren't the focus of everyone's attention. All day the citizens of Bradleton brimmed with excitement as conversations took place in every barbershop, diner, and convenience store about the team, the coach, and their chances against Highland Point's Fighting Eagles. Every hour on the hour, the local radio station spent ten minutes allowing people to call in and give their predictions and/or advice for the game.

"This is Chris, longtime listener and caller. Look, this is our homecoming game. We gotta win. I don't care what this new coach does. Our boys know what to do. So let's get it done!"

"Defense wins games. Everyone wants to see the long ball, but we gotta keep our eyes on the prize. Defense. That's where it's at!"

"This football team is important to us. As long as we win, I don't care where the coach is from. He could be from Mars, we just better get that W!"

Coach Alvin had a tremendous amount of pressure on him, something Wyatt didn't envy at all. He was happy to share the limelight.

And speaking of happiness . . .

Caila.

He'd craved seeing her since their kiss at the store that afternoon. It had been one of his most chaste in recent memory and yet it was also the one he couldn't stop thinking about. Images of her—her laugh, her eyes, the incredible way her ass looked in those jeans—ran on a constant loop in his mind. He knew he needed to keep her close for the sake of the plant and banish any ideas of a personal relationship. But when his brain recalled the feel of her full lips pressed against his, all rational thought flew right out the window.

And as he made his way to the front of the stadium, stopping every few minutes to shake hands and share a few words with his neighbors, he continued to lie to himself, to pretend the pounding of his heart and the anticipation that rolled in his gut was due to his interest in the game and not his hunger to see her.

Her back was to him when he finally spotted her, but even after only a few days, he'd be able to pick her silhouette out in a crowd. He was glad to see she'd taken his advice and dressed in jeans. He'd half expected her to show up in trousers and a blazer. Just to spite him.

He was also grateful she'd worn the second pair of jeans she'd tried on and not the last ones. His heart wasn't strong enough to handle the sight.

He snuck up behind her. "I'm sorry, ma'am. This entrance is for diehard Cougar fans only."

She gasped and spun around and he was struck anew at how beautiful she was. Her large eyes shone brightly and a smile curved her mouth.

"I may be in my early thirties but I have a ways to go before I need to worry about being called a cougar."

"You look stunning," he said, taking her hand and holding it aloft as he took in her blue and white striped top, green jacket, and tan ankle boots, her hair in a high ponytail.

"Thank you." Her lashes swept down momentarily. "I was going to buy some of the spirit merch, but I thought that might be a little much."

"You'd be surprised. You could've come in costume as Coop and you'd only be praised for your commitment to the team."

"Coop?"

"Cooper. The cougar. The school's mascot."

"Wow. You guys are hardcore."

"You're about to learn that truer words have never been spoken. Let's go in."

He placed a hand on the small of her back and headed toward the home side ticket gate where members from the boosters volunteered.

"Hey, Emma. This is Ms. Harris and she's my guest."

"Sure thing, Mayor." Emma handed Caila a wristband and a ticket stub.

"Congratulations," he told Emma. "I heard your daughter made homecoming court."

Emma beamed. "She did. We're so proud of her."

"You should be," he said, leading Caila inside the stadium and ignoring the curiosity in the older woman's eyes.

The stands were packed with people sporting their purple and gold gear. Fans held up homemade signs proclaiming, "Go, Cougars, Go!," "Can't Hide That Cougar Pride," and his personal favorite, "Your Mom Called, You Left Your Game at Home!" The cheerleaders were warming up the home crowd with rousing chants and spectacular flips, and the smell of popcorn and hot chocolate filled the air.

God, he loved this. Not only the game of football, which he'd played in high school, but the way the town came together to celebrate their team and support one another. Despite the responsibilities on his shoulders and the sacrifices he'd had to make, it was nights like these when it was all worth it. When he marveled at the sense of family and community Bradleton was lucky enough to possess.

And the woman standing next to him had the power to destroy it all with the stroke of her pen.

"Where did you park?"

"I grabbed a ride with Gwen and Kevin. I was surprised either of them planned to come, since Kevin isn't in high school anymore, but Gwen said most of the town attends." She gestured around them. "I see she was right."

"This crowd is larger than usual because it's homecoming."

Caila looked around her. "I never thought I'd attend another high school football game."

He smiled, picturing her in high school. With her looks and obvious intelligence, she'd probably been popular. "Let me guess, head cheerleader."

She tilted her head. "*Head* cheerleader?"

"Of course. You're too bossy to take orders from someone else."

She laughed. "I hate to burst your perverted bubble, but I was not a cheerleader."

"Color guard in the marching band?" he asked, mentally replacing his picture of her in a cheerleading uniform with her twirling a flag or a baton.

Still in a short skirt.

"Hardly." Caila pointed to a blond boy on the football field wearing sweatpants and a purple windbreaker, setting up an orange cooler and paper cups. "That was me. I was a student equipment manager."

"Really?" He hadn't been expecting that.

She exhaled loudly. "This all reminds me of where I grew up. The football team was a big deal and they got all the funding. I knew that participating with them would look good on my college transcript."

"It wasn't because you had your eye on the wide receiver?"

"Nope. I had plans that went beyond the borders of my town."

Town. Not city. So she hadn't told him the truth last night. The last time he'd checked, no one would call Baltimore a town. What was she holding back? And why?

"It's my turn to play 'guess your life.' I gather you like football?" she asked.

"I never miss a game," he said.

"High school, college, or pro?"

"Yes," he said, his heart skipping a beat at her laughter.

"You played in high school, didn't you?"

"I did."

"Quarterback."

It wasn't a question. He could feel a smile breaking across his lips. He found her confidence so sexy.

"Starting. My sophomore through senior years."

"Impressive," she said, though her tone seemed a bit subdued.

"Hey, Mayor," someone called out, "it's going to be one helluva game. I can feel it!"

He lifted a hand to acknowledge the statement, which seemed to initiate an avalanche of comments.

"Wyatt! Good to see you. When you get a chance, stop by the shop next week."

"How's your mother? Is she ill? She hasn't attended the last two service league meetings."

"Give your grandfather my regards. I head out to Charleston in the morning, but I'll stop over to see him when I get back."

Caila's expression remained pleasant, but he could feel her withdraw from him with each interaction and he didn't understand why.

When he saw a familiar profile, he grabbed Caila's hand. "I want to introduce you to someone."

Dan and his wife stood near the concession stand, practically disproving the concept of personal space and boundaries.

"All right you two, get a room. There are impressionable young people around."

"Jealousy isn't attractive on you," Dan said, turning with a smile on his face that stiffened when his gaze dropped to where Wyatt was holding Caila's hand.

She must've noticed Dan's expression because she let go of him and shoved her hands into the pockets of her jacket.

"Dan, you remember Caila Harris?"

"I do. Good to see you again."

She nodded, but her posture was tense and she looked more like the woman he'd first met in the diner and less like the one he'd just been flirting with minutes ago.

"And this lovely lady is Dan's wonderful wife, Laura, who owns the yoga studio in town. Wait, sorry, the new Bradleton Wellness Center. As smart as she is, I will always question her taste in choosing this one." He elbowed Dan in the belly.

"You're mad she saw through your bullshit and chose quality instead."

"Boys. Despite your current behavior, you are grown men with important positions in this community. Act like it," Laura said.

Her words were severe but they were offered with a loving smile and warm eyes. She leaned over and kissed Wyatt's cheek before turning her gaze to Caila. "It's a pleasure to meet you."

"Likewise."

Dan rubbed his hands together. "I'm looking forward to this game. Bradleton should win. We have a solid offensive backfield and our defense is getting better. But more importantly, Highland Point sucks!"

"Ugh!" Laura rolled her eyes and looked at Caila. "I may have vowed to love and cherish him forever, but that never included football."

"I hear you." Caila laughed.

"If I don't attend the games with him, I lose him for a quarter of the year. I'm not sure I would've married him if I'd understood the full picture." Laura pouted, but shot Caila a wink.

"That's why I always believe in getting as much information as you can beforehand," Caila said.

Although everyone laughed, Caila's comment was another reminder that this wasn't two couples hanging out at the football game. He and Caila weren't together. She was here to do a job. And his job required that he prevent that from happening.

Dan subtly jerked his head to the right and Wyatt almost sighed aloud. He might as well get this over with.

Wyatt turned to Caila. "Would you like some hot chocolate?"

Caila shrugged. "Sure. Thanks."

Dan looked at Laura. "Your usual?"

"You know it."

As Dan pressed a parting kiss to his wife's lips, Wyatt stared at Caila and wasn't surprised to see his own longing reflected back at him. But then she looked away and the moment was lost. He gave her forearm a brief squeeze before following Dan across the grass toward the line at the concession stand.

"What are you doing?" Dan asked.

He played dumb. "Waiting for our turn to order."

"You know that's not what I meant. What are you doing here with her?"

Wyatt bristled at the tone of Dan's voice when he referred to Caila, but he let it go. Addressing it would only lend credence to his friend's suspicions.

But Dan wasn't done. "You're playing with fire."

"You're making a big deal out of nothing. She needs to see how great Bradleton is, and what event showcases that better than homecoming?"

"This is all part of your plan?"

"Yes!"

"And everything you're doing is for the town? It's business, not personal?"

Wyatt clenched his jaw, quickly becoming annoyed with Dan's questions. "That's what I said."

"Then why are you both acting like you're on a first date and not like two people doing a business deal?"

"This isn't a date."

"Really? You always hold hands with your colleagues? I've never noticed you placing your hand on Jason Frye's lower back."

"I'm a Southern gentleman. It's what I do."

"No, it's not. You don't even hold hands with the women you usually date!"

Wyatt opened his mouth to respond, only to close it when he realized Dan was right. He'd never been a holding hands kind of guy.

Because the only hand you want to hold is hers.

"Just remember what you're supposed to be doing," Dan said, as they made their way back to the women, steaming cups of hot chocolate and bags of popcorn in their hands. "She's not your girlfriend. She's the enemy."

Easier said than done, he thought as Caila accepted the cup from him with a smile that arrowed straight to his chest.

A voice blared over the loudspeaker that the game was about to begin.

"If you'll excuse us, we're going to go take our seats," Wyatt said.

"It was good talking to you, Caila. Please stop by the center any time. Maybe we can grab lunch?" Laura said.

"I'd like that," Caila said, and Wyatt was grateful to see he wasn't the only one who'd taken a liking to the Endurance rep. Placing his hand on the small of her back, he started to guide her away until he caught Dan's eye.

Oh hell.

He moved his hand away and smiled to cover when Caila looked at him quizzically.

Dan was right. As much fun as it was to be here with her, to feel more comfortable with her than he had with anyone in a long time, that wasn't the purpose of this outing. He wished they'd met under different circumstances; when they could indulge whatever it was they were both feeling. But they couldn't. Caila seemed to know it. He needed to act like he knew it, too.

Leading Caila over to the stands, he saw an old man hunched over the chain-link fence that bordered the field, watching the teams running pregame drills. It seemed the perfect opportunity to bolster his plans had just presented itself.

"Smitty."

Smitty adjusted the cap on his wizened head and removed his ever-present toothpick from his lips. "Evenin', Mayor. Ma'am."

"You've known me since I was a baby. You don't have to call me mayor."

"That's your title, ain't it? I ain't calling you something you ain't. I'm showing you the respect your position deserves. Same as I did your grandfather. Same as I did your father."

Wyatt shook his head but smiled. "Caila, this is Owen Smith, but everyone calls him Smitty. He works at the hardware store downtown. He's been a fixture of Bradleton for as long as I can remember."

"It's nice to meet you, Mr. Smith."

Smitty nodded to her, then looked at Wyatt. "People aren't going to be happy if we lose homecoming."

"I know. We all want the boys to do well."

"I saw the coach's wife at the store the other day and I told her to make sure she reminds her husband that defense wins games. We don't need all that fancy long ball stuff. Just strengthen up that D-line and get those corners in and we should be good. That Jackson kid is fast. He needs to be starting."

"I'm sure she relayed that news," he said, unsure if he'd successfully concealed his sarcasm.

Or maybe she'd been hearing so much unsolicited advice that she'd discarded it as soon as it was offered. It was a tactic Wyatt sometimes employed.

"Now don't make me have to take you over my knee in front of your lady friend," Smitty said, turning back to the field, bracing his forearms on the top railing of the fence.

Guess not.

Caila laughed, and Wyatt's fingers curled into fists at his sides.

Do your job! You have a responsibility to your family and this town, not to some woman you just met.

"That wouldn't be a good look for the town and we're trying to make the right impression.

Caila is from Endurance. She's here to do an evaluation on the plant."

Caila stiffened, and Wyatt imagined a bricklayer setting up his trowel and mortar. Slowly but surely, he could feel the wall being erected between them. The weight of that disconnect laid heavy on his chest. He regretted doing that more than he'd regretted anything in a very long time.

"Ma'am," Smitty repeated.

"Smitty used to work at the plant," Wyatt said.

"Surprise, surprise," she muttered under her breath.

"Sure did," Smitty said. "Retired in '02. My son works there now. My granddaughter graduates from high school this year."

"That's wonderful. Is she going to college?" Caila asked.

"Oh no. We don't have no money for that. She'll go to work at the plant."

"I see."

"Three generations of your family working at Chro-Make," Wyatt summarized. Caila's narrowed gaze told him it'd been unnecessary. He pushed on. "But that's not unusual. A lot of families have worked there. That place has helped a lot of people."

"As everyone feels a need to tell me," she murmured, before taking a sip of her hot chocolate.

He'd made his point. They could take their leave.

"It's good to see you, Smitty. Enjoy the game."

Smitty nodded, put the toothpick back in his mouth, and returned his attention to the field.

"Let's go find our seats," he said, keen to put work behind him and ready to revel in the game and her good company.

Caila twisted her lips and shook her head. "I can't believe I fell for it."

"Fell for what?"

"You didn't invite me here so we could spend time together. You had an ulterior motive."

He wasn't the only one. She might claim she was here just to do an evaluation, but he couldn't shake the feeling there was more going on.

"I saw an opportunity and I seized it. That doesn't mean I wasn't excited about our date."

"I have news for you. I'm not sure what you usually do here, but a high school football game and a Styrofoam cup of powdered hot chocolate is *not* my idea of a date!"

She stared angrily at him, negative energy emanating from her in waves.

"Am I interrupting anything?" Holly Martin's thick New Jersey accent still took him aback when she spoke.

Caila smiled bitterly. "Nope. He's all yours."

"Caila, wait a minute." He grabbed her arm when she started to walk away.

She pulled away from his grasp. "Duty calls."

He let her go and held his hands up, palms out. "I want to talk about this. Please. I just need a minute."

"Fine." She crossed her arms over her chest and looked out toward the field.

People weren't shy about their interest and he was aware of the scintillating tableau they presented: him, two beautiful women, an air of agitation. Mayor McHottie strikes again, providing grist for the rumor mill.

He exhaled and called upon his vast reserves of patience. No matter what he was dealing with in his private life, he couldn't forget his public responsibilities. He steered Holly to a spot several feet away. "Is everything okay?"

Holly's smile wilted slightly, but she redoubled her efforts. "Of course! It's just that our schedules have been busy and we haven't had a chance to hang out again. I had so much fun the last time."

He knew; Holly had been open about expressing her continued interest. Unfortunately, twenty minutes into their date he'd realized she was interested in way more than he was willing to give. She constantly brought up her cousin back in Newark who'd just had a baby and asked him if he wanted children and what he would name them. But it had been her questions about his life as mayor and if his wife would be the "first lady" of Bradleton that had sealed the deal.

When they'd met for coffee a few days later, he thought he'd been just as clear in stating his wish that they remain friends.

"Holly, we talked about—"

She laughed loudly and tossed her blond curls, apparently uninterested in their conversation being semi-private. "Silly Wyatt, I don't recall much talking during our date," she said, her innuendo apparent.

He wasn't about to let that stand. "Actually, during dinner, we discussed your family, your recent move here, and your new job with Dr. Saunders, but, you're right, it was difficult to engage in conversation during the band's set."

After which he'd taken her home and passed on her offer of another drink.

Holly twisted her body from side to side and peered up at him from beneath her lashes. "All the more reason for us to get together."

He didn't believe he'd been ambiguous in his message, but it was possible he hadn't been firm enough in his delivery. It was an oversight he'd rectify . . . at a later date.

"This isn't a good time, Holly."

"Why?" she asked, a sneer suddenly marring her features. "Because you're here with her?"

He frowned, turned off by the ugly display. Not that he owed her an explanation, but he did want to defuse the soap opera–esqe situation this was devolving into. "Yes. Caila Harris. She's the company rep from Endurance."

"Oh." Holly's expression cleared. "This is about the plant?"

Thank God. Now that you get it, can you go away?
"Yes."

"Oh. Do you need any help? Because I'm here with my friends and we'd be happy to talk to her—"

Hell no! "I've got it under control. But thank you."

"I want to do my part to support the town. You go and do your mayor thing and I'll see you around."

Had she intended that to sound like a threat?

When he looked over, he was thankful and relieved to see Caila still standing there. She stared after Holly, then arched a brow. "She got dinner *and* a band? Good to know you're not always this cheap."

She walked away.

Dammit!

He hurried after her. "Where are you going?"

"To find Gwen. I knew I should've driven myself."

"Don't do that. I'll give you a ride back to the B&B."

She stopped again and faced him. He could've dealt with her anger, met it with his own, but the hurt he saw in the depths of her gaze gutted him.

"Why? You've already gotten what you want from me for tonight. Enjoy the game, Mayor Bradley."

Chapter Eleven

The pounding of her feet against the pavement in a rhythmic fashion sent a rush of peace through Caila. She shook out her hands, and rolled her shoulders, each step taking her closer to the zone.

She'd needed to do this; she hadn't run since she'd gotten to Bradleton. Maybe that was part of the problem, the reason she constantly felt off-kilter, like trying to stand on sand while wearing stilettos. Running was how she cleared her mind, how she focused her thoughts and her intentions. After five miles she was always stronger, more decisive, and more accomplished. She hadn't realized how much she'd needed those emotions until she'd awakened this morning after the homecoming game feeling listless, incompetent, and unsure of herself.

And it was all *his* fault.

If Nic had been here, she'd be laughing her ass off. *"Rookie mistake, Caila. You know better. Be clear on the terms."*

She'd thought she was. She'd believed the attraction was mutual. But she'd been embarrassed and made to look like a joke, and it was nothing less than she deserved.

She'd gone against her own beliefs. She never mixed business with pleasure, and her reason for being here was all business. In fact, it was arguably the most important piece of business in her life.

Instead of questioning the motive behind his invitations, she'd once again surrendered to the bedeviling emotions plaguing her in the past couple of months. Forget common sense, years of experience and logic. She'd chosen to believe a personal involvement with Wyatt wouldn't affect her mission.

And, though it now galled her to admit it, she'd had her own agenda.

If the football game was as big a draw as everyone claimed, she'd be surrounded by the very people she'd need to observe. And if she happened to see or overhear anything she could use to support Endurance's decision to break their contract with the plant . . .

A win-win situation for her.

But she hadn't been smart, and worse, she hadn't been clever. The moment he'd *casually* introduced her to Smitty, who'd *casually* begun talking about the generations of his family working at the plant, she'd felt like a first-class idiot. And not first class as in bigger-seats-separated-from-coach-by-a-curtain. Oh no. She'd rated as a luxurious-privately-enclosed-suite-with-double-bed nitwit!

It'd been a genius move. This time, he'd played her.

And she didn't like that fucking feeling one bit.

Irritation with her own shortsightedness fueled her as she continued beyond Sinclair House's neighborhood and on to another with large residences, immaculate lawns, and big trees. These homes were newer than the ones near her B&B, but they still retained the Southern colonial style, with two or three stories, a rectangular design, and a central front door. The addition of shutters, columns, or porches added some variation, but it was clear this was a traditional, well-established neighborhood.

No one who worked at the plant could afford to live here. Maybe that explained the absence of open hostility she experienced. She'd moved from the sidewalk to the street—to avoid colliding with mothers pushing strollers or people walking—and was surprised by the nods, waves, and calls of "Good morning!" she received as she went by. She enjoyed that small slice of camaraderie enough to acknowledge and return greetings of her own.

But her thoughts couldn't bear to be apart from their favorite subject for long. If she were honest with herself, she'd admit that part of her ire came from her inability to understand her reaction to Wyatt Bradley. It wasn't as if she rarely encountered attractive men. She lived in Chicago. She worked in the beauty industry. She was surrounded by boatloads of gorgeousness.

There was just something about him that pinged something within her. Despite the numerous pep talks and dire warnings against getting involved with him, she couldn't seem to help it. That deep, delicious drawl, those hazel eyes, the feel of his strong, callused hand when he'd grabbed hers last night, and when he looked at her and smiled, the action causing a flash of white to gleam against his dark stubble . . .

A shiver racked her body, causing her to stumble slightly.

She needed to get her shit together! He could possess the ability to give her toe-curling orgasms on demand but she still couldn't let it affect the job she came here to do.

The jarring sound of a horn jumpstarted her heart and she whipped her head around, certain she was inches from being hit. Fortunately, it was a man engaging his car's alarm half a block back, but it reminded her of the dangers involved in zoning out while running the streets of an unfamiliar town. If she'd been paying attention, she would've noticed she'd come to a cul-de-sac. A few more steps and she would've been standing on the driveway of the last house on the street.

She stopped and placed her hands on her hips, taking a moment to catch her breath. Upon closer inspection, she realized it couldn't be a driveway; there was no house before her. A road to nowhere? She jogged several feet to the right, and through a break in the trees she spied a huge brick and white-columned mansion sitting atop a hill. It was larger than the B&B and more ornate.

Man, there was some money in this town.

That thought reignited her irritation with Wyatt. All his talk of the plant being the lynchpin of the town and how closing it would destroy their economy. Please. From the look of these neighborhoods and that house in particular, she had the feeling the economy would be just fine.

Turning, she headed back in the direction from which she'd come.

Wyatt's help came with strings attached. And while she'd known that, she hadn't understood how far he would go in service of his agenda. She didn't intend to waste her time here following his rules or playing his games. *She* controlled her life, her destiny. Her successes or failures would happen because of her, not because of someone else dictating the terms.

If throwing her together with Wyatt Bradley was the universe's way of testing her, well, bring it on. She'd never failed a test in her life!

Glancing at her sports watch, she noted she hadn't run as far as she'd intended. If she went back to Sinclair House now, she'd end up two miles short of her five-mile goal. She needed a little more distance. At the next stop sign instead of keeping straight, she turned left and headed toward downtown.

Before long, the wide residential streets narrowed and single-family homes compressed into attached row homes and then businesses. Traffic picked up, and though she knew it wouldn't be good for her knees and risky for her ankles, she moved from running on the shoulder of the road to the brick-paved sidewalks.

Another couple of blocks and then she'd walk back.

Up ahead, a crowd of people browsed half a dozen tables covered with brightly colored cloths bearing an assortment of baked goods. As she got closer, flyers, poster boards, and large banners proclaimed she'd stumbled upon "The Harvest Festival's Community Bake Sale."

Inspiration struck. She'd missed the opportunity to observe the town at the homecoming game. The universe had heard her complaint; decided to give her a second chance. Despite what Wyatt had claimed when they'd first met, she didn't need his help.

She didn't need anything from him.

She slowed down as she reached the edges of the event. Men, women, and children ambled between the different tables, talking among themselves and purchasing treats. Once she ceased running, she fit right in. People wore jeans and sweaters, as well as sweatpants and sweatshirts. Her running pants and tee weren't out of place, as she'd feared, and if she got chilly, she could put on the windbreaker wrapped around her waist.

"That one-handed catch by Rondale Jackson was amazing!" she heard at one table.

She passed a group of women discussing the homecoming court.

"It's been better. Half of those girls were overweight."

"When we were in school, the court used to be based on looks."

"Not these days. It's more of a popularity contest."

"I'm sorry, but I prefer how it used to be."

"If I were eighteen I'd run for the court again, if only to have *this* Mayor Bradley crown me." One middle-aged woman, in a pink velour track suit, giggled with her friends.

Caila rolled her eyes. God save her from women fawning over Wyatt. She probably couldn't spit without hitting a member of his fan club.

But several tables down, she couldn't help smiling at the little girl shaking small pompoms and strutting up and down the sidewalk, doing her own version of a cheerleading-routine-slash-model-runway walk.

Caila's stomach rumbled at the mouthwatering smells emanating from the treats, so she stopped to peruse the pumpkin pies, rustic apple tarts, and cran-apple cobblers. Remembering Gwen's pumpkin cheesecake brownies, she thought the other woman should have a table out here. She'd make a killing!

Caila approached the redhead manning the nearest table. "These look amazing. What does the bake sale benefit?"

"Thank you!" The woman smiled. "It's for our local kids' club, specifically to help their before- and after-school programs for low-income families."

"That's such a worthy cause and you make it so easy to donate."

The other woman nodded. "The Harvest Festival bake sale is our most profitable fundraiser of the year. All of the desserts must be fall-themed. You won't find a lemon bar or a strawberry shortcake anywhere."

Caila pointed to the two-pack of puffy ginger cookies. "How much are those?"

"Two dollars each or three packs for five."

"I'll take three and a bottled water."

"Great." The woman took three packs of cookies and put them in a paper bag. "Janice Ross made these. She's one of the best bakers in town."

"Then I'm really looking forward to it."

The other woman held out her hand. "I don't think I've seen you around before. My name is Blair. Did you just move here?"

"I'm just visiting."

"But she's not a tourist." A woman with curly blond hair came to stand next to Blair. Caila recognized her as the woman from the football game the night before.

The woman Wyatt had taken on an actual date.

"This is Caila Harris. She was sent here by Endurance to close down the plant," Holly Martin announced in her best impersonation of a human megaphone.

The cacophony of voices surrounding her dulled as people turned to stare at her. Just moments before, she'd been enjoying the sense of camaraderie and affiliation small-town life offered. The warm feeling of welcome and the belief that people cared about your well-being.

That had all evaporated with Holly's words, leaving her privy to that other part of small-town life. The part she hated, that had sent her fleeing from Maryland. That sense of alienation. Of being different. Of being blamed for being an outsider.

You've done this before. You've dealt with hostile people. You know how to handle this.

Caila met Holly's unfriendly blue eyes and understood that this had nothing to do with her or even the closing of the factory and everything to do with Wyatt being with her the night before.

"She's partially correct. I *was* sent here, but to evaluate the plant, not close it down."

Technically true. It wasn't Caila's decision to close the plant. That decision had already been made by the higher-ups.

"Same thing," Holly sneered. "We see no one from your company for years. We do the best we can to get the orders out and then they send someone here to criticize the work we've done?"

A light-skinned black woman at the neighboring table pursed her lips and cocked her head. "We? You just moved here, Holly."

A flush mottled Holly's cheeks. She crossed her arms over her chest. "It's still true," she said, through clenched teeth.

Another woman looked annoyed, but she spoke up. "Holly has a point."

"If there's something you want to tell me, I'm willing to listen," Caila said, addressing the crowd around her.

"It may just be about facts and numbers to you, but to us, it's more than that. Our coworkers are like our families," a voice chimed in.

The floodgates opened.

"My mother worked on the line for twenty-five years. Five days a week, ten hours a day. She ate lunch with the same people. They celebrated their anniversaries and birthdays. Offered support when family members died. And now, they'll be gone. If they're lucky, they'll find other jobs."

"Do you people care what you leave behind? Or is it all about the profits? If you have a free minute during your 'evaluation,' drive to Grange a couple of counties over. See what happened to them when Allen Shoes left. It's a ghost town."

"How much money does your company need? You can't tell me Endurance isn't still making money. I bet the executives are still rich. They just want more and they're willing to ruin the lives of thousands of people if they can add another million to their bottom line."

Holly wasn't done. "She doesn't care about that stuff. She wants to know if someone is stealing product and selling it on the side or if people are lazy and not showing up for work."

Caila was shocked by the venom the other woman spewed.

Is this because Wyatt didn't ask you on a second date?

She needed to remain calm. Unlike Holly, this wasn't personal for her. She wasn't upset over some guy. Caila was here representing Endurance and she had to remember that in her response. "That's not the information I want to know."

Though it would help.

"We don't care what you want to know. We're not going to rat out our neighbors, because you buy a few baked goods," Holly said, her gaze sharp.

The pounding began in her forehead, just above her right eye. This hadn't turned out the way she'd planned. She'd wanted a little information about the town, not to be treated to the second coming of the Salem witch trials. By now, enough people were openly staring that Caila knew the Bradleton gossip mill would soon be active. Between the pinball machine challenge at the diner, the scene at the football game, and now this community confrontation, it wouldn't be long before this incident was discussed in every bakery and bar in town.

Resigned, she unzipped the small pocket on the side of her pants and pulled out the twenty-dollar bill she always carried with her ID when she ran. She held it out to Blair.

She knew when she'd overstayed her welcome.

Holly stopped Blair with a hand on her arm when the redhead reached for it. "It's on the house. We don't need your charity."

Caila almost laughed at the absurdity. "Yes, you do. It's a fundraiser, remember?"

"She's right," Blair said, shaking off Holly's touch and taking the money. She gave Caila the cookies and her water. "Thank you."

"You're welcome. And keep the change," Caila said, walking away.

Well, that had been a disaster. What had happened to her since she'd arrived in Bradleton went beyond a few people knowing who she was. She'd consistently made a spectacle of herself and lost any hope of maintaining anonymity.

Although it had been a while since she'd conducted an evaluation, she hadn't forgotten the rules. Keeping a low profile was key. No one wanted to make a lot of noise, especially when their presence might result in the loss of jobs. She'd need to—

What the fuck?

Only by the grace of God did she not face-plant on the street! That might have been satisfying for Holly, but it would've been an unfortunate image for both Caila and Endurance.

Caila turned to discover what large obstruction she'd failed to see that had almost broken her ankle—imagine that, stuck here and immobile!— and saw a teenage girl sitting on the curb, quickly drawing her legs to her chest.

Crap. Now she'd be accused of assaulting Bradleton's children.

"I'm sorry. I wasn't paying attention to where I was going. Are you okay?" Caila asked.

The girl rubbed her calf, then gazed up at Caila

through a mass of dark, tangled curls. "I'm fine, but—" Her gaze shifted to a book that was sprawled in the middle of the street.

Caila hurried over and grabbed it before it was trampled by the crowd, grateful it was a library book with a clear protective covering. Dusting it off, she was surprised by what she saw.

"*The Handmaid's Tale*," she read, impressed. She didn't think teenagers even read these days, let alone advanced stories that explored the dangers of governmental control over female reproduction. "That's some heavy stuff."

"Thank you," the girl said, accepting the book.

"You watch the show?"

"No. We don't have Hulu." She shrugged. "I just like to read."

The girl's defensive words caused an ache in Caila's throat. She remembered making a similar statement over and over during her own childhood. Certain places weren't kind to a kid who preferred the world of books to her own peer group. When her mother used to criticize her for keeping her "nose in those books" and missing out on life, Pop-Pop always defended her.

"Let her be, Mona. The girl's smart. And she'll benefit more from reading than she will hanging out with those knuckleheads."

Caila choked back impending tears and nodded to a spot on the sidewalk next to the girl. "May I?"

The young girl shrugged again. "It's a free country."

Caila sat down and crossed her legs. "What's your name?"

"Jada."

"Hi, Jada. I'm Caila."

"I know." Jada flipped through the pages of her book then looked at Caila and wrinkled her nose. "Is what they said true? Are you closing down the plant?"

I'm only doing an evaluation.

The canned response was on the tip of her tongue. But when she looked into the young girl's curious and intelligent light brown face, she found herself admitting something to her she hadn't told anyone else. "It's a possibility."

Jada's expression flickered and she looked down at the book in her hands.

Caila hesitated. "Were you planning to work at the plant?"

"God, no." Jada laughed, then covered her eyes with a hand. "That sounded awful. I shouldn't have said that. What I meant was my future plans don't include staying in Bradleton."

Caila experienced an inexplicable rush of relief. "And may I ask what those plans might be?"

"College. I just turned in my financial aid forms. I should hear from the places I applied to in the spring. People in my family work at the plant, but that's not for me. I want more. More than I can have staying here."

"Jada!" A little girl, with a similar mop of dark curls, rode up on a bike. "Mom said you need to come home so she can go to work."

Jada sighed and stood. "I have to go."

Caila shaded her eyes and looked up at her. "It was a pleasure meeting you, Jada."

"You too." Jada took a few steps, then turned back. "People around here may give you a hard time, and I understand why. But . . . I don't know. It's nice to see someone who looks like me doing well at life outside of town."

Caila understood the conflicting emotions. "Thanks. Here." She removed one of the three packs of cookies she'd bought from the bag and handed the rest to the teen. "For you and your sister."

Jada accepted the bag with a nod, then hurried after the little girl.

Caila watched until they'd disappeared from view. Then she stood, brushed the dirt and leaves from the back of her pants, and headed back to the B&B.

She'd thought she could complete this assignment on her own and get it done quickly. But she'd stumbled upon problem after roadblock mixed with complications.

As an analyst fresh out of B-school, she'd conducted dozens of evaluations, usually at company headquarters or regional offices, located in large or mid-sized cities. She hadn't been concerned about the consequences of restructuring departments or lost jobs. There'd been enough distance between her decisions and those who'd be impacted that she could focus on producing phenomenal work and making a good impression on her bosses, not so much the people behind the numbers.

But now . . .

Her job, and possibly her career, depended on her finessing information into a report that Endurance could use to get out of the Chro-Make contract. A contract that kept a third of the town employed.

In order to gain access to that information, it would appear that she'd need the help of the charming, sexy mayor. The man intent on convincing her company to honor that contract, who also managed to scramble her brain and stir her heart with one touch.

If she didn't find a way out of this predicament soon, she'd risk losing everything she'd ever worked for.

Because of a man.

Again.

Chapter Twelve

It hadn't taken Wyatt long to realize he'd fucked up. The challenge he now faced was what to do about it.

How had the situation gotten away from him so quickly? He'd been convinced he'd be able to enjoy his evening with Caila *and* do his job at the same time, without her catching on. And even if she did, she'd have to be impressed by his efforts, right? That had always been his experience in the past.

When he'd been younger and trying to evade Asher's attempts to take him on a hunting trip, he'd been able to persuade his mother or Violet to tell his grandfather he was sick and spend those days sequestered in his room, watching movies and playing video games.

In high school, when he'd missed taking his girlfriend to the Harvest Ball in favor of a road trip with his friends to see Matchbox Twenty in concert in Roanoke, he'd smoothed her ruffled feathers with an over-the-top apology in the cafeteria and a chauffeured limo ride the following weekend to Richmond.

Even at the football game, he'd managed to handle the scene with Holly so that it didn't end with a dramatic blowup or her hating him. But with Caila, it had been the first time in a long while when he hadn't been able to sweet-talk his way out of a situation with a woman.

And somehow, he didn't think some flowers picked from the Bradley Estate's garden and a correctly calibrated smile would be enough to solve this problem.

Why couldn't he ignore his attraction to her? Why couldn't he keep his hands to himself? Why had he given in to his need to kiss her? Despite his best intentions, the boundaries between their personal and professional relationships were bleeding into each other and causing a hell of a lot of havoc. And now Chro-Make and the entire town could end up paying the price.

If he'd had any thoughts about seeking guidance from his family—not that he would, but if he'd wanted to—that notion had been laid to rest the moment he'd arrived to breakfast that morning . . .

"Did the homecoming game go well?" Asher had asked, shaking out his copy of the *Bradleton Herald* and folding it closed.

"It did," he'd said, kissing his mother on the cheek. "We won and the boys played well. Coach Alvin may actually have a peaceful week."

Peaceful, but not quiet. People would always have an opinion about football, especially in the days leading up to each game, but maybe the words Coach heard would be more supportive and less critical.

"I was curious," Asher said, "since every phone call I received last night was about the spectacle you made with that woman from Endurance."

Wyatt clenched his jaw and took a seat at the table. He might need to skip this little family ritual as long as Caila was in town.

"I think 'spectacle' is overselling it a tad."

"Do you think it was smart to parade her around?" Renee asked. "People who consort with the enemy usually do so in private."

Wyatt took a deep breath and held it in for a few seconds before letting it out. "I came up with a plan to give us a fighting chance and keep her here instead of back in Chicago, recommending another factory to Endurance. No one has standing to criticize the choices I make."

"Yes, they do. Your constituents. And they do it by voting," Asher said. "We may have a bit of an advantage because of our last name, but if the town's citizens believe you aren't acting in their best interests, you won't get a second opportunity."

"Taking Caila to the football game was part of the plan. She needed to be around us and hear from people who would be directly affected by the plant losing the Flair/Endurance contract."

"It's Caila now? I see. And did part of that plan also require you to hold Caila's hand?"

Damn! Did his grandfather hire retired CIA spies to do his surveillance?

Wyatt accepted the cup of coffee Violet placed before him, waving away her offer for breakfast, having lost his appetite. "What is this really about?"

His mother sighed and put her fork down. "You have a reputation in this town—"

"Oh, come on—"

"Mayor McHottie."

He didn't think there was anything he disliked more than that horrible nickname, but he was wrong. Hearing his mother utter it was way worse.

"And as distasteful as I find that moniker, you needed some time to sow your oats."

Wyatt cringed. "No one says that anymore."

"Better he does it before he gets married." Asher buttered a piece of rye toast. "Get it out of his system. I'm sure he could overcome a cheating scandal, but I'd rather not have to test that theory."

"What are you talking about? There's no cheating scandal. And I'm not discussing my private life over the breakfast table."

"It doesn't require a discussion. Only a statement. When the time comes for you to settle down, you will need to pick a woman who's appropriate," Asher informed him.

His grandfather's implication set his blood simmering. "She's smart, she's beautiful, and she's successful. What makes her inappropriate? The fact that she's black?"

Asher bristled. "Was that one scene last night with Ms. Harris and the dental hygienist not enough? Are you aiming for another one? Do you expect me to deny it in some aggrieved outburst?"

Wyatt eyed him levelly. "I asked the question because I wanted to know."

"I'm not racist, I'm a realist. Her being black is a factor, but no, that's not why I consider her inappropriate for you."

Bullshit.

"You need to think about your position in this town. Ms. Harris is from the city. She's here temporarily to do a job and then she'll leave."

They could assert their city-slicker rationale as loud as they wanted, but everyone at that table knew what their primary complaint was.

His mother jumped in. "Your wife needs to be someone who will put this family first. Whose sole concern lies in being a great first lady for the town and, eventually, Virginia."

"Like you, Mother?"

Color tinted his mother's cheeks and he immediately regretted the acidity with which he'd asked the question.

"Yes," Renee responded, jerkily readjusting her napkin in her lap. "When I married your father, I understood what my role would be. I came from a good Virginia family. It was how I was raised."

His brief moment of contrition didn't stop irritation from tightening his jaw. "Why are we talking about this? I just met her three days ago!"

"And yet her presence has affected you in a way we've never seen before."

"Why? Because I'm questioning your belief that you have veto power over whomever I decide to marry?"

"Because you want to forget that being the scion of this family requires you to put our history and legacy above your personal desires."

"Shouldn't the main criterion for the woman I marry be that we love each other? That we care for and support one another?"

Asher was stone-faced. "Your father neglected his responsibilities and we all know how that turned out. Do you—"

"Mayor? Mayor Bradley? Wyatt!"

The sharp tone of Bradleton's city manager yanked him—thankfully—from that painful reverie. He snapped forward in his chair. "Yeah?"

As his city manager, Denise coordinated departments, supervised department heads, and reported directly to him. "Did you hear anything I just said?"

He had a vague notion of her mentioning shelters and landscape architects, but the specifics . . .

Nada.

Still, he hazarded a guess. "Happy Creek Park?"

Her lashes flickered. "You got lucky. Yes, Happy Creek. Now that we've voted down the road extension, we really should update the facilities."

"I know. Nothing has been done since the town first built it out after the Randalls donated the land." He rapped his knuckles on his desk. "We need to start soliciting bids for the project."

His action must've drawn Denise's attention to the furniture. She trailed her fingers across the smooth surface. "You know I've always loved this desk. It's a custom piece, right?"

He nodded. He'd made the rustic executive desk using reclaimed wood from a barn several counties over. It had taken him four months, and when it was done, he knew it would look great in his office. He'd received many compliments on it and evaded questions about where he'd procured it, unwilling to admit that he was the one who'd built it.

"Don't tell me any more. The town won't pay for it and I surely can't afford it." She sighed. "I'll start gathering the information we'll need."

"Great," he said, relieved they'd left the subject of the desk behind. "Write it up and submit it to me for final approval."

"Will do." She stood then paused. "Is everything okay?"

"Yes, of course." He gestured to her jeans and sweater. "I appreciate you coming in on a Saturday morning for a quick meeting."

"You've had a lot on your plate dealing with the possible closure of Chro-Make. It wasn't a big deal. Stan took the kids to the bake sale and I'm on my way to meet them downtown. Unless you want to talk?"

"Nah, it's not necessary. I'll see you on Monday. Have a good weekend. And tell Stan I said hello."

After Denise left, Wyatt was preparing to leave when he heard her voice in the outer office as if she was speaking to someone.

Hadn't she said she was meeting Stan downtown?

The mystery was solved when Vince popped his head in the door. "Working on a Saturday? Who are you brown-nosing for? *You're* in charge!"

"I know it's hard for you to understand, but being mayor is a full-time job."

"Right. You're doing the everyman act today." Vince strolled in, dressed in his usual Southern-gentleman-slash-bro uniform: faded red chinos, white button-down shirt with the sleeves rolled up, Vineyard Vines canvas belt, Ray-Bans on a neoprene strap around his neck. He sat in the chair Denise had just vacated. "Great game last night. We killed Highland Park. I almost felt bad for them."

"That win was crucial. We need *something* to celebrate right now."

"True. And we'll win even more if the coach learns to make adjustments during the game. He's gotta be ready to make changes on the fly! We can't run the same plays over and over again."

No one would ever be satisfied with what the coach did. Bradleton could have Bill Belichick, the best football coach in recent history, and they'd still have a need to second-guess every decision he made.

"Give the coach a chance. This is only his first year here."

Vince crossed his legs, resting an ankle on the opposite knee. "The contest on the field wasn't the only entertainment last night. People were talking about you bringing the woman from Endurance to the game."

Wyatt flicked his gaze to the ceiling. He'd been clear that the plan was to show Caila around town. How did they think it was going to be done? A self-guided headphones tour?

The woman from Endurance.

"Her name is Caila Harris."

"I thought you were going to introduce her to people," Vince said in an accusatory tone. "Kind of manage her experience."

So Vince *had* been listening. "I am."

"Then where were you this morning?"

"Excuse me?"

"You don't know?" Vince asked, almost chortling. "It's all over town."

Wyatt gritted his teeth. "What are you yammering about?"

"Apparently she'd been out on a run this morning and . . . you know, I don't get running. It doesn't even look fun. Although it probably explains her killer body."

"If you don't get to the fucking point . . ."

"I'm just saying the only time I'd ever run is if someone was chasing me. But, if *she* was chasing me, I'd stop running and let her catch me."

"Vince!"

"All right! Damn! I heard she stopped by the bake sale—"

Wyatt frowned. She did? He hadn't expected that.

"I mean, if that was your plan and you thought she'd see the good side of Bradleton, that didn't work out."

Wyatt was two seconds from leaping over this desk . . . He forced himself to calmly ask, "What. Happened?"

"I heard Holly Martin was there and gave her a really hard time. Called her out in front of the crowd and told her we weren't going to stand for her closing our plant down. Then everyone turned on her."

Son of a bitch! What did Holly think she was doing? He'd wanted Caila to see the best of the town. See how they were a family, how they cared for one another, the hope being it would engender some sympathy in her about the number of people who would lose their jobs.

But if her thoughts about Bradleton were colored by what had happened this morning, where it came off as bullying instead of protecting . . . they were screwed.

"My mom said Holly was jealous seeing you with the wo—Caila," Vince said. "Maybe you shouldn't have gone out with Holly. Maybe you should've given someone else a chance."

Wyatt shot Vince a look on the way out of the door.

This town was going to talk itself into economic destruction.

Twenty minutes later, he stood on the bottom step of Sinclair House and watched Caila sway to and fro on the white wicker porch swing, her eyes closed, her chin tipped skyward.

Every nerve ending in his body jumped to attention, causing his grip to tighten on the black wrought-iron railing. She was so lovely. Even in workout gear, her face devoid of makeup, he couldn't take his eyes off her.

"Stop staring," she murmured in that low, sexy voice that haunted his dreams, begging him to make her come over and over again.

He exhaled audibly. "I wish I could."

Had she heard the desperation he'd been unable to hide? Her eyes flew open and she rolled her head to look at him, her own expression showcasing a relatable combination of yearning and weariness.

His heart shifted in his chest. "Are you okay?"

She let her lashes fall and brought her head straight again. "I'm starting to wonder if I'll ever be okay again."

The pain in her voice gutted him. It was raw and potent and . . . older than the night before. Entrenched. Something in him, some foreign part he didn't recognize, wanted to know the origin of that pain. Wanted to face it and conquer it for her, like a dragon slayer of old.

He climbed the steps and sat down next to her. "What's going on?"

She didn't move or change her position. "Why do you care?"

He shifted to face her, placing his arm along the back of the swing. "I shouldn't. It'd be easier if I didn't. But I do."

They hadn't used many words, but it felt as if they both recognized they'd admitted more than they'd intended. He also knew if he pushed her to divulge more, she'd come right back at him and he wasn't ready to share his feelings, especially since he'd yet to understand them.

"You must be happy today," she said.

Considering he felt anything but at this moment, he asked, "Why would you say that?"

"The game. Your team won."

He exhaled, grateful for the lighter change in subject. "Yeah, it was a blowout."

"I'd hoped the other team would come out after halftime and make it somewhat interesting."

He frowned. "You saw the game? I thought you left."

"I ended up staying." She shrugged. "Gwen and Kevin were having a good time."

Disappointment churned in his midsection. After she'd left, he hadn't been able to think of anything else. He'd called himself all kinds of fool for not going after her, but what could he do? He'd had to preside over the halftime homecoming festivities. It wasn't the first time his responsibilities had gotten in the way of what he'd personally wanted. But it was the first time he'd honestly questioned if the cost was worth it.

But she hadn't left. She'd been there. And if he'd known he would've talked to her. Made her understand. And spent the rest of the time in her company, the way he'd wanted.

"What about you? Did you end up having a good time?"

Had the men near her in the bleachers fallen all over themselves to talk to her, to be the recipient of one of her smiles? Had she met someone with less baggage? Someone not in conflict with her purpose for being here? Who didn't have women he'd previously dated showing up and leading a town revolt against her?

She wrinkled her nose. "I'm not a big football fan."

"But you worked on your high school team."

And she'd agreed to go to the game with you. Even though she didn't like the sport.

"That was about academics. I don't watch it now."

"Why? I know the rules can be difficult to understand, but—"

"I understand the rules just fine." She sighed and sat up straight, shifting to face him. "You've seen the studies that link football with long-term brain disease, right? Knowing that, how can I watch these young men constantly hitting each other, aware that each contact contributes to the likelihood they'll experience some sort of neurological damage?"

The full power of those eyes, up close . . . they took his breath away.

"A lot of schools, including ours, have changed the way we coach the game. We're teaching our boys to tackle head up and use their shoulder, to minimize impact to the head."

"Minimize, but not erase. The danger is still there. Why put people at risk when it's not necessary?"

"For some, it *is* necessary. Take kids who live in dangerous conditions," he said, warming to the topic. "Football gives them an activity to stay safe and out of bad situations at home. It builds character, teaches lessons on accountability and leadership and gives boys the opportunity to become successful."

"Come on! What percentage of boys actually turn pro?"

"Maybe not pro, but they're able to go to college and try to obtain a better life for them and their families."

"Okay, okay. Yes, for those who use the scholarship and take the opportunity seriously. But is that what's really going on? If they're playing college ball, in some part of their mind they want to go pro. They're not thinking about their majors or classes or careers beyond football. And then, what if they get hurt? Their scholarship is yanked and they're sent back with no diploma, no other viable skills, *and* an injury. Meanwhile, the school has made millions off them."

He tapped two fingers on her shoulder, pleased when she didn't move away. "Sounds like you're advocating for paying college athletes."

"I'm not advocating anything." She shook her head. "How did we even get into this conversation?"

"I don't know. I think I just asked if you enjoyed the game. Note to self: Don't ask Caila about sports ever again."

She laughed. "Pin it, too, so it remains at the top."

He smiled and continued trailing his fingers in little circles at the nape of her neck and back and forth across the ridge of her shoulder. She didn't tense, shift, or ask him to remove his hand, but he watched her closely for any sign of unease.

"I heard you went to the bake sale this morning."

He felt her stiffen, but her tone was still light. "If you get a chance to stop by, try Janice Ross's ginger cookies. They were the bomb."

He laughed. "Janice is one of the best bakers in town."

"Reputation is completely earned. Though Gwen is really good, too."

Her eyes sparkled now, free from their earlier despondency. He didn't want to dim their light, but he wasn't here just to make her feel better.

"I'm sorry. Holly had no right to do what she did."

She laid a hand on his knee, and the caress seared through the material of his jeans and branded his skin. "You don't need to apologize for her."

"Well, I'm sorry it happened."

"Be real. You despise her approach, not her message."

"Caila—"

"That's why you invited me to the football game and introduced me to Smitty. That's why she said what she did. Community activism. I've dealt with it before."

"Yes," he interrupted her, when she would've said more, "it's the reason I introduced you to Smitty. But it was never meant to be confrontational. Only to show we're more than numbers on a spreadsheet; we're a community, too."

"You guys should get that on a fucking T-shirt." He missed her touch when she crossed her arms over her chest. "The economic health of your community is not my responsibility."

"Did your way work for you?" At her blank look, he elaborated. "When you talked to people at the bake sale? Did you get the response you wanted?"

Her gaze flicked away. "No."

"Your method may work some places, but this is a small, tight-knit community. People won't just talk to you because you ask."

"And if you asked them to?"

"They would. But I gather you'd prefer information that was actually helpful to you."

She sighed. "Then what do you suggest? Yoga at Laura's studio followed by a rousing town chorus of 'Kumbaya'?"

He laughed. "Nothing that dramatic. The Harvest Festival 5K is tomorrow. It's a color run. Have you done one before?"

"I've done several 5Ks, but I don't know what a color run is."

"It'll be fun. Seeing you there, with your guard down, enjoying yourself . . . People may open up to you." He looked over his shoulder to the street and saw that, once again, they were the focus of some not-so-subtle nosiness. "Take advantage of the time you have until Joe comes back from his trip with his family. What do you say?"

She bit her bottom lip.

Stay focused, Wyatt!

Finally, she nodded. "Okay."

"Great." He clapped his hands together, ridiculously elated. "I guess you'll want to meet me at the starting line, right?"

She nodded and smiled.

"Since I don't want to push my luck, I'll go ahead and leave. Nine a.m., Concourse Park, downtown."

He jogged down the steps but stopped before he reached the pavement. He turned back, one foot braced on the step above.

"One more thing. Earlier you said I invited you to the game for 'community activism.'"

She tilted her chin. "Yeah."

"You're wrong. I *should've* asked you to the football game for the town. But I didn't. I asked you to the game for me."

Chapter Thirteen

It took Caila about five minutes to realize what the "color" in color run meant. She hadn't given it much thought when Wyatt had asked her to join him. She'd assumed people wore brightly colored clothes during the race, hence "color run." She'd shown up in a white windbreaker with reflective strips for nighttime running and a hot pink headband, the best she could do considering she didn't own fluorescent running gear. She thought she'd blend in nicely with everyone else, rather than stick out, one of the main reasons she'd decided to participate.

She did not expect her expensive white jacket to be doused with a bright powdered color that would not only ruin it, but would get in her face—and her hair!—pollute the air around her, and become so dense that she'd choke on it.

She learned this the hard way, about a kilometer in, when she noticed two people standing just off the running path holding large plastic bottles of a baby blue substance. When the person in front of her neared them, they stepped onto the trail and squeezed the bottles, emitting a cloud of color that painted the runner's shirt, face, and arms.

It happened too quickly for Caila to avoid them and she, too, ran face-first into a cloud of blue chalk. Choking and cursing, she vowed to avoid the other color stations and she did her best, but she couldn't avoid the yellow, green, pink, and purple mist at each subsequent station. In the end, she looked like she'd been vomited on by a dozen troll dolls, but she'd had a lot of fun, and everyone involved appeared to be in good spirits.

When she crossed the finish line, she accepted the wet towel and bottle of water a volunteer offered her. After carefully wiping the chalk residue from her face and hands, she moved to the side and began stretching, waiting for Wyatt to complete the race.

From the moment the race began, families, parents with running strollers, and cliques of friends flocked to him. They all wanted to be around him and she understood why. He cracked jokes, alternated between groups, and cheered on older walkers. He kept everyone near him in good spirits, creating a fun atmosphere.

But a mile into the run, she'd been antsy with pent-up energy. She'd never considered herself a sprinter, but her pace was definitely faster than that of the people around her.

During her first few races, she'd begin in the wrong group and find herself with people who ran either too fast for her or too slow. Over time, she'd learned a very important rule: Run your own race. She couldn't concentrate on the runners around her; it would be a mistake to try to match her pace to theirs. The best she could do was to stay true to how she'd trained. To run the pace that was best for her.

And she stuck with that motto, because it served her well. When she knew she couldn't hold herself back any longer, she'd gestured to Wyatt and he'd waved her on with a smile. She took off, finishing the race pretty close to the front of the pack.

About fifteen minutes later, she saw him, running alongside a young boy of about eight or nine. They crossed the finish line and threw their hands in the air as if they'd just won a gold medal in the Olympics. The sense of accomplishment on the little boy's face was evident, and watching Wyatt acknowledge it and pat the kid on his shoulders, caused a sizable crack in the protective shell around her heart.

Wyatt looked up and scanned the area until he found her. It seemed impossible, but his gaze grew brighter. Or maybe it was a trick of the sunlight. He tousled the boy's hair, then jogged over to where she waited.

"You're fast as hell," he said, still breathing heavily. "After you left us, I turned to respond to Carl's question and when I looked back, all I could see was your dust."

"That wasn't me, that was this stuff," she

said, gesturing to her now tie-dyed jacket. "But I appreciate you not giving me a hard time for running ahead."

Through his newfound chalky pallor, his hazel eyes burned. "I'd never want to be responsible for holding you back."

His words, combined with his stare, heated her insides.

She glanced away, not ready to face his suggestion. "They were handing out towels and water."

"I'll be right back," he said, jogging away.

The space gave her a moment to catch her breath, his presence doing more than the race to task her lung capacity. He returned moments later with a wet towel and a half-empty water bottle.

"What's that commercial, 'Taste the rainbow'?" His mouth worked as if perceiving something bitter. "Let's not."

Caila laughed. "I think you left out a key detail from this invite. For future reference, if you're going to invite a black woman to an event where her hair is going to get messed up, inform her of that fact in advance. If I'd had all the information, I'm not sure I would've shown up."

A small smile curled his lip. "Noted. But since you're here, I think I made the right call this time."

"Easy for you to say. Do you know how long it'll take me to deal with this?" She patted her hair, beyond annoyed when a Pig-Pen–like dust cloud rose from the strands. "All you'll need is some soap and water."

He touched his cheek. "Soap? Is it that bad?"

Did she really want to tell him no? That it'd take more than a dusting of powder to render him unattractive?

Misreading the look on her face, he took the towel and did a cursory swipe over his face. "Better?"

She smiled and shook her head, then gestured as if to encompass her entire face.

He wiped again and raised a brow.

She pursed her lips and held out her hand for the damp material. When he gave it to her, she stepped closer to him, reached up, and began wiping the powder off his skin. With sure, steady strokes, she removed the colored particles from his forehead, his brow line, around his straight nose, down his cheeks, across his jaw, over his lips . . .

Her hands trembled slightly as she handed the towel back to him.

"That's most of it," she said, her voice pitched higher than usual.

His nostrils flared slightly. "Thanks."

Nervousness fluttered in the pit of her stomach. She swallowed and held out her arms. "This jacket is probably ruined and I'm a mess! I hate to even take this into Gwen's lovely house. And her bathroom? I don't want to ruin it with this horror show. Maybe I can climb a trellis or she could hose me off in the backyard?"

"You can come to my house," he said, his tone as calm as if they were just discussing the weather and he hadn't dropped a bomb into their conversation.

Had he really said that? More importantly, had he meant it?

"I don't want to get your house messy, either."

He waved a hand. "It'll be fine."

"Are you kidding? Look at me."

Her words were like flint against steel and produced sparks. His gaze started at her head and flowed down to her feet, leaving a trail of heated brush fires in its wake.

"I've been renovating it since I bought it a little while ago," he said, his lids at half mast, his drawl more pronounced. "A little powdered chalk won't affect the areas we'd go through."

She licked her lips, seeking moisture that had fled. Was she ready to do this? They both knew that a trip to his house was more than a regular invite. In the privacy of his home, away from prying eyes, they'd be at the mercy of temptations they'd been fighting since they first met.

"If you're sure . . ."

He nodded, resolute. "I am. Did you drive?"

So was she. "No, I walked."

His hazel eyes widened. "Even though you knew you were going to run a 5K?"

She shrugged. "I run five miles several times a week. I could handle a twenty-minute walk and a three-mile run."

"My house isn't far from here. A ten-minute walk. Can you handle that?"

She wasn't imagining the double meaning behind his question. Not when his gaze was locked on hers.

"Let's go."

The chilly fall morning had given way to sunshine and a warm breeze. Leaves fluttered around their feet as they strolled along the brick-paved sidewalks in a comfortable but expectant silence. They waved, pointed, and laughed at their fellow color run participants, who were easy to spot, since they all looked as if they'd taken part in a colorful, G-rated version of a *Walking Dead* reenactment. Caila loved the bustle of Chicago; it energized her, gave her a sense of purpose. But she couldn't deny the contentment settling in her bones caused by her current surroundings.

And through it all, the man at her side consumed her senses.

Hers and everyone else's.

She didn't miss the sidelong glances in his direction. Even with his chalk-stained face and hair, he was a stunningly handsome man. And he wore the hell out of the gray windbreaker that molded to his chest with each whiff of wind and blue joggers with white stripes down the sides.

He wasn't a runner—she'd known that within the first five minutes on the course—but he was in great shape, with a body most men would sell their souls for.

Wyatt Bradley was gorgeous, charming, smart, and considerate. And he appeared to want her, aside from their work issue. She didn't believe in mixing business with pleasure, and if she did, it was a really bad idea in this situation.

Then why did you accept his invitation? What are you doing here?

Oh, shut up.

They turned onto a street populated with craftsman bungalows. At the end of the block he stopped in front of a cute two-story blue house with contrasting white trim.

"This is yours?" she asked.

"No, I brought you to a stranger's place so we could stand outside and stare at it," he teased.

She punched his shoulder. "Ha-ha."

"Yes, it's mine," he said, his voice tinged with pride.

Caila admired the small manicured lawn, covered wide porch, and columns that tapered from chunky stone bottoms to leaner plastered tops. "It's a beautiful house."

"I think so, too. Come on in."

Inside, the foyer was still a work in progress and she understood what Wyatt had meant when he'd said her chalky mess wouldn't mar his decor. The finish on the wood floors was scuffed and vacuumed, and wallpaper had been stripped from the walls. A tall ladder stood in one corner, and several large white buckets were scattered around the room.

"Should I leave my shoes here?" she asked, eyeing the floor.

"For now. I'll rinse them off and set them out on the porch to dry."

She undid her laces and toed off her sneakers before following him into the next room.

"Wow!" She turned in a circle, attempting to take in all of the details.

Where the foyer was clearly in the early stages of renovation, the living room was further along. The sunlight burnished the traditional wood moldings of the room divider and turned the stained glass in the transom windows above it into works of art. The colors danced upon the warm cream walls and created spotlights on the gleaming hardwood floors.

But the main focal point was the beautifully carved staircase.

She gasped. "I've never seen anything like this. It's amazing."

In most staircases, the spindles ran vertically, but on Wyatt's some of the spindles were horizontal, creating a unique design that added extra interest to the space. Like a functional sculpture.

She ran her fingers over the grooves carved into the post. "You were lucky to find this in such great shape."

"It wasn't."

She stared closely at the intricate details on the post's cap. "Then the people you hired did an amazing job."

"I didn't hire anyone. I did it."

The end of her ponytail hit her cheek when she whipped around to face him. "You did what?"

He dropped his head and squeezed the back of his neck. "The banister. I carved it."

She was blown away, both by him and by his work. "You built it?"

A flush darkened his cheeks. "Yes."

Adorable.

This big, strong man had created a beautiful object with his bare hands, yet he seemed embarrassed by her praise. Pop-Pop used to act the same way when she'd compliment him on something he'd done.

A sudden swell of emotion threatened to knock her over. Her chest ached and her throat burned. Tears scalded her eyes, rendering his once-clear image blurry.

He rushed to her side. "What's wrong?"

She closed her eyes and shook her head slightly. *Don't do this here. This is not the time or place for you to get emotional!*

He bent down in front of her. "Did you step on something?"

"No, no. Get up." She pulled on his arm until he rose. "I—you just reminded me of someone for a second."

"Someone who made you cry?" He wiped his thumb across her cheeks, and she was surprised to see moisture on the pad of his finger. "I don't like the sound of that."

"Not in the way you're thinking. He . . . was good with his hands, too. He could fix anything."

Like the old car he'd bought and restored for her sixteenth birthday.

She'd awakened that morning to find car floor mats outside her bedroom door. When she'd walked into the hall bathroom to brush her teeth, pine tree air fresheners had been attached to her toothbrush. And when she'd gone down to get breakfast, it was to see Pop-Pop sitting at the kitchen table, a cup of coffee in his hand, a wide grin splitting his kind face, a set of car keys in front of him.

"Happy birthday, sweetheart."

That car had meant independence at a time when she'd craved it. Her town didn't have a public transit system. For two years, she'd been stuck at her grandfather's home ten miles outside town, dependent on him or her mother if she'd wanted to go anywhere other than school, church, or the Sav-Mart.

But that red 1986 Saab 900 had changed her life. It had allowed her to stay after school for activities or spend time at the library in town. She'd gotten a job and begun earning money. When she'd started planning for college, she'd been able to visit nearby campuses to gather as much information as possible.

Pop-Pop had given her the ability to gain some control over her life, and that gesture had begun to erode the resentment she'd fostered against him for taking her away from her life.

A piercing insight, almost as strong as her earlier sentiment: Pop-Pop would've liked Wyatt Bradley. He possessed a high regard for men who could create something out of nothing and took the time and effort to do so. Said it required vision and courage.

How do you think he'd feel about what you're doing in Bradleton, a town similar to his own? You're not creating anything here; your actions could possibly destroy it.

Unsure of what to do with that knowledge—of Pop-Pop approving of Wyatt and possibly disapproving of the reason for her presence here—or how to feel about it, she forced a bright smile. "So, you're doing all of the renovations by yourself?"

He continued to eye her for a long moment before answering. "Most of it. Whatever I can't handle, I contract out."

"How long have you been making things?" she asked, bracing a hand on the banister.

"I started when I was a little boy. My dad was an artist. I remember sitting and watching him paint these canvases, sometimes for hours on end. One day, when I was ten, I went with him to visit this guy who made custom frames. The guy gave me a piece of wood and a sheet of sandpaper to play with while they talked business. By the end of that visit, I'd sanded the edges and made a block! I was hooked."

She grinned, easily able to imagine him proudly holding up his creation for his father to see. "Did you become your dad's official framer after that?"

His smile didn't change in size, but it became less vibrant. The genuine joy from seconds earlier had vacated his eyes. "It took some time to get to that point, but . . . yeah, I made a few."

She could tell there was more to the story, but she didn't want to press him. Especially since she hadn't wanted to talk about her own issues.

"Have you made anything else?"

She'd expected him to rattle off a list of items, so she was surprised when he said, "Come with me."

She took his outstretched hand, and he led her through another room and a kitchen, in the beginning stages of being restored, to a door that led down to the basement.

"Be careful," he said, as they descended the darkened space. "The light switch at the top of the stairs doesn't work. I'll be calling in an electrician soon."

"If you're thinking you'll save your plant if you get rid of me, you should know Endurance would just send another rep," she joked—kind of—aware that no one knew she was here.

He tossed a smile over his shoulder. "Considering you're the only person I've shown this to, my motive to get rid of you would be to protect my secret."

He flipped a switch, and Caila thought she'd been transported to the island of wooden furniture. Tables, chests, cabinets, a headboard, several benches, and other pieces filled up the unfinished space.

She saw one table in the corner, its contrasting light- and dark-colored planks partially covered by boxes. She gasped and ran over to it, spreading her arms and laying her upper body on it. "It's an Olivia Pope table!"

He laughed. "I don't know what that means."

She turned her head to look up at him. "Olivia Pope? From the TV show *Scandal*? She has a conference table in her office that's just like this."

"I'll take your word for it." He leaned back against the table, crossing his arms over his chest.

She knew she couldn't lie on this table all day. Especially because it was highly unflattering. She stood and attempted to reclaim her dignity. "Well, you do good work. The table is very . . . uh, sturdy."

His lips twitched. "Thank you. I try. I'm very serious about structural integrity."

"It shows."

She blew out a breath, then slid him a sidelong glance. The amusement on his face made it difficult to hold back her own. She burst out laughing, and her heart leaped in her chest when his deep chuckle joined hers. It felt good to share that moment of levity with him.

Moments, plural. When she thought she'd gotten herself under control, he'd thrown himself down on the table and kissed it, and the absurdity of the picture he presented set her off again.

"Seriously, you're so prolific," she managed, when the giggles finally subsided. "Do you make them for people? Sell them? You could make a killing."

His gaze flitted over her features, as if mapping the image for his brain. "I've never sold my pieces, but I've given a few away. To Dan and Laura, mostly. Not a lot of people know what I do."

"Why? You're very talented."

He looked away and scratched his cheek. "It's complicated."

"Your family knows, right?"

"My family isn't interested in what I do in my spare time, as long as it doesn't interfere with being mayor and doesn't embarrass them. So, I make sure it doesn't." He straightened. "And that's the end of this episode of *Mayor Wyatt's Woodworking*. I'm sure you're ready to clean up. Let me show you to a bathroom you can use."

The second floor of the house was in much better shape than the main floor.

When she pointed that out, he said, "I started up here, with the master suite and the other bed-rooms."

They reached a closed door in the hallway. "This bathroom is next, but I haven't touched it yet. It's in full working order. Everything you need is in there and towels are under the sink."

He opened the door and stepped into the room. It was small, barely able to house the tiny vanity, tub with shower, and toilet. Only after she'd followed him had she realized it wasn't made for two people. If she spread her arms out to her sides, she'd be able to touch the vintage green tile that covered the walls above the vanity and the tub.

He turned to face her and there was little space between them. Her lashes flew up and her eyes met his. He swallowed.

"Okay, so I'm going to go . . ." he said, pointing over her shoulder.

They shimmied to switch positions. Her nipples brushed against his chest and pebbled inside her sports bra. He exhaled loudly, then pulled the door closed.

"Wait!"

The door flew open and he stood there, his broad shoulders filling the frame, a muscle ticking in his jaw. "Yes?"

Damn. Why did he have to be so sexy and funny and smart and talented? This would've been much easier had he been anyone else but him.

She cleared her throat. "After I clean up, I don't have anything to change into."

He blinked, then cleared his throat. "I—uh, I have something you can change into."

She wrinkled her nose. "No, thank you. I'm not keen to wear the discarded clothes left behind by an ex-girlfriend or random hookup."

He flinched and took a step back. He started to leave, then hesitated. "I don't bring people to my house. In the two years since I bought it, the only people who've been here are Dan and Laura."

The import of his words ripped the air out of her lungs, and the vulnerability expressed left them both exposed, with nothing to hide behind.

"But you invited me here."

"Yes."

"Why?"

He reached out and tucked an errant lock of hair back into her ponytail. "I don't know."

She licked her lips. "We shouldn't do this."

He moved closer until the vanity was at her back and he . . . Good Lord, he was in front of her. "I know."

She was powerless to resist the surge of pleasure coursing through her. Her fingers tingled, her heart raced, her pussy pulsed. She hadn't felt this much . . . wanting in such a long time. She'd begun to wonder if she'd ever feel that way again.

She put trembling hands on his shoulders. "There are so many reasons this is a bad idea."

His hands gripped her hips. "I agree."

She shivered. "I'm here to evaluate the plant."

He leaned forward, pressed his cheek to her temple. "Of course."

His words stirred her hair. She slid her arms around and squeezed the muscles in his upper back. "I won't be here long."

He slowly and sensuously moved his face against hers. "I know."

Their lips met, clung, then pulled away once, twice before his hand gripped the back of her neck and he took her mouth in a deep, hungry, and possessive kiss. Her heart seized, then thudded in her chest, and a liquid pool of desire settled low and thick in her belly. He kissed her with a skill and expertise that left her weak in the knees, like she was a fevered fantasy, like he'd devour her whole if she let him.

And in this moment, with the way he was making her feel, she'd let him. She honest to God fucking would. Every molecule in her body strained toward him, as if they, too, understood her urgent need to be joined with him. His arm was a steel band around her waist, anchoring her to him. Everything about him made her crave him more: his scent, his feel, his taste. His tongue curved and brushed the roof of her mouth, and she moaned, letting her thighs spread.

Right *here*. Right *now*.

The hardness of his cock prodded her hip through the thin material of his pants, and she couldn't wait to get her hands on it. To run her thumb over the lubricated head, wrap her fingers around the shaft, and guide him into her. She slid her hand down and cupped one firm ass cheek, shivering in delicious anticipation of doing that again when they were both naked.

But he abruptly broke their kiss, leaving her dazed and bereft. And angry.

What the fuck?

He rested his forehead against hers, their harsh breathing the only sound. She tried to drag in more air, if only to voice her question aloud or to pull him back for more, but her body wouldn't cooperate. Like the strength of their combined desire had short-circuited her central nervous system.

And it had only been a kiss.

After a long, slightly unbearable moment, he untangled himself from her and backed out of the space.

The muscle in his jaw was working overtime. "Take your shower. When you're done, leave your clothes in a pile on the floor. I'll get a bag for them. Oh, and feel free to use all the hot water you want."

His implication was clear.

He'd only need the cold.

Chapter Fourteen

Wyatt didn't flinch as the cold water hit his heated skin.

Caila Harris would be the death of him.

He rested his forehead against the shower wall and let the icy flow stream down his back. When he'd invited her to his house he'd had honest intentions.

Mostly.

He hadn't consciously planned for anything to happen, but he'd wanted to spend some time with her. He'd regretted how their evening had ended at the homecoming game, and getting her to participate in the race had seemed like an opportunity for both him and the town to get what they wanted. And he'd invited her back to his house because, frankly, he wasn't ready to say good-bye to her.

What harm could come from it?

That kiss had changed everything. Pulling away from her had been the second most difficult thing he'd endured in his life.

Yeah, dude. What in the hell were you thinking?

He'd been thinking their kiss must've made her wet and wondering if he should check with one finger or two.

He'd been thinking he could come just from the luscious rasp of her tongue against his.

And he'd been thinking these feelings—for her—were unlike any he'd ever known or experienced.

If this were just sex, him scratching an itch, he would've continued kissing her. They were two intelligent, consenting adults who found each other attractive and wanted to let nature take its course.

But this was more. And as much as he wished their situation was different, his wants weren't his only concern. They couldn't be. He had the expectations of his family and thousands of people resting on his shoulders. They didn't care that Caila had the softest skin or the sweetest lips or the most bewitching scent. They wanted to know if Chro-Make would continue to operate. They wanted to know if they would have jobs. They wanted to know if the town would continue to function as they raised their families and lived their lives in Bradleton.

In comparison, his feelings for Caila seemed selfish and inconsequential. They'd passed the point where he could have his cake and eat it, too. He could no longer fool himself into believing he could pursue a personal relationship with her separate from their business one. The lines drawn were clear: He could have her or he could help the town. He couldn't do both.

He'd had the privilege of being a Bradley and of being mayor. Now, he needed to tend to the responsibilities being both entailed.

He turned off the shower and reached for a towel to dry off. How long had he been in there? Too long. He'd promised to provide Caila clothes to change into. Once he did, he'd apologize for the kiss and his previous inappropriate behavior, politely but firmly explain that it would be better for both of them if they kept everything on a business level, and offer to drive her back to Sinclair House. He'd call Joe and tell him to head back to Bradleton, and then Wyatt would do everything in his power to help Nate prove to Endurance why it would be a mistake to remove their business from Chro-Make.

He threw on a T-shirt and a pair of sweats and grabbed another one of his shirts and some yoga pants Laura had left the last time she and Dan had dropped by to help with the house, and headed to the hallway bathroom. He stooped down to leave them by the door so she'd see them when—

The door opened. Swirls of steam slipped past him unheeded as he came face to towel-covered belly. Droplets of water dotted her slim calves and muscled thighs. He swallowed as one bead of moisture near her knee decided to traverse the miles of supple brown skin down her legs to dissolve at her ankle.

Lucky bastard.

Are you fucking kidding me? I'm trying to do the right thing. How much temptation am I supposed to endure?

She stared down at him, her eyes wide. "I—I was looking for clothes and some lotion."

His chest rose and fell as he stared up at her, his heartbeat drowning out any ambient sounds. Her gaze burned into his, and just when he thought he'd burst out of his skin, the pink tip of her tongue darted out and left her lower lip wet. She took a step toward him.

Like a moth to a flame . . .

Fuck responsibility.

With one fluid motion he stood, slid his hand beneath the weight of her wet strands to cup her neck, and claimed her mouth with all of the pent-up yearning that had enveloped him from the moment they'd met.

She moaned and clawed at his back, meeting him kiss for frenzied kiss. He backed her into the steamy bathroom and lifted her until she was sitting on the sink. Her legs clamped around his hips and pulled him closer, the heat from her core calling to him.

He was powerless to refuse.

He fisted his hand in her hair and pulled her head back. He drew his lips across the skin of her neck, its dewy softness yielding to his tongue and his teeth. She smelled amazing, her own scent mixed with his soap. Giving in to a heretofore unknown flight of fancy, he licked her collarbone. He didn't know why. Just another way to be close to her. She moaned and dug greedy fingers into his scalp.

He wanted to see her, to feel all of her, but the

damn towel impeded him. He snagged the knot between her breasts and pulled, his heart racing as the pima cotton slid open and bared her naked body to him, like a special gift being unveiled.

He exhaled slowly. "You're beautiful."

Her eyes glowed. "Keep looking at me like that and I might believe you."

Her breasts were the perfect handful, with dark, puffy nipples that reminded him of chocolate thumbprint cookies. He cupped their smooth roundness and kissed their tops, his tongue traveling all over the orbs but never going near their tips.

It didn't matter.

Her peaks hardened as if he'd lavished them with all of his attention, and when she finally squirmed in his arms and squeezed his hips with her thighs, he gave her what she wanted, puckering his lips and treating the bud with long, slow pulls that left her responsive, lithe body trembling in his arms.

"Yessssss," she moaned.

She arched her back, and he followed the lines of her body as it led him down a path to her navel, her hipbone, the crease at her inner thigh, and then her curl-capped mons. He pressed a kiss on the wiry thatch of hair and reverently spread her thighs so he could gaze upon the treasure awaiting him.

"So pretty," he whispered, breathing in her warm, aroused scent.

With one hand he separated her lips while he sucked the index finger of his other hand in his mouth, then pressed it against her nub.

Her toes dug into his upper back and she pushed herself against his finger, grinding against the pad. Her breathy sigh of ecstasy welcomed him home and created a sex slave. He wanted nothing more than to give her as much pleasure as she could tolerate.

Then show her she could take more.

He lavished her outer lips with nibbles and kisses, running the tip of his tongue up and down the furrows between her outer and inner lips. She tilted her pelvis up, allowing him better access, and he took full advantage of it. The floor was hard beneath his knees and his jaw got tired, but he didn't care. He'd stay locked in this position, loving her, for as long as it took.

"I thought about this," she said, her words punctuated by moans.

So had he. And his dreams could never have lived up to the reality.

Her hands palmed the strands at the nape of his neck. "That first night we met," she continued, "I wanted your mouth on me. Even then."

God damn.

Her words were like gasoline on a brush fire; it set everything ablaze. He licked, sucked, tickled, and lapped every part of her pussy. It was like finally eating a juicy peach when the ripe fruit was all you'd craved for days. With his tongue, lips, and fingers, he savored each delectable taste until she grabbed a handful of his hair and gasped his name.

He smiled against her as she came, hips arching and bucking, inner thighs quivering. He softly nuzzled her and rubbed his nose against her skin as her tremors subsided. He kissed her gleaming lips one more time, then stood and kissed her properly. She didn't recoil from him; on the contrary, she greedily ran her tongue over his lips and his chin, sampling her altered essence from him.

"Like how you taste?" he murmured.

"I do," she said, her voice a soft purr.

"Can I tell you something?"

She nodded.

He nibbled his way to her ear. "You're the best thing I've had in my mouth in a long time."

He drew her earlobe into his mouth and bit it.

"Now, Wyatt," she commanded, her husky voice teetering on the edge.

His dick grew so hard he imagined it ripping through the fabric of his pants.

Not needing to be told a second time, he fumbled open a side drawer and frantically sifted through the contents. Not finding what he sought, he shut it and opened another one.

"What are you doing?" she whined. Not in an annoying way. In a totally sexy I-need-you-to-fuck-me-now kind of way.

He understood the feeling.

"I keep condoms in here," he said, his voice slightly distracted as he continued.

"Why?"

He tilted his head. "You really want to discuss that right now?"

She bit her lip. "Not really."

She was so cute.

He kissed her quickly before resuming his search. "Found them."

"Finally."

He pulled one out and ripped it open with his teeth.

"Allow me," she said, then gestured to his shirt. "Take that off."

He hauled the fabric over his head while she reached into his sweatpants and grabbed hold of his cock. He gripped the sides of the sink to keep from coming in her palm like some inexperienced teenager. She slid the condom on, leaving him with barely a modicum of self-control. He trailed his fingers down her arms, clasped their fingers together, then pinned both hands above her head and stared into her eyes.

"Are you sure?"

She nodded, and to emphasize her desire, prodded him closer with the heel of her foot on his ass.

He didn't rush, though. He took his time, wanting to enjoy the feeling of her enveloping him inch by exquisite inch.

"Oh God, oh God," she muttered.

Her pussy walls clenched around and clamped down on him and it was all so fucking unbelievable.

He closed his eyes. "Don't. Move."

He honestly didn't know how long he could last. He hadn't expected it to be this . . .

He exhaled, and the sharp bite of pleasure receded slightly. He took a moment, and when he opened his eyes, it was to find her watching him. They were so close he could see where the dark brown of her pupil ended and the black of her iris began. He couldn't stop staring at her, memorizing every feature, every mole. The bow in the center of her upper lip, the curly hairs at her temple.

As he began to move—to withdraw and dip back in—she never looked away from him. Over and over as his hips thrust, building up the slick friction between his cock and her pussy, her lashes flickered, her lids lowered slightly, but she kept her gaze trained on his.

It drove him out of his mind.

She bit her lip, and when it emerged wet and swollen, he released her hands and surged into her. She braced a hand against the side of the sink and slid her other one down between them to rub her clit.

His knees threatened to buckle and fell them both.

"Do you mind if I do that?" she asked, with a tiny smile.

"Fuck no," he grunted, his fingers digging into her hips. "I know you like it."

"How?"

"Your pussy tells me."

It did. Her inner walls massaged his dick with each pulse of pleasure she experienced.

She tossed her hair back and closed her eyes. "What are you doing to me?"

He could ask her that very same question. It was gratifying to know they were in sync with regard to their feelings.

"Wyatt . . . Wyatt . . . I'm coming."

"Come on, baby. Come on," he begged, his voice hoarse, his muscles straining. "Let me feel it."

Please.

She did and it blew his world apart.

SEVERAL HOURS LATER, Wyatt entered his bedroom carrying two glasses of water.

"We need to stay hydrated," he said. "Between the 5K and what you just put me through, water is a must."

Caila laughed and pushed herself into a sitting position on his bed, holding the white sheet against her naked chest.

"You getting modest on me now?" he growled, handing her a glass.

He'd tasted every inch of those breasts. He knew they were sensitive, that he could get her halfway there just by focusing on them. He knew she liked when he paid attention to her entire breast and not just the nipple. But when he did lock in on that bud of pleasure, look out! He'd also been thrilled to learn she got really turned on when he caressed her nipple with the head of his cock.

Just thinking about that last one . . .

He shivered.

And even with all he learned, he could spend years discovering more.

He raised his own glass to his lips and downed more than half its contents in several long swallows.

"One of us should be," she said, placing her glass on the nightstand and tipping her chin toward his cock straining against the confines of the boxer briefs he wore . . . and nothing else.

Water dripped from the glass to rest on his chest. Before he could brush it away, she rose onto her knees and captured the drops with her tongue. Then she took the occasion to pay a little attention to *his* nipples.

Heat flooded him. It hadn't been that long since they'd finished round two, but his body didn't seem to care about that small, pesky detail.

With a final flick of her tongue, she fell back to the bed and smiled languidly. "I'd never considered myself modest, but when the girls are free, you tend to lose focus. And you were all about your water. Hydration, remember?"

He grabbed her ankle and hauled her to him. "You're about to see why."

Giggling, she kicked away from him and scooted across the king-sized mattress. "You're insatiable!"

"Only for you."

"Well, I need a break. My legs may be strong from running, but that last position put a lot of strain on them."

He leaned back against the headboard and pulled her into his arms. "I guess a little rest will do us both some good."

Her fingers brushed the wood behind him. "This is gorgeous."

He'd carved designs into three large rectangular panels of pine and mounted them to the wall above his bed. "Thanks."

"Your work?"

He nodded. "One of the first things I worked on after I bought the house."

"You really are talented."

He shrugged, not wanting to discuss his woodworking. That would bring in the outside world, the broken promise he'd made to himself, and the need to figure out where to go from here.

"It's probably the only time I truly feel at peace."

Except the past few hours he'd spent here with her.

"I know you said you haven't sold them in the past, but have you ever considered it? Selling your furniture as a business, I mean?"

Maybe if things were different, if he were someone else or lived somewhere else, but—

"That's not something I can pursue now."

"I understand," she said, squeezing him tighter. He reveled in being close to her, in feeling she wanted it as much as he did.

She trailed her fingers through his chest hair. "Wyatt, we need to talk."

He stiffened. Every guy knew nothing good ever followed those four words.

"About what?"

"What just happened between us."

"Which time?"

He felt her smile against his skin. "Both. I didn't plan this."

He played with her hair. "You think I did?"

"Of course not. What I meant was I'd thought about it, I'd even tried to convince myself it wouldn't be an issue, but I never thought it would actually happen between us."

"Do you regret it?" He held his breath and waited.

It felt like an eternity before she answered. "No. But I need you to understand that it doesn't change anything. This isn't going to stop me from doing my job. And once it's done, I'm leaving."

He winced at the pain that darted through him at her words, but he knew she was right. Because he felt the same way. "It's possible I blacked out a couple of times because it was *that* good, but I'm pretty sure I didn't propose, right?"

"Right," she said, her tone uncertain.

"Although . . ." He moved quickly and pulled her across his lap, spanking her backside. "I'd definitely propose to this ass. It's perfect!"

She squeaked in surprise, then slapped his chest. "You're such a jerk! You scared me half to death!"

He growled against her neck and she laughed and bent her head, trying to dislodge him.

Another thing about her body he'd recently discovered. She was extremely ticklish.

"You're not the only one in a difficult situation. I'm still the mayor of Bradleton and I have to advocate for my town." He stared into eyes that had gone somber with his words. He cupped her cheek. "But can you deny we've been drawn to each other from the moment we met?"

She could. But she'd be lying.

She nestled into his palm. "No."

"And this . . . this was incredible, right?"

A slight smile curved her lips, and she shrugged. "It was all right."

She'd pay for that later. "Then what's the harm in us enjoying what's between us while you're here?"

He'd asked and answered this question hours before. He knew the harm. It was the reason he'd decided to pump the brakes on a personal relationship between them.

But that was before. Now that he'd had a taste of her, he couldn't give her up.

He wouldn't.

She pushed away from him. "But can we do that? Can we 'enjoy what's between us' and not let it affect the reason I'm here? How do I know you won't use what we do in here against me out there?"

"Hey. Caila. No. I would never do that to you."

She exhaled. "Even if you don't like my . . . recommendation?"

Fuck! This was getting way too complicated.

But he didn't care what he'd thought earlier. He wanted her and he had to help his town. He'd figure out a way to have both.

Later.

"Even then. But we can cross that bridge if we ever come to it. Right now, it's miles away." Or two weeks, give or take a day. "I say we have some fun."

Her brows pulled together and she looked away from him.

He could feel the conflict warring inside her. Fear reached into his chest and constricted his lungs, making it difficult for him to breathe. She could say no, say this wasn't worth it.

He wasn't worth it.

She shook her head softly.

He blinked as the acidic scrape of bile teased the back of his throat—

She trailed a finger down his arm. Tilted her head so her hair fell over one shoulder. Smiled. "What do you have in mind?"

Thank God! The giddy rush of relief rendered him momentarily speechless.

But when it came to her, he seemed to recuperate quickly. He reached into the glass on the nightstand and pulled out an ice cube.

"How about a little frosty foreplay?"

Chapter Fifteen

Walking through the kitchen back at Sinclair House on Monday afternoon, Caila caught sight of her reflection in the microwave. Thankfully, her hair looked decent, even though she hadn't followed her normal conditioning and detangling routine after her shower.

She'd been . . . delightfully preoccupied.

Wyatt didn't seem to have an issue with being involved with a black woman, but she wasn't ready to give him the orientation on black hair care. Especially when she could think of a much better use for their time together.

Oh my God. Stop grinning like some giddy teenager who's been asked out by the most popular boy in school!

Though how could she stop smiling after the previous day and a half spent with Wyatt? The man's skills in the bedroom were the stuff of legends.

And she didn't regret any of it. Even if it never happened again, she knew the memories of that night would stay with her for the rest of her life. Something to reflect on when she got back to Chicago and her twelve- to fourteen-hour days.

Or maybe she'd listen to Ava and her friends and family and start dating again. Clearly, her strong response to Wyatt was fueled, in part, by her lackadaisical love life.

What if what she felt with Wyatt was unique to him? He made her feel sexy and cherished and desired, and if she didn't watch herself, she'd become addicted to the way he looked at her.

Ten days. She had ten more days until Joe came back and she'd get access to the financial reports. And once Endurance got her report and backed out of their contract with Chro-Make, Wyatt wouldn't want to see her again.

Which was fine. All of the complications just proved why it had to be temporary between them. That was all it could ever be. Long-term, her focus had to be on getting her life back on track.

One mistake. One night when she'd let disappointment get the best of her. She worked so hard for everything she'd had. She couldn't lose it. Not because of a man.

That would make her no better than her mother.

Though she allowed herself a moment to indulge in the scenario where she brought Wyatt Bradley home to meet her mother. Mona would probably work herself into a feminine flutter reacting to all of that male fineness.

And she truly believed that Pop-Pop would've loved him. Wyatt reminded her of her grandfather in so many ways. He was smart and considerate and he cared about others.

And those gorgeous pieces he'd created. She wondered if he'd sell that *Scandal* table to her. It would look great in her office.

Who would've guessed the pretty boy had such depth? She remembered when they'd first met. She'd assumed the calluses were due to golf, tennis, or some other gentlemanly sport. Instead, he'd gotten them shaping wood, and the hotness of that imagery seared into her brain, making her incapable of thinking of anything else but his hands on her body.

Her phone's text ringtone broke through her reverie. She pulled the phone from the pocket of her running pants and checked the screen. A message from Wyatt stole her breath.

I can still taste you on my tongue.

Heat rushed into her cheeks and, look, that smile was back. She typed in her response. Is that a good or bad thing?

His response was quick. It's good because you tasted so sweet, but bad because I can't focus on anything until I have you again.

I wish I could help you in some way.

You can. I want to see you tonight.

She poked her tongue into her cheek. See me? Is that all you want to do?

Hell, no. But it'll be a start. Say you'll come. It'll be fun. Intimate.

Dragonflies dipped, then soared inside her belly. I'm looking forward to it.

Maybe she *was* a giddy teenager. Is this what it had felt like? She wouldn't know; she'd been too focused on her schoolwork to indulge in relationships. The same with college and her job after she'd graduated. She'd had sex and she'd enjoyed it. But this playfulness, this aching yearning, the keen anticipation of seeing him again . . . This was all new.

And she rather liked it.

She was laughing at the tongue out and peach emojis he'd texted back when the doorbell rang.

"Jada!" Caila was surprised to see the teenager from the bake sale.

"Hi." Jada looked down at her shoes.

"What are you doing here?"

"I don't know. I shouldn't have come." Jada turned to go.

"No, it's okay." Caila gestured to the porch swing. "You want to sit and talk?"

Jada closed her eyes and nodded. "If you don't mind?"

"Of course not."

They sat. Jada placed a tattered string backpack next to the porch railing, the beautiful wild curls tamed into a pouf on top of her head, bouncing with her movement.

"Shouldn't you be in school?"

"The week after homecoming we're always on fall break."

"That must be nice."

"Not really. At home, I have to take care of my little sister and brother. I prefer school."

"I did, too. Most kids aren't like us, though."

Jada rolled her eyes and shoved her hands into the pockets of her Bradleton High Cougars sweatshirt. "All they care about is who's hooking up with whom and trying to get famous through YouTube or Instagram."

The correct usage of "whom." Caila smiled, remembering her high school years. The hard work and pressure to make good grades; the nights spent studying while everyone else was drinking and partying; the teasing and bullying because she hadn't been like the other kids.

It had all been worth it. If there was one thing she wanted Jada to understand, it was that she wasn't alone. High school was tough, but if she remained focused and didn't let anything distract her, she'd achieve any goal she set for herself.

"For me, it was kids trying to get on *The Real World* or *America's Next Top Model*."

"So stupid."

Yeah, it was.

"How's *Handmaid's Tale* going?"

"I finished it yesterday. I'm reading this now." Jada reached into her bag and pulled out a book.

"*Y: The Last Man*?"

"It's this graphic novel series about a guy and his pet monkey who are the only two males to survive a global event that killed all other living mammals with the Y chromosome."

A world without men? There were times when Caila didn't think that would be such a bad thing. Although after yesterday, she didn't feel like she could completely commit to the notion.

She tapped the cover of the book. "Your reading habits are very eclectic."

"Don't look down on comic books," Jada said. "Comics theory is an actual field of study offered in colleges."

Huh. At the price of a college education these days, Caila wasn't sure she'd waste the credits on something that frivolous.

"Is that what you're interested in?"

"Oh no." Jada dismissed that idea with a wave of her hand. "I want a career where I make money, so I can help my family. I'm going to be a lawyer."

"One of my best friends was just appointed to the bench in California."

Jada's eyes widened as if Caila had announced she personally knew Beyoncé. "You're friends with a judge?"

"I am." A thought occurred to Caila. "Do you have an email account? If so, I can pass it on to her. If you want to talk to her or ask questions. She'd be a great resource."

"Really?" Jada's gaze was bright and hopeful. "You'd do that? For me?"

Caila's heart melted a little.

"Of course. Plus, us book nerds have to stick together," she said, bumping the girl's shoulder.

"That's so cool. Thank you, Ms. Harris."

"Call me Caila. In fact, I think I have one of her cards with me. How about I give that to you, and you can contact her when you're ready? I'll let her know to expect you."

She stood just as the screen door opened, and Kevin stood in the doorway, his cheeks stained with that perpetual flush, his blue eyes glossy. "Mom made some strawberry pecan bread last night and I made sure to save you some. I can bring you a piece . . ."

The kid was sweet, but sensitively dealing with the never-ending adoration was draining.

"I've already eaten, but thank you. Maybe later. Kevin, do you know Jada?"

Kevin frowned. "I think so. I mean, we haven't met but I saw you around school."

Jada nodded. "I'm a year behind you."

"You graduate in the spring?"

"That's the plan," Jada said.

Kevin's gaze slid to Jada's lap. "Did you know they're turning that into a TV show?"

"They're turning everything into a show." Jada leaned forward. "Have you read it?"

"Uh, yeah!" He shoveled fingers through his blond curls. "Have you read *Saga* or *Southern Bastards*?"

"*Saga*'s on my list but I've never heard of *Southern Bastards*." Jada paused. "Outside of my grandma cursing."

Kevin laughed. "It's about life in a small town where football is everything. Sound familiar?"

"Shockingly so." Jada sat back and shook her head. "I live it, so I don't know if I want to read about it."

"It's an interesting critique of Southern culture. It also has a kick-ass heroine. Try the first issue; see what you think."

Caila tilted her head to the side. This was the first time she'd seen Kevin natural and relaxed and not in "puppy-dog eager" mode. He was actually pretty cute when his face wasn't cycling through the colors on the outer spectrum of the rainbow.

Caila motioned over her shoulder. "Jada, I'm going to get that card. I'll be back."

She left them deep in discussion and headed to her room to find Ava's business card. Her friend had sent her several from the first printing for her new position: The Honorable Ava Taylor, Superior Court of California.

Ava had been so proud of those cards, almost as proud as she was of her new judgeship, especially as it came in the first year she was eligible to be appointed.

When she called Ava about Jada, should she also mention what had happened with Wyatt?

No, not yet. The other woman didn't need another reason to believe in her infallibility when it came to other people's lives.

CAILA SIGHED AND slid her free hand in the front pocket of her jeans. "When you used the word 'intimate,' this isn't what I had in mind."

Not that she wasn't charmed by the venue. The red barn and silo wouldn't have looked out of place on a storybook farm. In real life, the effect was enchanting. Although the large wooden cut-out jack-o'-lantern, with its slightly creepy gap-toothed smile, added a touch of kitsch to their surroundings.

"I know what you had in mind and I promise, we'll get to that," Wyatt said, the conviction in his low, deep voice bolstering his vow. He raised their clasped hands and brushed his lips over her knuckles.

Her nipples tightened into buds.

She gave in to the loopy grin that fought to break loose. "You can't do that. People might see you."

"That's why we're standing over here, behind the Fun Barn."

"Is it really called that or are you being facetious?"

He chuckled, and goose bumps danced along her skin. "I didn't make it up. That's what it's called."

She wasn't sure she believed him, but she appreciated the segue. "The name may be real, but what about our reason for being here? Are we going to casually bump into the owner of the farm, who'll tell me that this land has been in his family for generations?"

"Well, it has."

"Uh-huh. And then will he let it drop that there's a plot of land where they harvest the raw materials Chro-Make uses for the makeup?"

Wyatt maneuvered them so her back was against the barn and he stood in front of her, a hand braced above her head. "Do you get pleasure out of constantly busting my balls?"

"I thought we both got pleasure out of what I did to your balls." She tapped a finger against his chin. "But seriously, my questions are legit. With you, there's always an agenda."

His expression was serious. "I just wanted to spend time with you in my town without hundreds of people watching."

Oh.

Crap. Now she felt like a bitch. Not ready to meet his gaze or think about what he'd just said, she looked up. Away from the city, the stars sparkled bright against the velvet night sky. She could never see them that clearly in Chicago. It was an awe-inspiring sight.

Unlike the image over Wyatt's shoulder. In the distance, tall corn stalks and another creepy wooden cutout, this time of a cartoonish ear of corn, proclaimed the entrance to a corn maze that gave Caila *Children of the Corn* vibes.

Nope, not doing that.

Wyatt sighed. "I love coming here. Each year, the Andersons open their working farm during the week of the Harvest Festival and offer pumpkin picking, corn mazes, a pumpkin mountain slide and"—he patted the wall above her head—"the Fun Barn."

Sounded like something the children of the town probably enjoyed. And yet—

"Where are all the kids?" She hadn't seen any since they'd arrived about twenty minutes ago.

"During the day, they're everywhere, especially since schools are on fall break. But after eight p.m. you have to be twenty-one or older to get in."

"Adults only? Is this where all the Bradleton swingers meet up during the holidays?"

His mouth dropped open. "If I were drinking something, I would've actually spit it out."

"No orgies in small towns?"

"Not in public. But if you're interested, I'll see what I can find out." He leaned his upper body away from her to peer around the building. Then he raised his hand. "Mr. Miller?"

What the hell? He wasn't really—?

She pushed, ineffectively, against his chest and followed the direction of his gaze to an older couple standing several yards away. The position of Wyatt's body over hers and the barn hid her from their view.

As long as they didn't start walking this way.

Wyatt waved. "I was wondering—"

She ducked back against the barn. "What are you doing?" she hissed.

"—if you could tell me—"

"Don't you dare," she muttered.

"—where I might find the events of—"

"Stop it!" She laughed and pulled on his arm.

He stared down at her, and in the warm glow of the surrounding light, his hazel eyes gleamed. "Are you sure? Because I'm pretty sure they know where all the kinky stuff goes on. I've thought that about them for years . . ."

She couldn't control her laughter. "You are ridiculous."

He shrugged. "You had your chance. Never mind, Mr. Miller. It's wonderful to see you both. Have a good night."

She let her head fall back against the barn. "I can't believe you did that."

"I can't, either." He smoothed a lock of hair behind her ear and brushed his thumb across her cheek. "You make me do things I've never done before."

The way he looked at her . . .

Heat suffused her body and her heart rebounded against her chest. "Like what?"

"Like kiss a smart, beautiful woman behind the Anderson family barn."

"I don't want to be responsible for your corruption." She fisted her hands in his sweater and claimed his lips.

The man could kiss like nobody's business. If it were a subject, he'd have a doctorate. If it were a sport, he'd be in the hall of fame.

Quite simply, he took her breath away.

A bell-like ringtone penetrated their heated embrace. Wyatt broke their kiss and pressed his cheek against hers.

"Sorry about this," he breathed into her ear, as he pulled a cell from his jeans and answered the call.

"Hey," he said, his eyes boring into hers. "No, we're here." He cupped her shoulder and slid his hand down her arm. "We're over by the Fun Barn." He twined his fingers with hers. "Mind your damn business. We'll be there in a sec."

He hung up.

"Come on. Got us tickets for the private hayride."

Privacy sounded promising. "What's that?"

They walked over to a large wooden structure built to resemble a miniature outdoor train station, complete with a shedlike roof.

"Small parties can take a half-hour hayride through the farm and end up in a private section where there's a campfire and treats and you get to hang out for ninety minutes before they come back to get you."

When they reached the hayride depot, Caila saw Dan and his wife, Laura, standing close to each other, engaged in a deep conversation.

She slid him a sidelong glance. "You called in reinforcements?"

"This probably isn't the time for me to get caught having sex with the Endurance rep in the middle of a field. And if it were just the two of us, I wouldn't be able to say no. I find you irresistible." He winked at her.

It was her turn to be shocked as Wyatt greeted his friends. She addressed Dan cordially—she didn't get a warm, welcoming vibe from him—but was surprised when Laura hugged her. She didn't mind returning it; she liked the other woman.

A red farm truck with a wooden flatbed pulled in. Wyatt hopped into the back and helped her up. Piles of hay were stacked around the bed for comfortable seating. Caila took the spot next to Wyatt; Laura and Dan sat across from them.

The wind kicked up and she snuggled into the fall jacket she'd purchased on her shopping spree. The air was crisp, scented with hints of cinnamon and cloves. Caila did her best to take it all in, to remember the idyllic scene exactly as it—

She sneezed. She sneezed. She sneezed again. When Caila opened her eyes, all three people were staring at her.

"Bless you," Laura said.

Caila smiled. "Thanks."

Wyatt turned his body toward her. "It didn't even occur to me to ask if you were allergic to hay."

"I wouldn't know. I don't have lots of occasions to be exposed to it. I do have seasonal allergies." There was an annoying tickle in her nose, but her throat wasn't scratchy and her eyes felt fine. "If I am, it's only slightly."

"I'm so sorry." Wyatt clawed a hand through his dark strands. He stood. "We don't have to do this. Let's get you some medicine and—"

She tugged on the hem of his maroon sweater. "Sit down. I'll be fine."

His brows drew together. "You're not fine."

"I want to go. Come on, I'm good."

He stared down at her before he took two steps and jumped off the truck.

"Wyatt!"

Dammit.

Annoyance at the scene he was making, affection that he cared, and lust at the way his body moved when he leaped down, warred within her. She didn't know which to allow to the forefront.

She looked over to find Dan and Laura studying her. She tried to lighten the mood. "Did he just ditch me?"

"No. Far from it." Dan frowned and peered after his friend.

Cryptic much, Officer Daniel?

"Sooo." Caila switched her attention to Laura. "How long have you two known each other?"

Laura smiled. "Since high school. My family moved here when I was in the ninth grade."

"Where from?"

"Virginia Beach."

Caila sat forward, responding to an experience that seemed similar to her own. "That must've been jarring."

"Oh, it was. My father was in the navy and when he retired, he wanted to move closer to family. My grandparents lived here, so we moved back."

"I'm another transplant," Dan added. "We moved here when I was five."

"Wow. I guess I didn't think of Bradleton as a place that people moved to." She closed her eyes when she heard her own words. "Shit. That sounded more bitchy than I intended."

Laura's bark of laughter caught Caila by surprise. "No, I understand what you're saying. But it's the biggest town in three counties, so people come here to do their shopping or to visit and spend the day. Nearby towns haven't fared as well."

"Can I ask you a personal question?"

"You can ask, but we may not answer," Laura said, a smile softening her words.

Caila took a deep breath. "Why do you stay?"

They glanced at each other before Dan said, "We all left to attend college; couldn't wait to get away. But as you get older and start thinking about having a family, you want to give them the same experience you had growing up."

I don't, Caila thought.

"We have history here. We know the people here." Dan took Laura's hand. "Eventually, we'll want to raise our children here."

Laura nodded. "Bradleton may never be what it was, but it won't have the chance to morph into something new if everyone leaves."

An easy decision for them to make. *They* fit in here, were straight out of central casting for Small Town, America. Laura ran a wellness center. Dan was a cop. No offense, but they could live in a small town. Hell, they could thrive.

"Have you always been into wellness?" she asked, several moments later, when Wyatt hadn't returned.

"No." Laura laughed and rolled her eyes. "I worked in politics in D.C. When we left, there wasn't an opportunity for me to work remotely."

"And how did that translate into wellness?"

"I'd practiced yoga and Pilates for years, and when we came to visit, before we moved, I'd always complain about the lack of a proper studio in town. Once we'd officially relocated, I looked into opening my own."

Caila remembered Wyatt's correction at the game. *Laura, who owns the yoga studio in town. Wait, sorry, the new Bradleton Wellness Center.* "The wellness center is a recent development? You opened a yoga studio first?"

Laura nodded. "In my practice I often referred clients to our local massage and physical therapists, and they were doing the same. Then, about eighteen months ago, we all got to talking at the monthly business mixer and we realized we could save money and provide better, more comprehensive service, if we combined under one umbrella. So, we did."

They'd made a really smart move. By merging, they could share accommodations, thereby reducing their expenses and creating built-in cross promotion with their existing clientele.

Something about that blueprint pinged a latent part of her brain, but before she could explore it further, Wyatt ran up, a black and blue plaid blanket thrown over his arm. He hopped in the truck—Lord, have mercy, he could move!—and spread the fabric over the hay. He gestured for her to sit on it.

"Maybe that'll help." He pulled a small pouch from his jacket pocket. "I also have tissues."

"Where did you get all of this?" Caila asked.

He grinned sheepishly and rubbed the back of his neck. He looked so damn adorable. "I kinda pulled rank at the box office. I figured they'd have something useful around here." He sat down next to her. "It's a working farm and the Andersons' house isn't far. I asked one of them to help me."

Her heart shifted, settled into place, and began racing at the speed of light. She placed a hand on his knee. Squeezed. "That's the sweetest thing anyone has ever done for me. Thank you."

Wyatt covered her hand with his. "You're very welcome."

A voice screeched through the loudspeaker attached to the back of the truck, breaking the mood. "Now that everyone's aboard, let's get you guys going."

Warmed by Wyatt's concern, Caila sat back and tried not to read meaning into the look that Dan and Laura exchanged.

Chapter Sixteen

Wyatt closed his eyes, and in the dark, everything was more intense. The softness of her skin, the sound of her moans, the smell of their sex.

It overwhelmed him.

He opened his eyes, and the visual onslaught didn't help.

Fuck! It didn't matter. He wasn't going to last much longer.

Caila's body was arched above him, one hand braced behind her, the other holding the device that was driving them both insane. She held the vibrator against her clit and undulated her hips, the muscles in her sleek thighs rippling with her exertions. He could feel the reverberations inside her pussy, and the all-encompassing sensations drove him insane with desire.

He slid a hand up her sweat-slicked torso and caught a nipple between his thumb and forefinger, rolling it.

"God, Wyatt, yes. Harder."

Her husky voice lowered in pleasure? There was no better sound on this earth.

He rose up to suck on the hard peak and press it against the roof of his mouth. She cried out and ground vigorously against him. Her moans?

The second-best sound.

"That's it, baby. Ride me. Ride my cock."

He gripped her hips and thrust into her until he couldn't see straight and her eyes rolled back in her head. She gripped the sheets between her fingers and screamed as she came, rhythmic bands of pressure swathing his cock.

His heart galloped in his chest and pleasure tightened into a knot at the base of his spine. A second later, it was his turn, and he roared as his balls contracted and waves of paralyzing energy coursed hot and thick through his body.

She collapsed on top of him, and the vibrator rolled from her fingers to rest on the blanket.

He exhaled shakily and hugged her close, pressing a kiss to her damp forehead.

Several moments later, when he'd caught his breath, he chuckled. "Evelyn Nash sells sex toys? I won't be able to look her in the face the next time I see her."

Caila snuggled into his side and slid her knee over his thigh, lazily stroking his calf with her foot. "The next time you see her, you should thank her. It was worth every penny I spent."

Had he ever felt so at peace? Like he was finally home? Holding her in his arms, her warm feminine scent both stimulating his senses and soothing his soul . . .

He never wanted it to end.

Caila's fingers idly combed through the hair on his chest. "Dan and Laura kept staring at us."

"I noticed," he said, grabbing her hand when her wandering thumb brushed too close to his nipple. He needed a little more time before round two. "They weren't trying to be subtle about it."

"They probably thought I was the rudest person on earth."

He smiled against her hair. "Earth might be stretching it a little, but . . ."

She groaned and hid her face. "I know."

"Baby, I'm kidding."

She pushed back against his arm and stared up at him. "I basically questioned why she'd give up a career as a policy analyst in D.C. to own a yoga studio in Bradleton."

That pretty much summed it up. But Laura hadn't taken offense at her questions. In fact, she'd taken him aside a little later and told him how much she liked Caila.

"She doesn't tolerate bullshit and I respect that," Laura had said.

Wyatt did, too. He cared for Caila. A lot. Beyond that, he wasn't ready to quantify his feelings, though he couldn't escape her growing importance to him.

At one point during their outing, while making s'mores and talking to Dan, he'd caught sight of Caila in his periphery. She'd looked stunning with the firelight flickering across her brown skin and a bright smile curving her lips at something Laura said. Emotion had swamped his chest, making it hard for him to breathe.

This is what I want. More evenings like this . . . with Caila.

"Dude, I like my marshmallows burnt, but that one is incinerated." Dan had smirked, lifting a bottle of beer to his lips.

Wyatt had tried to remain casual and act like nothing had changed. He'd flipped Dan the bird, then discarded the alien-looking clump of charred sugar.

But once the thought had formed, it refused to go away.

He wanted more with Caila. Beyond her temporary stay in Bradleton.

But how could that work? She had her life and career in Chicago; he had his family and responsibilities here in Virginia. Not to mention the biggest obstacle between them: the role she might play in Chro-Make losing the Endurance contract.

Uncertainty sank like a stone in his stomach. He didn't want to worry about any of that right now. He had ten more days with her until Joe came back, and he wanted nothing more than to spend them just like this: her in his arms, the outside world at bay.

No talk of factories, contracts, or the future.

Caila kissed his chest. "This is great."

"I agree."

"And you're wonderful."

He smiled and tried to shake off any lingering anxiety. "I like to think so."

Her laughter was his heart's siren song. "But I couldn't do what she did. As much as I respect what Laura and Dan have, it isn't for me. I'm never getting married."

He stilled. "Why not?"

She shifted her upper body to fold her arms across his chest and prop up her chin. "Because I'll never allow myself to be dependent on a man. For anything."

The harshness of her words initially chilled him, until he saw past his own shock and caught the pain saturating her eyes.

"That kind of proclamation requires a story."

"It really doesn't."

She didn't want to talk about it, so he'd let it go. For now. It was good to know how she felt. Maybe it would stem the rising tide of his affections.

He stroked her hair and forced himself to speak past the sudden obstruction in his throat. "I appreciate your candor and I'm glad you told me. Because someday, I'll have to get married."

She tensed and looked away from him. "Why do you say 'have' instead of 'want'?"

He allowed the distance and imbued his tone with a breeziness at odds with his mood. "It's my responsibility to carry on the Bradley name."

"You're talking like you're a Rockefeller or a Kennedy."

"Down here, I am. Objectively speaking, the Bradleys are a big deal in Virginia. For as long as I can remember, my family has drilled into me that carrying on our legacy is my foremost duty."

She turned back to face him. "It seems to me you're doing exactly that. You're the popular mayor of the town named after your family. What more could they want from you?"

Everything.

"I've had a very privileged upbringing and I was granted a lot more leeway than other members of my family, but now the bill for that freedom is due. My grandfather wants me to run for the Virginia House of Delegates next year, with an eye toward the governorship."

Caila sat up and pushed her hair out of her face. "That's major. Is that what you want to do?"

Had what he'd wanted ever been a consideration? Or had they all assumed his wishes didn't matter? That he'd do what was expected of him?

"Why were you given more leeway?" she asked when he didn't respond.

He folded an arm behind his head. "My dad. Do you remember how I told you I got my interest in woodworking from him?"

"Yes."

"Since becoming mayor, I've been able to balance fulfilling my responsibilities to my family and pursuing what interests me. My dad didn't. To him, staying true to his art was the most important thing." *More important than me.* He swallowed those unsaid words. "He left when I was twelve."

"Have you seen him since then?"

"No. My grandfather wouldn't allow it."

"Why was that his call to make? What about your mother?"

"I guess she agreed." He shrugged. "When I was a senior in high school, we found out he'd died while living in an artist colony in California."

"Oh, Wyatt, I'm so sorry." Her caress on his chest was soothing this time instead of titillating. "Have you ever considered leaving like your father did?"

"No!" He actually recoiled from the thought. "I'm sure it sounds old-fashioned, but I'd never shirk my duty. I'm an only child. It all falls on me."

"That's a lot for you to shoulder. You don't think it's unfair?"

"I shouldn't complain."

"Yes, you should. You're a gifted artist. That should be nurtured. Especially if it's what you want. When you're governor, I seriously doubt anyone is going to let you set up your bench and chainsaw in the official office."

That surprised a bark of laughter from him.

"Chainsaw? I'm not Leatherface," he said.

She narrowed her eyes. "People use chainsaws to cut down trees."

She was so adorable.

"I don't. I'm not a lumberjack."

"Okay." She crossed her arms over her bare chest. "What do you use?"

The action blocked his view of her breasts. *Not cool!*

He tugged one of her hands and her arms unfolded, like a bow on a gift. *Better.* "A wood chisel."

"Fine. Wood chisel. Is that better?" she asked, rolling her eyes.

If only. He wished all his problems could be solved with flirty banter.

"My grandfather wants me to announce that I'll run for state delegate at the Harvest Ball on Saturday."

"Isn't that premature? Don't you have to declare it to the state or something first?"

"There are forms to fill out, but they aren't due until March."

"Then there's no rush. You don't have to do anything until you're ready."

The way she came to his defense warmed him. "My grandfather is ready."

She frowned. "Your grandfather sounds like a . . . commanding man."

"Is that a compliment?" he asked, unused to hearing someone refer to Asher with anything less than deference and awe.

"Not really," she murmured. "What's the Harvest Ball?"

"It's the annual dance we have to mark the end of the festival. It's usually a lot of fun."

"Are you going to do it?"

"I don't have a choice," he murmured, though for the first time, he wondered how true that statement was.

"Not having a choice. I know that feeling."

"You do? How?"

Her eyes widened, as if she'd realized she'd spoken aloud. She waved her hand. "Nothing."

He rolled over and propped himself up on an elbow. "Do you think I'm going to let you get away with that? I bared my soul to you. You've got to give me something."

Her expression softened and she leaned forward and kissed him, running her tongue along his lower lip. "I thought that's what I spent the past hour doing."

"Caila . . ."

She straightened and turned her shoulder away from him, the fall of her hair hiding her face from his searching gaze. He smoothed the strands behind her ear and stared at her profile.

"No, baby. Don't shut me out. What did you mean about not having a choice?"

She continued looking down, her fingers plucking at the fitted white sheet. He stroked a hand down her back and waited.

"I don't even know where to start." She shook her head. "There have been two men that I've counted on in my life. Daddy and Pop-Pop."

Wyatt was almost afraid to breathe. She was opening up to him, and if the emotion pulsing through her was any indication, what she was sharing was very important.

"I was a daddy's girl. We lived in Baltimore and he was a professor at a local college. He was so invested in my future. We used to spend hours in his study talking and planning: What activities I'd pursue. What college I'd go to. What I'd major in. What I'd do with my life. And our plans had worked. I received a scholarship to the top prep school in the state. But before I could start, he died." She drew in a shuddering breath. "After the funeral, we moved to a small town in rural Maryland to live with my grandfather."

Damn. "That must've been quite a culture shock for you."

"You have no idea. It was tough. Unlike my mother and sisters, I didn't want to go, but that didn't seem to matter to anyone else. My plans weren't important. What I'd worked for wasn't important. We had relatives who lived in the city; I could've stayed with them. But my grandfather wouldn't consider it. Said the family had to stay together. And my mother stand up to a man?"

Caila's tone made it clear that was highly unlikely.

He didn't miss the striking similarities in their lives. But he didn't comment on it. He just listened. He had the distinct feeling that she didn't tell many people what she was choosing to share with him.

"We moved the following week and I had to give up my scholarship. It all happened so fast that I left a lot of my stuff behind, including some of my favorite books and my dream box."

She was brittle with tension. He was afraid to touch her, afraid she'd shatter into pieces.

"Dream box?"

"It was this little fabric-covered box my dad had given me on my tenth birthday. I would write down my goals and dreams on a piece of paper and put it inside. Every night I'd pick it up and think about my future. It was my way of manifesting the life I wanted, before I even understood what that meant."

It wasn't difficult for him to picture a young, intense Caila defining her ambition and willing it to happen. He smiled, the image causing warmth to expand throughout his chest.

"I was so angry with everyone, especially Pop-Pop, and I wanted to hate him. But I couldn't. He wasn't an educated man like Daddy. He only had a high school education and he worked with his hands. But he was like my dad in all the ways that mattered. He understood me. He supported me. He taught me so much."

He could feel the deep affection in her words and wanted to know more about this man she clearly loved.

"Like what?"

"About a month after school started, he picked me up early. I was having a hard time, mainly because I still hadn't let go of my bitterness over the move. I was in full-on brat mode, but he didn't say anything, just drove us over to the Sav-Mart. We got two milkshakes and sat at a table near the window. At first, I was quiet, like I couldn't be bothered."

She shrugged. "But when he started talking about my dad, I lost it. I let him have it. I told him he didn't know a thing about Daddy, because if he did, he wouldn't have taken me from Baltimore. I railed about losing my scholarship and told him everything Daddy and I had planned, which he'd ruined by bringing me to Backwardsville. I was such a little shit.

"He listened to it all and never said a word. When I was done, he leaned forward, looked me in the eye, and told me that was the only time he'd let me get away with disrespecting him. And then he said he didn't see why I still couldn't pursue my goals from there. He promised to help me. And he was true to his word. Every week, we'd meet at the Sav-Mart, have a milkshake, and go over my short-term strategic plan." A slight grin curved her lips. "The weeks when we didn't have much to discuss, I spent a few hours playing pinball."

His mouth dropped open and he pointed a finger at her. "I knew it! You *were* a ringer!"

"You weren't innocent! You suggested pinball because you assumed I couldn't play!" Her laughter ended abruptly, and her smile faded.

Dread formed a knot in his stomach. "Caila?"

She started trembling, and when he reached to cover her hand with his, she jerked.

Something bad was coming.

She closed her eyes again and whispered, "Pop-Pop died this summer."

There it was.

Fuck!

"I thought I was fine. That I'd handled it. But I . . . I let it affect my performance at work."

Her suffering rolled off her in waves, and he felt it physically.

"That's understandable. You're still grieving—"

"No." She shook her head and turned fevered eyes to face him. "I hadn't talked to him in months! I avoided his calls. It seems so stupid now, but I was angry. He'd gotten on me about missing my sister's baby shower because of work. I couldn't understand why he was saying that to me. He knew how I felt about my job. And I thought, if he cares so much about *her* feelings, then he could talk to *her* about the Orioles and the latest thing he was working on. Oh God! Why? Why didn't I call him back? Why didn't I just apologize . . ."

Her sobs got the best of her and he pulled her into his arms. Her body shuddered violently, and she struggled to catch her breath. He couldn't stand her pain; the rawness of it was near to breaking him. In that moment he knew he'd do whatever it took to ease her suffering, even if it meant going against everything he believed.

"The man you described loved you to pieces. He knew you were upset. I'm sure he didn't hold that against you."

She shook her head, as if she didn't believe him, and the despair of the gesture shattered him. He tightened his hold.

"I'm sorry," she said several moments later, grabbing the sheet and wiping the moisture off his chest. "I didn't know all of *that* was going to happen."

He brushed his thumb beneath her eye, capturing a lingering tear. "You don't have to apologize."

"With work and this assignment, I . . . I haven't allowed myself to cry like that. Not even when I found out he'd passed away."

"Aw, baby . . ." He hated knowing she'd kept all of that pain and sorrow inside. "How do you feel now?"

She exhaled shakily and laughed. "Like a wrung-out rag doll."

"If you're a rag doll, you're the most beautiful one I've ever seen." Unable to resist touching her, he kissed her shoulder and pressed his cheek against her. "It couldn't have been easy holding on to that. I'm just glad you've finally expressed it, and honored you felt you could share it with me."

"Hey." She shifted, and when their gazes finally met, he knew he'd lost a bit of his soul to her. "Thank you. Not only for allowing me to use you as a human handkerchief, but for what you did earlier. Our date at the farm. The company, the drinks, and the s'mores. I haven't enjoyed a relaxing evening like that in a very long time."

"It was my pleasure. If I could, I'd make sure you took more time to relax. You know"—he traced the fullness of her lips with his finger—"if things were different we could do—"

"Don't." She covered his hand with hers. "There's no use wishing our situation was different. Things are what they are. I'll go back to my job and you . . . you'll make a great governor of Virginia."

"Caila—"

"You will," she stated emphatically. "You're a great leader. You've already proved it as mayor. You're a good communicator, you're fearless, you have vision and integrity. I'd vote for you."

His cheeks burned, and guilt gave his heart another twist.

Integrity.

Not even close.

But he couldn't dwell on the shortcomings of his principles. Not now. His time with Caila was limited. He intended to make the most of it.

"Is that how you see me?" he teased. "It sounds like you're describing a legend."

She laughed, and his heart leaped in his chest.

"A legend? Please. What you are is a handful."

He maneuvered until she was beneath him, nestling his hardening cock in the heat at her core.

"Then it's a good thing you have two hands."

WYATT SAT IN his car after dropping Caila off at Sinclair House. He pressed a contact on his phone.

"Mayor?" Nate picked up on the fourth ring, his voice leaden with sleep. "What time is it?"

"Late or early, depending on your view. Sorry to bother you, but . . . have you talked to Joe?"

Nate yawned. "Not since our meeting with Ms. Harris on Thursday."

You can still change your mind. You don't have to do this.

"Give him a call. Tell him we need him to come back a week early."

"Why?"

"We don't need the extra time."

"But your plan is working. She's been to the football game, the bake sale, the color run. She's talking to people. Isn't that what you wanted?"

"It'll have to be enough."

There was a long pause, then Nate said, "People are talking about the two of you. They say you took her out to Anderson Farm tonight. Are you sure you're doing what's best for Bradleton and not letting your feelings for her get in the way?"

No he wasn't, and that was the fucking problem.

Chapter Seventeen

$\mathcal{F}$or the third time in ten minutes, Caila caught herself staring into space. She closed her eyes and smiled.

Admit it, girl. You're feeling him.

She was. She'd tried to keep it casual, but something had shifted between her and Wyatt a couple of nights ago. She'd told him about Pop-Pop and had felt safe enough to grieve for her grandfather in a way she hadn't allowed herself to before. And he'd responded with kindness, compassion, and some of the best sex she'd ever had. She was starting to wish they could pursue something beyond her time here.

But those emotions were dangerous. Because while she felt better, like a shroud had been removed from her spirit, she was still keeping her true intentions hidden. Her actions in Bradleton had the potential to destroy his town. And as long as that remained true . . .

Still, nothing said sex-only pals, with no strings attached, like dinner with the family.

She shouldn't have agreed to it, but when he'd asked, she'd been caught up in the good feelings he'd evoked and unable to say no. She didn't know what to expect this evening, but she couldn't deny she was excited to see him.

She was putting the finishing touches on her makeup when her phone rang. Hurrying to where it lay on the table, she saw her assistant's face and answered it.

"What's up?" she asked, pressing the speaker button and sitting down on the adjacent chair.

"Why am I looking at the ceiling?" Diane asked.

"Because I'm busy," Caila said, sliding her foot into a black heel and hooking the strap around her ankle. "You're working late tonight."

"I'm leaving soon, but I wanted to wait. In case you needed me."

A discordant tone in Diane's voice stopped her. She straightened and grabbed her phone. Hills and valleys dotted the usually smooth space between her assistant's brows.

Ah, hell. "What's wrong?"

Diane's blue eyes softened briefly. "Awww, you look amazing! That can only help."

"Help what?"

"Ms. Mitchell wants to talk to you in five minutes!"

"Are you kidding?"

"It was ten, but it took me five minutes to get back to my desk. Damn slow elevator."

Caila's stomach churned and she bit her lip. "Do you know what she wants?"

"No, but something's happening with the C-level executives. When she called me up, the atmosphere was more tense than usual. She kept me waiting a long time and when she finally brought me in, she was extremely agitated. She never even looked at me, floating between her cell and her computer. She told me to get you on the line and then she immediately took another call."

That didn't sound good.

"Give me one minute before you transfer her."

Caila sat down at the table, opened her laptop, and engaged her camera. A few seconds later, an image of her boss's face flashed on her screen. Caila inhaled sharply and clicked on the green icon.

"Timeline has changed," Kendra said, forego-ing pleasantries, her dark brown eyes intense. "I'm going to need your report by Tuesday."

"Tuesday?" Her stomach roiled. "That's only five days away. Joe isn't due back until a week from tomorrow."

"Then find the information some other way."

"Kendra." Caila kept her expression neutral but clenched her hands in her lap. "We talked about thi—"

"Someone has the ear of Fogarty and Watson," Kendra said, referring to the CFO and the general counsel. "And they've convinced them to move up the meeting on the national rollout to next week."

Fuck!

A few months ago, being responsible for the marketing of the new organic makeup line was all she'd wanted. She still wanted it, but it was harder to blithely dismiss the impending fallout when you constantly saw the faces of the people who'd be affected by your actions.

"*. . . we realized we could save money and provide better, more comprehensive service, if we combined under one umbrella . . .*"

Her conversation with Laura broke free from her subconscious and floated to the fore.

"Do we have to break the contract?"

Kendra sighed and pinched the bridge of her nose.

"No, hear me out," Caila said, hurrying to make her point when it looked as if her boss would dismiss her out of hand. "What if there's a way we can make it work? Where we could make it cost-effective to continue using Chro-Make? I can come up with a plan that would work for all—"

"That's not what the board wants. You've been given an assignment. We need the information to successfully argue that it'll be detrimental for us to stay with Chro-Make. I want that report in my hand so I can highlight how you saved us millions of dollars. It'll be good to have something to point to when I put your name up for consideration."

Have something? What about the ten years of her life that she'd given to the company? When she'd worked eighty-hour workweeks and holidays? Was that not enough?

Caila shoveled a hand through her hair, mussing in a second the sleek strands she'd spent half an hour arranging. "I understand."

"Good." Having delivered her directive, Kendra seemed ready to end the call. "I believe in you and I'm fighting hard for you. But by doing so, I've entwined our fates. Don't make me regret that decision."

Caila received the message loud and clear:

Get it done or else.

CAILA GASPED WHEN the car crested the hill and the palatial estate came into view.

Wyatt's family lived in the house she'd seen during her run!

The Georgian architecture was more impressive up close, with its two-story portico entrance, wide symmetrical structure, and numerous black-shuttered windows. Against the lush pastoral surrounds, including the sculpted shrubbery and running stone fountain in the front yard, the house trumpeted the status of its occupants.

Wyatt came around and opened her door.

She took his outstretched hand. "Why did I agree to this again?"

"Because they're my family and they asked."

"But they didn't ask. I believe the word you used was 'summoned.'"

Wyatt shrugged. "Rather polite for them, actually."

Caila studied him. He always looked great, but

she'd never seen him so polished. He was flawless in a well-fitted black suit and open-collared white shirt. Heat pooled heavy and thick in her belly. The moment she'd seen him walking up the B&B's sidewalk, she'd wanted to drag him to her room, strip him naked, and run her tongue over every inch of his body.

She glanced down at her deep red V-neck sheath dress. It was one of her favorites for business presentations, but for tonight . . . "I should've worn something else."

He moved closer to her and lowered his voice. "You look beautiful. You elevate everything you wear."

That accent. Those eyes. Still as potent as ever.

She took a deep breath. Exhaled. "I don't understand why they need to see me. They know we're not a couple, right?"

"We may not be a couple, but you hold the fate of this town in your lovely hands. I'm only surprised it took this long."

"No pressure or anything," she murmured.

"It'll be fine," he said, bringing their entwined fingers to his lips and brushing several lingering kisses along her knuckles. "Let's go. I'm sure they know we're here."

She expected to go up the brick front steps so she was surprised when he ushered her around the side and led her through a glass-paneled door.

"Is this how you snuck all the girls up to your room?" she whispered.

"Nope, I met them in the pool house." He winked at her. "I hate using the front door. It always feels too formal for entering a home."

He led her down a long hallway with expensive-looking paintings on the wall, and turned into an exquisitely decorated room on the left. A woman with light brown hair and flawless makeup sat in a high-backed chair, holding a glass of amber liquid. She wore a cream sweater, fawn pants, and sensible heels, and her legs were crossed at the ankles.

He went over and kissed her cheek. "Hello, Mother."

"Wyatt." The woman smiled and studied him from head to toe. "You look wonderful. Very dashing."

"And you're beautiful as always," he said.

He turned to the tall, slim, older man who possessed the straightest posture Caila had ever seen.

"Grandfather."

He returned to Caila's side and placed a hand on the small of her back. "I'd like you both to meet Caila Harris. Caila, this is my mother, Renee Bradley, and my grandfather, Asher Bradley."

Asher stood with an arm braced on the fireplace's mantel, his expression holding a hint of disapproval. "So, you're the young woman who's thrown my town into a tizzy."

Caila bristled, but she'd been raised better than to go to someone's home and treat them rudely. "I guess, but that wasn't my intention."

"Intentions are irrelevant," Asher said crisply. "Perception is what counts."

"Grandfather!" Wyatt snapped.

Caila rested a calming hand on Wyatt's arm, but kept her gaze on Asher. She knew men like him, knew that sussing out weakness in a person was akin to breathing.

She arched a brow. "Then yes, I am *that* woman."

"Where are you from, Ms. Harris?" Renee asked, taking a sip of her drink.

"I live in Chicago. And please, call me Caila." Caila envied her the alcohol. She didn't know if she'd make it through the dinner without a drink.

As if sensing her thoughts, Wyatt asked, "Would you like a drink?"

Bless you! She smiled. "I'll take a glass of whatever red wine you have."

He squeezed her hand and strode to a gold ornate bar cart against the wall.

Renee brightened. "I love Chicago. The shopping on Michigan Avenue is amazing."

"Yes, it is."

The smile Renee directed her way was a few degrees warmer. "And your family is there?"

"No, I moved to Chicago after business school."

Renee waited, as if she expected more, but Caila, keeping her expression pleasant, offered nothing. She didn't feel a need to provide more information about her family. They had nothing to do with her reasons for being here.

"Here you are," Wyatt said, handing her a glass of wine.

"Dinner is served," a voice behind Caila said.

She turned to see an older black woman wearing a simple dress and a crisp white apron, holding a silver serving tray in one hand.

Dizziness disoriented her, and Caila clenched her fingers to keep from dropping the crystal glass in her hand. Why was she surprised? She shouldn't be. Renee Bradley wasn't cleaning this big-ass house and she certainly wasn't cooking in the kitchen. Who else would they have hired to be keeping house?

Thankfully, no one appeared to notice her lapse. Asher walked over to Renee and offered her an arm. Renee deposited her empty glass on the tray and they left the room, like some couple in a Jane Austen novel.

Wyatt kissed the maid on the cheek and motioned for Caila to join them.

"Violet, this is Caila Harris."

Violet's eyes shot back and forth between the two of them. She looked as uncomfortable as Caila felt, but she nodded. "Ma'am."

"Violet's worked for my family for years."

Of course she has.

"It's a pleasure to meet you."

Violet's face softened and she took Caila's extended hand. They smiled, both acknowledging the awkwardness of the situation while standing next to the man they both . . . cared for.

Excusing them, Wyatt cupped Caila's elbow and steered her across the hall to the formal dining room. Asher and Renee were already seated at the beautiful dining table, Asher at the head, Renee to his right. Wyatt held out the chair next to his for Caila, then took his own place across from his mother.

"I read the minutes from the last meeting, Wyatt. Good job on keeping things from escalating."

"Thank you, sir," Wyatt said.

Beneath the table, his fingers trailed over the bare skin of her knee, sending sparks up her thigh. She crossed her legs, trapping his hand, and squeezed, sending a silent admonishment.

Stop that!

"That type of leadership will eventually serve you well as governor," Asher said. "Which reminds me—"

Segue, party of one!

"—did you sign the forms required by the Department of Elections?"

Wyatt smoothly slid his hand from between her thighs. "Not yet."

"What are you waiting for? If we don't jump on this opportunity, it'll set our plans back another six years."

"We don't have to discuss this right now. I know what I have to do. You've been lecturing me about my duties and responsibilities since I was a little boy." Wyatt rested his hand on the table.

"If I don't continue to guide you, you'll go off course." Asher's face tightened. "I made that mistake with your father and look how that turned out."

Ouch! Caila widened her eyes at the older man. That was a low blow.

Wyatt's hand tightened into a fist, at odds with the tablecloth, silver, china, and crystal. "I'm not my father."

"Thank God for that."

Damn.

She'd attended her fair share of awkward family dinners, but the coldness and formality of this superseded anything she'd ever been forced to endure.

"This all looks lovely, Mrs. Bradley," she said, trying to change the mood. "The lamb is wonderful."

"Thank you, dear. That's all Violet's work. She's a wonderful cook."

"I'm sure," Caila said, a tickle of disquiet in the back of her throat.

"You work in business," Renee said, appearing to want to do her part to disperse some of the strain between the two men. "That must be fascinating. Where did you go to college?"

"UVA," Caila said, using the abbreviation that everyone in the state would know.

"Ah, the University of Virginia. An excellent school," Asher said. "Wyatt's refusal to attend VMI wouldn't have been so bad if he'd decided on Virginia. But no, he had to go to some school up north."

Wyatt rolled his eyes. "You're right. I threw my life away deciding to attend Princeton."

"It was expensive and it won't help you as much politically as if you'd stayed here and gone to Virginia," his mother said.

"Seriously?" he asked, throwing Caila a conspiratorial can-you-believe-them look.

"Sorry," she said, shrugging her shoulder. "I agree with your family on this one." Her love for her alma mater was strong. After all, it's where the Ladies of Lefevre first met.

"Outnumbered, even when I bring a guest." He laughed.

The tension seemed to ease a little with the exchange, and Caila breathed a silent sigh of relief.

Wyatt pointed to his mother. "It had nothing to do with the cost. You just wanted to keep an eye on me."

"Of course. I know my son."

Silence descended again, but this time it was more relaxed. It wasn't the warmest dinner she'd ever attended, but the food was outstanding, and Wyatt had gone back to making small, delicious circles on her inner thigh.

Caila was trying her best to keep it together. All she wanted to do was jump him. And be with him. And laugh with him. And talk to him.

To tell him that he needs to get you that information now? That you're leaving early? And to speed up the time when he finds out what you've done?

The thought completely stole her remaining appetite.

"The Harvest Ball should be fun this year," Renee said. "The planning committee did a wonderful job. And holding it at the lodge is always a hit. Are you going to attend, Caila?"

Caila glanced at Wyatt before responding. "I don't know, but it seems the entire town is excited about it."

"It's one of the most popular events each—"

"I can't take another moment of this inane conversation," Asher exploded.

"Asher!" Renee said, her eyes going wide.

"No! This has gone on long enough! We're going to sit here and pretend everything is normal? That this isn't the first time Wyatt has brought a woman home to have dinner with us?"

Wait, what?

Caila turned to Wyatt. "I thought you said they invited me."

He was staring at his grandfather. "They did."

"Of course we did. You haven't been seen with the same woman more than twice in public in years. And now the only person you're ever seen with is her."

"Do you not remember why she's here? I'm the mayor, which I *know* you haven't forgotten. It's my job. I'm showing her around town."

Caila flinched. He wasn't saying anything she didn't already know, but hearing the words out loud, after what they'd shared, felt stark and wrong.

Asher narrowed his eyes. "I've hosted important people in this town. I know how it's done. And I don't think I've ever taken any of them on a private hayride at Anderson Farm!"

"Are you spying on me?"

"I don't have to spy on you. This is my town. I've been governing here longer than you've been alive. I have the right to know what's going on in it, especially when it pertains to my family."

Caila was over the drama. She certainly didn't intend to sit quietly and let them talk about her as if she wasn't here and able to speak for herself.

"With all due respect, sir, that may be true for Wyatt, but that doesn't extend to me."

Asher squinted at her. "I beg your pardon?"

"You should," Caila said coldly. "Wyatt may have given you the right to check on him, but I didn't. You have no right to spy on me."

"I do when you're dating my grandson!"

"We are not dating."

"That's enough!" Wyatt slammed his hand down on the table. "Who I choose to be involved with is none of your damn business."

"So you *are* involved with her!" Asher said, pointing a finger in triumph.

"Oh, for Christ's sake," Wyatt said.

"Don't you take the Lord's name in vain at my table," Renee chimed in.

Caila swiveled her head to stare at the other woman in disbelief. *That's* what's stood out to her in this conversation?

"We are a very important family. You can't bring just anyone home," Asher said.

Caila's blood heated. "I'm not 'just anyone.' I'm an independent, successful woman who doesn't require anyone's approval for the things I do or the decisions I make."

She took her napkin off her lap and placed it on the table.

Asher ignored her comment, focusing on Wyatt. "You've been a playboy for years and we've allowed it because we believed once the time came to settle down, you'd understand your responsibility to this family."

"I'm so sorry," Wyatt said to Caila.

"Wyatt, I'm speaking to you!"

"Great job, Grandfather. Way to insult the woman who holds the fate of this town in her hands."

"If Ms. Harris is as successful and professional as she claims, then this family conversation won't factor into her decision-making process."

His smugness was as evident as his perfect posture.

Well played, Mr. Bradley.

Either she held her tongue and allowed him to continue insulting her, or she spoke up, and if she decided to pull the contract, Wyatt would forever wonder if his constituents lost their jobs because of her hurt feelings.

Either way, Asher Bradley got what he wanted.

It would've been a genius move if her mission hadn't already been set before she got here. And if she'd believed in the possibility of a relationship with Wyatt.

In a strange way, this scenario reminded her of her own family. Why were the people who were supposed to love you always trying to change you? Make you into something you're not?

"You seem like a lovely woman, Caila," Renee said. "Truly. This isn't about you. It's about what this family requires. Wyatt is going to be the next governor of Virginia, with possible plans beyond that. You don't seem to be first lady material. That doesn't appear to be where you want to go. You have a career in Chicago. It would never work."

Everything Renee said was true. So why did Caila feel as if her heart were being smashed into a million pieces?

"This conversation is over," Wyatt roared. He threw down his napkin and stood. "You both have gone too far. Let's go."

Caila stared up at him, stunned. She'd never seen him so angry.

She took Wyatt's outstretched hand and followed him out of the room, amid calls from his family to return.

What in the hell had just happened?

He was quiet as they drove through the darkened streets and she was surprised when he pulled up in front of the B&B instead of his house.

"Do you mind? That was fucked up, and"—he sighed—"I need to clear my head."

What was she supposed to say? She did mind, but if she'd just gone through a familial ambush of that magnitude, she'd probably want to be alone, too.

"Sure."

He stared straight ahead, as if in a daze, and when he didn't respond, she got out of the car. She'd taken a few steps when she heard his car door open.

"Caila, wait."

She turned, and he scooped a hand beneath her head and drew her to him for a hot, searing kiss. She clutched him tight, fueled by a desperation she didn't understand.

He pulled away and stared into her eyes. "I'm sorry."

She touched her mouth. "For the kiss?"

"No, for how they treated you. And for not putting a stop to it sooner. I'll call you tomorrow."

WYATT SLOUCHED IN the leather club chair in Dan's study, his coat long discarded, his legs spread out in front of him, a tumbler of scotch dangling from his fingers.

"It was insane. They went from attacking me to attacking her. How dare they say our marriage wouldn't work?"

From the adjacent club chair, Dan frowned. "Wait, who's talking marriage?"

"They were! I thought they'd invited her because of the situation with the factory. But no, it was my family asserting control over my life."

The ice clinked against the glass as he took a drink and let his arm fall back beside the chair.

Dan pointed a finger at him. "If you let that drink fall onto this new area rug, Laura will kill you. And then I'd be required to arrest her, but I won't. We'd have to go on the run together, which would be tough. All of that to say, get a better grip on that glass."

Wyatt's laugh was halfhearted. He knew it was a joke, but he could see the conviction in Dan's eyes.

"You'd do it though, wouldn't you?"

"Let her kill you?" Dan tilted his head as if to ponder it. "Nah, I'd stop her. It's hard to make new best friends at our age."

Wyatt ignored the wisecrack. "You'd give up everything you've worked toward? For her?"

"Without batting a lash." Dan finished his drink and sat it on the side table between them.

"But what about your responsibilities?"

Dan shrugged. "Doesn't matter?"

"How can you say that?"

"Easily. Because it's the truth. I love her."

Dan said it as if the reason was obvious and the only one that mattered. He continued. "Laura left her job to come back here with me. If I had to give up everything for her, I would."

"But what about your mother? I always thought she was the reason you came back?"

"She was. Once she got sick, I wanted to be close to her. But if Laura hadn't been willing to move back to Bradleton, I wouldn't have done it. We would've figured out an alternative. Maybe move Mom to wherever we lived. But Laura being with me was essential. There was nothing without her."

"I wish it were that simple for me. I have generations of Bradleys staring down on me."

The pressure of being in his family and fulfilling the familial legacy was overwhelming.

"I couldn't possibly understand your situation, and it's easy for me to say choose your happiness, but can't you have both?"

Wyatt thought of his family and what they wanted him to do. And then he thought of Caila and what he'd learned about her upbringing and her career. She'd already had to give up so much that was important to her. He couldn't ask her to do it again.

And maybe a part of him was scared that if he did, she wouldn't choose him.

Like his father.

"No."

Dan sighed. "Then you have a decision to make, my friend. And I don't envy you one bit."

Chapter Eighteen

Seven hundred feet. The end of the block and you're done.

Caila shifted into another gear and pushed herself until she'd reached the fire hydrant she'd set as her goalpost. Slowing to a stop, she jammed her hands on her hips and attempted to haul in as much fresh air as possible to relieve her burning lungs.

It hadn't been a question of *if* she'd run this morning. More like how many miles she'd go.

Between the call from Kendra, dinner with Wyatt's family, and his dropping her off afterward, she'd been left feeling unsettled and full of uncertainty. Something she didn't like.

Kendra apparently wanted her to devise a report out of thin air. Not that creating it would be difficult; she'd done so many starting out, she could write them in her sleep. But they tended to be more effective when she had access to the proper information.

Add to that the ever-growing, inconvenient thought that she might be able to salvage the situation for Endurance without recommending the closure of Chro-Make, and the possibility of losing her job should be causing her to hyperventilate more than this run. And yet the problem currently tasking the majority of her mental energy was Wyatt . . .

They'd spent every night since the color run together, though she always made sure to get back to the B&B before morning. Last night, not seeing him or speaking to him after the confrontation with his family . . .

It hadn't felt right.

Better get used to it.

Getting used to it wasn't the issue. Whether she *wanted* to get used to it, that was the question.

When she was able to breathe without wincing, she continued walking another block, before turning the corner and quickly covering the distance to the B&B. She hustled up the steps, pausing when she saw the person waiting on the porch.

"Hey, Jada. How are you?"

Jada rose from the porch swing. "Hi, Caila. I'm good. Did you enjoy your run?"

Caila laughed. "The first mile? No. Thankfully, it got better after that. What's up? Did you stop by to talk?"

"No." Jada blushed. "I'm waiting for Kevin."

"Oh." Caila hadn't been expecting that.

"We're going over to the park to hang out."

"Sounds like fun."

"Uh-huh." Jada shoved her hands in the back pockets of her jeans. "I sent an email to your friend Judge Taylor, asking her about being a lawyer."

"Oh, good. Did she respond?"

"She did! She's sending me some information to read and a list of documentaries to check out."

Caila's heart warmed at the time and effort Ava had made for the teen. She really did have extraordinary friends.

"That's wonderful. I hope it helps."

The screen door flew open and Kevin emerged, a backpack slung over his shoulder.

"Oh, hey, Caila. I just left you a note. My mom had to run out, but she wanted me to tell you she left you something delicious on the counter."

Gone was the awkward, flushed-face boy who usually interacted with her.

"Thanks, Kevin," she said. "You two have fun."

Kevin gave Caila a friendly smile, but his eyes brightened when they landed on Jada.

"No problem," Kevin tossed over his shoulder as they trotted down the steps.

"We will!" Jada waved, and the two headed in the direction of downtown.

She was going to miss them, especially Jada. The teen had impressed her; she was smart, focused, and driven. Caila was going to make sure they stayed in touch. Smiling, she pulled out her phone and sent a quick text to Ava, thanking her for responding to Jada, as she went into the house. She grabbed a bottle of water from the fridge and snatched a slice of warm chocolate chip pumpkin bread from the plate Gwen had left on the counter. She was heading to her room to stretch and cool down before her shower when the doorbell rang.

Answering it, she found Wyatt standing there, backlit by the mid-morning sun. He wore jeans, a white T-shirt, and a blue V-neck sweater that made his hazel eyes pop.

Would there ever be a time that the sight of him wouldn't birth a corresponding ache for him?

"Hey," she said softly.

"May I come in?"

She held open the door. He entered the house, and she closed the door behind him.

"I saw Kevin heading downtown. Is Gwen here?"

"No. She was gone when I got back."

The words were barely out of her mouth before he was pulling her close.

She tried to hold him off. "I just came from a run. I'm all sweaty."

"I've kissed every inch of your body. I think I can handle a little sweat."

Well, when he put it that way . . .

She relented and relaxed into his embrace, sighing when he wrapped his arms around her. She loved his hugs. They made her feel cherished, protected, cared for.

Like she could take on the world by herself but she didn't have to.

She led him into the kitchen and he stood, leaning his hip against the counter.

"You hungry? Gwen's been baking again. I was just getting ready to have some when you arrived."

He waved off her offer of food. "I wanted to apologize again for my family. That dinner was . . . fucking nuts."

"You weren't kidding when you said your family takes the legacy stuff seriously."

"I wish I was." He sighed and crossed his arms over his chest.

She didn't want to discuss his family or the implications of their assumptions that led to the assault.

"Where'd you go last night?" she asked, taking a drink of water.

"I went over to Dan's. I needed to think. To talk some things through."

With him. Not with her.

What do you expect? Dan's his best friend and you're leaving on Monday.

She covered up her irrational hurt. "Did it help?"

"It did. And I have some news I think you'll like."

"Really? Will Dan stop glaring at me when we cross paths?"

He stiffened and leaned forward. "Has he said something to you?"

"Settle down, Edward Cullen. Don't go into protector mode. I was making a joke." A bad one, apparently. "What news?"

"Joe Keslar will be back on Sunday."

She gasped and her hand flew to her mouth. "Are you serious?"

"Yes. And he's prepared to be available to you at Chro-Make all day, if necessary."

Euphoria bubbled within her. "How? Why?"

"Let's just say I wanted to be the third man you could count on."

Tenderness overwhelmed her at the realization that he'd remembered what she'd said about Daddy and Pop-Pop. Her heart raced into overdrive. "If I wasn't so sweaty, I'd jump you right now."

One corner of his mouth lifted in a wicked grin. "I thought we'd already dealt with the sweat issue."

"You're right." She cupped his cheeks and laid a big openmouthed kiss on him, darting her tongue inside to briefly duel with his, before retreating. "Thank you."

His lids dropped low and a flush stained his cheeks. "If I have more good news, can I get another one of those?"

What else could he tell her that would be better than his news about Joe Keslar? "Maybe."

He snagged a tendril of her hair and twirled it around his index finger. "I also made a few phone calls, and if you're free right now, there are several people waiting to talk to you over at the plant."

Her eyes widened. Talking to some of the workers would be extremely helpful. Especially for some of the options she'd been working through. She knew what Endurance wanted her report to contain, but if she could provide viable alternatives to the board, maybe she could get her promotion and save Chro-Make and Bradleton. "Of course I'm free. I just need to grab a shower."

She hurried out of the kitchen.

He followed her. "Aren't you forgetting something?"

Stopping with her hand on the doorknob, she turned, tilted her head, and eyed him skeptically. "I thought I needed to hurry."

"There's always time for a kiss."

Sandwiched between the door at her back and his warm, hard body at her front, she surrendered to the deep, wet, slow exploration of his tongue. Her belly dipped and twisted in a viable approximation of an amusement park ride, and she clutched his broad shoulders in an attempt at equilibrium.

It wasn't to be. He slid his hard, jean-clad thigh between her legs, pressing upward until she was practically riding him, the friction against her clit creating a seductive lethargy that enveloped her limbs. He was easily the best kisser she'd ever known. Hell, he was the best lover she'd ever had. And if she didn't do something, Gwen would find them fucking on her hallway floor.

She pushed against his chest, and when they broke apart, they were both glassy-eyed and breathing heavily. He straightened his leg and she shivered at the withdrawal.

"Damn, Caila." His voice was low, his accent pronounced in that luscious way she liked. He leaned his forehead against hers. "Will you be my date to the Harvest Ball?"

She gazed into his eyes. "That's supposed to be a big night for your family."

"I know. And I want you there."

She shouldn't. She would meet with workers today and Joe on Sunday; there was no professional benefit to attending the ball. But her time with Wyatt was drawing to a close and selfishly, she wasn't ready to let go. Her answering smile contained a touch of sadness. "Okay. It'll be a nice bookend to my time here."

Furrows materialized on his forehead. "What?"

"My boss called. I have to be back in Chicago on Tuesday."

"That's four days from now!"

She lowered her lashes. "I know."

"Fuck!" He shoved away from the door and raked a hand through his hair. "When were you going to tell me?"

"I found out before dinner with your family. I would've told you last night, but . . ." She shrugged.

A muscle ticked in his jaw. "What's the hurry? Why can't they wait a few more days?"

She sympathized with his anger, and maybe her own, mixed with an underlying guilt, was why she confided further in him. "Remember when I told you I let Pop-Pop's passing affect my performance at work?"

His expression softened and he nodded.

"I'm not responsible for evaluations anymore, but Endurance sent me here to do this one as a last-ditch effort not only to prove that I should keep my job, but to show I'm worthy of an upcoming promotion. The board moved their meeting up to next week and my boss wants the report before then." She grasped his hand between hers, willing him to understand, hoping he'd recall this moment when he found out what she'd done. "My job is all I have left. I've poured my heart and soul into that company for ten years and I'm so close to fulfilling the dreams my dad and I had talked about all those years ago."

"What would you have done if I hadn't given you the news?"

"I'd planned to tell you that we'd have to revisit the issue of calling Joe and interrupting his vacation."

"Well, you don't have to worry about that now. I took care of it."

Is that what he thought? That he was saving her?

Her smile slid from her face and she dropped his hand. "I don't need you to take care of anything. You're just getting me the information I should've already had."

"That's not what I—" He squeezed his eyes shut and pinched the bridge of his nose. "You're right. I'm sorry."

"No, no, *I'm* sorry." She rested her forehead on his shoulder. "I didn't mean to snap at you. It's just . . . I haven't had the best track record depending on men to help me. But I am grateful for this."

His arms came around her. "Like you said, you should've already had this information."

The mood had changed so often in the past few minutes it had given her emotional whiplash. She remained in his embrace for a few moments longer, before moving away and scrubbing her hands on the sides of her thighs. "I'm going to shower and change. I don't want to keep the people waiting any longer than necessary."

"Do you need any help scrubbing your back?"

She laughed, appreciating his attempt to lighten the tension between them. "Gwen could be back at any minute. Just because I'm her only guest doesn't mean we should act like this is my house. Why don't you wait in the parlor? I'll be quick."

When she closed the door on his overly dramatic, disappointed expression, her excitement at this new development quickly morphed into anguish.

His plan had involved showing her all that Bradleton had to offer, in the hopes that it would filter into her recommendation. And yet, because of her own issues, he'd put that aside and was doing everything he could to help her.

He'd actually come through for her.

And if it doesn't work out, he's going to hate your fucking guts.

THE HARVEST BALL was held in a beautiful lodge at the edge of town. String lights hung from every available fixture, imbuing the ballroom with a warm intimate glow. Strands of gold, orange, and maroon leaves wound around wooden columns and beams, emphasizing the autumn theme. At one end of the large space, a band was set up on a stage, playing an assortment of music that kept the dance floor packed.

"Pretty nice, huh?" Laura asked, taking a sip of her pomegranate rum punch.

Caila grinned sheepishly. "It is."

She and Laura stood near the bar, on the side of the room where the tables and chairs had been arranged. Fall-themed tablecloths added variety and color, as did the centerpieces, comprised of pumpkin vases filled with sunflowers, orange roses, autumn mums, and apples.

"Let me guess, you thought there'd be bales of hay, scarecrows, and barrels stocked with apples?"

"Something like that. But if you share that with anyone, Laura Yates, I will vehemently deny it!"

Laura laughed and squeezed her arm. "Your secret is safe with me."

Caila had enjoyed her brief conversations with the other woman. In a different situation, she would've enjoyed continuing their acquaintance to see if it could develop into a friendship. In this instance, she didn't see that happening, and it saddened her more than she'd expected.

She felt that way about many of the people she'd met during her time in Bradleton. Gwen, Jada, Kevin, Laura, Shirley at Turk's; she was going to miss them all. And her stomach churned at the thought of them hating her once the news of Endurance withdrawing their contract broke.

"I've been meaning to tell you, I love your dress." Laura flicked the flared skirt of Caila's golden yellow dress, with its fitted floral embroidered bodice and long sheer sleeves. "And that color looks gorgeous against your skin. I know you didn't buy that here."

"Thank you. It's something I started doing years ago. I always pack one cocktail dress when I travel."

Laura's brows furrowed. "Everywhere?"

"Everywhere. It's habit now. When I first started traveling for work, I'd only pack work clothes. Inevitably, I'd get invited to a function that required something nicer than business suits. I'd go shopping, buy a dress, and take it home. A couple of trips later, it would happen again and the cycle would repeat. It took four years and a closet full of cocktail and formal dresses for me to just start packing one each time I traveled, whether I knew I'd need it or not."

"I don't miss much about working in politics, or my life back in D.C., but I do miss the galas and dressing up," Laura said, her tone wistful. "Not much cause for that here, so when I do get the chance to dress up, I go all out."

Laura twirled, showing off the short, multicolored sequined dress with kimono sleeves that looked fabulous with her blond hair.

"And it was worth it," Caila told her. "That dress is fierce and you look amazing in it."

"Thanks. You know who else thinks you look beautiful tonight?"

"Who?"

"Wyatt." Laura inclined her head over to where Wyatt stood with a group of other men, including Dan and the drunk bro-dude from the diner. "What are the two of you going to do?"

"About what?"

Laura pursed her lips. "Are you going to continue seeing each other after you leave?"

Caila's pulse jump-started but she forced herself to remain calm.

"I have no idea what you're talking about," she said, carefully.

"Really? You do recall I was there for the hayride and the private bonfire, right?"

Where they'd been completely circumspect, just a host showing a guest around the town.

"And that I'm married to his best friend?"

Caila dropped her head and chuckled softly.

Busted!

"I've watched him watch you tonight, and he doesn't look at you like a man getting ready to say good-bye in two days."

Caila's heart twisted. She wasn't prepared to say good-bye to him, either. "It's complicated."

"If I were you, I'd brace myself. It can get uncomplicated pretty damn quick when a man goes after what he wants." She took a sip of her drink and promptly started coughing.

"Are you okay?" Caila asked, looking around and grabbing a napkin from the closest table.

"No!" Laura took the napkin and handed Caila her drink. "There's Charlotte Edgerton. She's been trying to talk me into adding a Himalayan salt grotto to the yoga studio. I need to disappear for a second. I'll be back."

Laura hurried away and Caila laughed, totally convinced that was something Lacey would do. She took Laura's abandoned drink over to the bar and placed it on the tray with the other empty, discarded glasses. She was wiping her fingers on a napkin when she felt a tap on her shoulder. She turned to see the redhead from the bake sale.

Caila searched her memory. "Blair, right?"

"Hi. I just wanted to come over and apologize for what happened at the bake sale. I felt so bad after you left."

"Thanks." Caila shook her head slightly. "But you didn't do anything."

Blair's chin trembled and her fair skin burned. "I know. And that's the problem. I should've spoken up. Holly's been bad-talking you because the mayor has been spending time with you. I tried to tell her it's his job, but she wouldn't listen."

Holly might've been hostile, but the woman wasn't stupid.

Caila placed a hand on the other woman's arm. "I appreciate you coming over to say hello. Your apology wasn't necessary."

Blair's relief was evident in her smile. "Enjoy your evening." She walked away, then turned back and clasped her hands in front of her chest. "I hope you don't mind me saying this, but don't let Holly, or any other bad seeds, cloud your opinion of Bradleton. It's a great town. My husband and I are among those who didn't grow up here. We moved to town about ten years ago and we love it. People care about each other here. They work hard, and there's a sense of community that's truly wonderful. I hope you take that into consideration."

She waved and headed off to join a group of people seated at a table.

Caila stared after her, dazed. When she'd first come to Bradleton, she hadn't been excited about her assignment or what it would require her to do, but she'd planned to do it in her typical efficient and exemplary manner. It was the only way she'd keep her job and get the promotion she deserved.

But now, looking around her and seeing all of the people here, knowing they'd all be affected by what she'd been asked to do . . .

The enormity of that burden weighed heavily on her shoulders.

"The band finally took a break," Wyatt said, sidling up behind her, his voice low in her ear. "If they played one more song, I don't think I'd be able to refuse Mrs. Martinez. She may be in her seventies, but she's grabby."

She inhaled his clean male scent. Her lashes fluttered and her mouth watered. He smelled divine.

"Do you think they take requests? How about Beyoncé? Drake?"

He laughed as he came around to face her. His hazel eyes warmed as they scanned her from the top of her updo to the tips of her Manolo Blahniks.

"You're the most beautiful woman in this room."

Pleasure at his words darted through her.

"I have to keep up with you," she said.

He would've fit in at any Hollywood event in his navy slim-cut suit, white shirt, and brown belt and shoes. He was undeniably gorgeous. Did the man ever look bad? Was it even possible?

"You've never had an issue keeping up with me," he said, his accent sexy and pronounced. "I want to lift that pretty skirt up to your waist, unzip my pants, and slide my cock into your wet pussy."

Said pussy quivered, and that familiar thick, liquid heat pooled between her thighs. Her lids lowered. "That wouldn't go over too well."

She knew they were already garnering quite a bit of attention. Some people pretended to be involved in their own conversations, while others stared outright. She'd convinced him it would be better if they arrived separately and she'd done her best to keep her distance. He hadn't made it easy, always appearing just within her periphery.

"That's okay. I'll just think about it until I can do it later." He moved closer to her, and she felt his hand brush hers where it hung at her side. His pinkie clasped hers. "I can't believe you're leaving in two days."

"I know. It's going to be hard to say good-bye."

Wanting to hold her hand, knowing that they couldn't be seen doing it? Wyatt Bradley wasn't just a woodworker, he was a demolition expert, too. Because he was single-handedly wrecking the walls she'd built around her heart.

"I was thinking: Do we have to?"

Her mouth fell open. "What do you mean?"

"I certainly didn't expect this when you first arrived, but I don't want to say good-bye to you."

Could he see the sudden spike in her pulse? "I live in Chicago. You live here. You're going to be governor of Virginia. This can't work."

"We don't know if we never try," he said, his tone urgent, his gaze determined. "You make me feel things I've never felt before. Ever. But it's not just about how I feel. Do you want to walk away from me?"

Every fiber of her being rejected that notion in one unanimous urge to heave.

She shuddered. "No, but—"

"Wyatt, hi." Holly Martin joined them, stunning in a tight black dress that showed off her figure and made her blond ringlets pop.

"Holly," Wyatt said through clenched teeth, his irritation at the interruption clear.

Holly was either blind to all social cues save those she wanted to see, or she was incapable of deviating from a mission once set.

She wrapped her claws around Wyatt's elbow. "When the band comes back, would you like to dance?"

Wyatt's eyes narrowed. "Actually, you can—"

Caila interrupted him. "I'm really thirsty. Can you get me something to drink?"

He glanced at her, his brow furrowed, his aggression immediately melting. "Now?"

"Yes, I'm quite parched." She smacked her tongue against the roof of her mouth to emphasize her point. "I'll take a cup of their hot spiced wine."

Arching a brow, he left to fulfill her request.

Holly curled her bright red lip. "If you think I'm going away, think again."

Caila frowned at her. "What are you doing?"

"You may have Wyatt fooled, but I know—"

"Hol-ly," she said, drawing out the syllables in her name, "what are you doing?"

Holly's head snapped back, and she closed her mouth.

"Wyatt couldn't have made it any clearer that he isn't interested in you."

"We went out—"

"When you first moved to town. I know. I also know that after that date, he never asked you out again."

"Did he tell you that?" She sneered.

"No, you did. You said so at the football game."

Holly's face bloomed with color.

"And in the ten days that I've been here, he's either been with me or Dan, or at work. Not with you."

"You're leaving soon."

"True. And he's a free agent," Caila said, though the words nearly caught in her throat. "He can date whomever he pleases."

"Then I'll have my chance."

Sympathy for Holly overrode any prior feelings of dislike. "But do you want it? You're chasing after a man who isn't interested in you. Even if I'm not here, that won't change. Don't you feel like you deserve better?"

Holly's jaw tightened, but Caila didn't know if it was in response to Caila's words or some truths sinking in.

"It's none of my business—well, it is right now because I'm trying to enjoy this event and you are interrupting us—but it seems to me you need to work some of this out. You should find someone who wants to be with you. Someone you don't have to chase, but who'll always be next to you."

Caila firmed her lips and left before Holly could respond, running into Wyatt, who held her drink. He looked beyond her, then back to her.

"Is everything okay?"

She nodded. "It's fine."

"You know I'm not interested in her, right?"

"I know that and you know that, but maybe now *Holly* will accept it." The music started and Caila smiled. "Would you dance with me?"

He put the glass of spiced wine on a nearby table. "I guess you weren't that thirsty."

"More like hungry," she said, taking his hand and leading him onto the floor.

He pulled her into his arms, but they kept distance between them, though his hand was hot on the small of her back.

He stared deep into her eyes. "I want to finish our conversation."

She knew what he wanted. She wanted it, too. But there was no way it could happen, not with this lie about Endurance and the contract between them.

Tell him the truth.

She started.

"Are you okay?" Wyatt asked.

Was that even a possibility? She'd told him about her upbringing. About how important her job was to her. If she explained about Kendra and the assignment, would he understand? Could he find a way to forgive her?

"Caila? What are you thinking?"

Her heart hammered so hard she couldn't catch her breath. Had it been only ten days since they'd met? How had he become indispensable to her in such a short amount of time? He was the first thing she thought of in the morning and the last thing at night. Seeing him always made her feel better, and she loved being with him. So much so that the thought of walking away from him felt like losing a limb.

He'd become a part of her.

And he was going to hate her.

Oh God. Oh God. Oh God.

She closed her eyes and squeezed his hand before she stopped dancing. "I have to tell you something."

"What?"

Nausea hovered in the back of her throat. She pulled her hand from his and wiped it on her skirt. She bit her lip and let her gaze flit over the room.

Shit, she should've pulled him to the side. Or waited to talk to him when they were alone.

"Caila, you're scaring me." He cupped her shoulder. "What's going on?"

Fuck! Just say it. Right now, before she lost her nerve. She could do it. She had to. He'd gone out of his way to get her the information she'd need for the report. The report that might cripple his town's economy. Even if he never forgave her, he needed to know what was going to happen. So he could find a way to prepare.

She clung to his forearm, wanting to strengthen their connection as much as possible. "Wyatt, I wasn't honest—"

"Well, isn't this cozy."

A booming voice startled her and sent her heart hurtling into the depths of her stomach.

Caila glanced away from Wyatt and into the face of Gerald fucking Thorpe, the other regional manager in the running for the promotion at Endurance.

Chapter Nineteen

Caila stared at the other man, his mere presence anachronistic in this setting.

"Gerald? What the hell are you doing here?"

"Clearly not having as much fun as you are," Gerald said, his smile tinged with nastiness. He looked at Wyatt. "And you are?"

Her stomach roiled but she made the introductions. "Gerald Thorpe, this is Wyatt Bradley, mayor of Bradleton."

Gerald chortled, his face flushed. "Mayor? Well, it appears I underestimated how far you were willing to go for that promotion, Caila."

Bastard.

Wyatt took a menacing step forward.

"Don't do it, Wyatt. Ignore him," she said, grabbing his arm. She tugged on the band of steel until she gained his attention. "Can you give us a second, please?"

"Who is this clown?" Wyatt asked, the muscle in his jaw ticking like a time bomb.

Nausea threatened and she fought to keep the panic at bay. "He's from Endurance. Someone I work with. I just need to talk to him. I'll be back."

Wyatt nodded, but his expression showcased his reluctance to let her walk away.

Caila took a deep breath, then turned and gestured for Gerald to follow her. She located a small alcove away from the ballroom.

"How did you find me?"

"Easy. I went to the place you were staying and the boy told me you and most of the town would be at this event," he said, glancing around with a sneer on his lips.

"What do you want?"

"Are you serious? You've been leading Kendra on for a week. The other executives got tired of her excuses and they sent me to fix the situation."

"You son of a bitch! You're the one who got the board to move up the date of the vote!"

Gerald's smile was too wide, too bright, and way too self-congratulatory. "It didn't take much to convince them that you being here longer than a few days was a waste of money."

"I talked to Kendra and she knows what's going on. I just found out the key person I've been waiting for will be here tomorrow."

"You *are* losing it." Gerald shook his head. "I never thought I'd see the day when the great Caila Harris would be played."

Gerald was extremely annoying and a black belt brown-noser, but he was good at his job and he wasn't prone to flights of fancy. He knew *something*.

Her chest tightened. "What are you talking about?"

"I can't wait to tell all of the executives, but especially Kendra. She's been singing your praises for years now. Acts like you practically walk on water."

Caila's hands curled into fists at her sides. "Fucking spit it out, Gerald!"

"The guy you've been waiting for?"

"Joe Keslar. Like I said, he's been away on vacation in Wisconsin. But he'll be back tomorrow and I'm meeting with him then."

Gerald shook his head. "He's here."

"Okay. Then he just got back."

"No, I mean he's here in Virginia. At a campground with his family several hours away."

She frowned. "What is he doing there?"

"That's where his family vacations. Every year."

But Wyatt said . . . "You're making no sense."

"I'm the first bit of sense you've had since you got to this town. It wasn't hard to track the guy down. It was all part of their plan. He was supposed to get back the weekend after you got here, but the mayor paid him off to stay away."

A buzzing saturated her ears. She stumbled backward and held up her hands, palms out. "No."

"Yes. You came here looking for information to shut them down and the entire time, your mayor had his own plan. He was keeping the one person you needed away. Like I said, I never thought I'd see the day when you got played."

His eyes flicked over her shoulder before settling back on her. He laughed. "You can kiss that promotion good-bye. How are the executives supposed to trust you with the national rollout of a product?"

Gerald couldn't have been happier if he'd also been granted the privilege of firing her.

It all flooded back to her. The plant being in turnaround. No one available to talk to her. Wyatt taking her to events and showing her around town. Random people telling her how essential the plant was to Bradleton. Joe's sudden willingness to end his vacation and come back.

Gerald was telling the truth.

Motherfucker!

How much of the truth, she didn't know. But the important part about Wyatt keeping her here unnecessarily to benefit his own plan, she believed wholeheartedly.

Caila's body wanted to cave in on itself in despair. She'd trusted him, depended on him to help her, and he'd destroyed her chance for her promotion, and probably cost her job. She'd told him: That job was the most important thing in the world to her.

It took every ounce of willpower she possessed, but she pulled it all back from the void. She held it together. She wouldn't let any of them defeat her or make her look like a fool. There was a lot she needed to do, but first, she had to call Kendra and immediately do damage control.

Gerald shoved his hands in his pants pocket and rolled up on the balls of his feet. "For years, you've walked around like—"

"Gerald, if you say one more fucking word to me, I'm going to bury my stiletto heel in someplace fleshy on your body."

Anger burning through her insides, she turned and bumped into Wyatt.

"Caila—"

"No." She pointed at him. "Not now. Not after what you did. I've got to call my boss and try to make her understand—"

She brushed past him, but he stopped her with a firm grip on her arm.

His face was carved from a slab of granite. "You came here to shut us down."

"You knew that."

"I thought you came here to evaluate the factory. According to your coworker, you came here with a hidden agenda."

Was he seriously going to stand there and lecture her about having a "hidden agenda"?

She jerked her arm from his grasp. "Let's talk about ulterior motives. You lied to me. Joe Keslar would've been here a week ago! You paid him to stay away."

"It's a good thing I did!" Wyatt raised his voice, his anger appearing to match hers. "You were never going to give us a fair shake, were you? The evaluation was already done. You just needed evidence to back up your conclusion!"

Her pulse raced, there was a pounding in her ears, and her muscles tensed with a continuous source of anger.

The veins in his neck twitched, his legs were planted wide, and his eyes were the coldest she'd ever seen them.

"You can't do this, Caila! You've spent ten days getting to know these people. If you close this factory, you're going to put them out of work. You'll decimate this town."

"You! You! You! *I'm* not doing it. The company is. I'm just doing my job. The numbers don't lie. The factory is losing money and Endurance doesn't want to take that on. They're not closing the factory. They've decided not to renew their co-packing contract. Chro-Make can stay in business."

"Except they'd lose the only client they have."

"That isn't my fault!"

"When Flair's profits continued to decline, they cut their orders. Nate couldn't fire people, especially when they weren't at fault. We're like a family and that's what you do. You take care of family."

"You've been throwing that word around ever since I got here. *Family* can also be an albatross around your neck, pulling you down. Keeping you from reaching your full potential."

Wyatt jammed a hand on his hip and shoved fingers through his hair. "I know you're dealing with grief and issues with your family. I guess I hoped you'd put that behind you and do what was right for the town."

She winced. He'd brought up what she'd shared with him and used it against her. "So lose my job and everything I've worked for to save a bunch of people I barely know?"

"Yes! It's the right thing to do!"

"Is it the right thing to hide behind the idea of family rather than be who you are? You're so concerned about the truth, why don't you tell your family how you really feel? Be honest with the people in this town. Your *family*." She wrinkled her nose. "You talk a good game about duty and responsibility, but that's not why you do it. You do it because you're afraid if you tell them what you really want, they won't accept you. That doesn't make you better than me. It just makes you a coward."

The words hung there between them.

"I find it interesting that's what you think of me," he said, quietly. "You're the one who's so busy living in the past you're afraid to step forward. It's not family that's holding you back. It's you. And some idealized version of childhood dreams that's hindered you from letting go and moving on."

Oh, she could let go and move on. Watch her.

She firmed her trembling lower lip. "Then I guess we're both too cowardly to be together?"

The muscle ticked in his cheek. "I guess so."

"STOP IT! YOU can't goad me into doing what you want me to do. I'll go when I'm good and ready," Caila said.

Her running shoes just sat there, condemning her in silence.

She dropped back onto her sofa. She needed to do something.

Go for a run.

Go to the grocery store.

Shower.

It'd been a week since she'd returned home from Bradleton. A week since her heart-crushing encounter with Wyatt. On Monday, she was expected at Endurance to learn the fate of her future at the company. Kendra had been too busy to take her calls and Diane had told her the executives didn't want her in the office. Some were even advocating for her dismissal.

Not willing to give up without a fight, she'd followed through on the idea that had been coming to her over the past couple of weeks and she'd drafted a report on how Endurance might benefit from honoring Flair's contract with Chro-Make. It wasn't the report the board wanted, but the more she considered it, the more she was convinced it was the strategy her company needed. After two days of almost nonstop drafting, she'd sent it to Kendra and an hour later, her boss had called to inform her that she'd received the report.

"It's brilliant. You might just manage to pull your ass back from the brink. Sit tight while I figure out the best way to spin this and contain the situation as best I can."

That had been four days ago.

She was so fucked! And the knowledge that she was on the verge of losing everything she'd worked for had dragged her into a depression.

That's all it was. Work. It couldn't be because she missed him.

Wyatt.

Dammit! She threw the pillow she was holding across the room and watched it bounce against her bookshelf before falling to the floor.

He'd lied to her. He'd betrayed her. But her heart didn't care. She still cried herself to sleep each night, missing his arms around her.

The sound of the buzzer pulled her from the dismal quicksand of her thoughts. She wished she could ignore it and stay wallowed in her melancholy, but she'd run out of food this morning, and since she wasn't inclined to go to the grocery store, she'd ordered takeout from the restaurant down the street.

Food. She'd get up for food.

Pushing herself off the couch, she trudged over to the intercom unit by the front door and pressed the button.

"Ms. Harris, you have a visitor."

She frowned. That's not how they usually announced her takeout.

"Is it my Chinese food?"

A pause. "No. It's a woman. She said, quote, She's no five-foot-four white stripper, but she hopes she'll do, end quote."

The tears were rolling down Caila's face before she pressed the button to respond. "Send her up."

A few minutes later she opened the door to find Ava standing there, a suitcase by her side, a paper bag in her hand. "Lunch is served."

But at Caila's distress, Ava's smile vanished. She hurried in, dropped the food on the counter, and pulled her into a hug.

Caila clung to her friend, having cried more in the past two weeks than she had in the past two decades.

"It's okay. Go on and let it out. I've got you," Ava said, holding her and murmuring the words over and over in a soothing voice.

When her howls subsided to whimpers, Caila drew in a deep, shuddering breath. "I'm sorry."

"Don't be." Ava looked around for tissues and handed one to Caila. "Clearly you needed it."

Caila sniffed and blew her nose. "What are you doing here?"

"How could I not come?" Ava asked. "When we talked after you got back from Bradleton, you sounded terrible. I would've come sooner but I had a one-day trial turn into three days. I got here as soon as I could. Go sit down and I'll fix you a plate."

There was no use arguing and she didn't want to. Caila sank down on her sofa and pulled her feet beneath her.

Ava knew her way around a kitchen and it wasn't long before she'd gotten out plates, silverware, and cloth napkins that hadn't been used since Ava's last visit.

"What happened?" Ava asked, dishing out the food.

"It was a disaster. I took my eyes off my goal and everything went to shit."

"I find that hard to believe. You're the most focused person I know. Wine?"

Caila nodded her assent then responded, "I usually am. You know how important it was that I do a great job on that project. But from the moment I met Wyatt everything went downhill."

Ava brought their food and drinks into the living room and sat down next to Caila. "That's an interesting way to describe it. When we texted, you didn't talk like things were bad. You sounded . . . happy."

She had been. But had it been worth it?

"It cost me everything. I've worked hard to get where I am. How can it all be over?"

"Caila, before you went to Bradleton, you worked fifteen-hour days. You didn't date and you didn't have a life outside of Endurance. On our vacation you worked the entire time. We were worried about you."

"You don't understand."

"Don't tell me I don't understand. I've known you almost half your life. You've been striving toward some invisible goal from the moment I met you."

Caila set her plate on the coffee table, her appetite gone. "I know what I want. It isn't invisible to me."

Ava sighed and put her fork down. "Invisible isn't the right word. Unattainable, maybe? All I mean is that it'll never be enough. I don't think you have any idea of the level you'd need to reach to make you secure."

"So now you're trying to Oprah me?"

Ava rolled her eyes. "It's not hard. I think it's always simplistic to blame stuff on your childhood, but in this instance . . ."

"I had a life in Baltimore. I had plans and goals that were more than getting married and having babies. And they took it all away from me!"

"Girl, get over it!" Ava jostled her plate and some food fell on the floor. "Your selfishness was understandable when you were fourteen. But you're over thirty."

"There's a time limit on my pain?"

"Feeling it, no. But using it to blame people for the understandable choices they made in the past? Yeah, there is. Your mother didn't make those decisions to hurt you. Have you ever put yourself in her shoes? Imagined what it was like for her?"

Caila opened her mouth to respond, then closed it. Shame spiraled through her. She'd never thought about her mother in that situation. Only herself. But Mona Harris had been a housewife and a wonderful one at that. Caila had never understood her mother, probably because she was more like her father, but she couldn't deny that she'd been cared for and had everything she'd needed.

And her father had loved her mother very much.

"Her husband died, and this woman, who hadn't worked outside the home in over a decade, was suddenly responsible for three girls. She was probably upset, overwhelmed, and frightened about her future." Ava looked her up and down. "Sound familiar?"

It did. It was how Caila was feeling right now.

"Someone she loved reached out to her and offered to help."

And Caila had judged her mother for accepting that help ever since. She hadn't thanked her mother for keeping their family together, or for giving Caila a stable home and a strong male role model. She'd been angry she'd had to leave her charter school, her scholarship, and all of her own activities.

She sighed, what little food she'd eaten now sitting like a load of bricks in her stomach. "I was such a bitch."

She'd been working to get to this place where she'd be able to make her own decisions. Where she'd depend on no one but herself. But Ava was right.

When would it be enough?

"For almost ten years you've devoted yourself to Endurance. And now, yeah, you might lose it. But you're not losing everything. You still have your family. You still have us, your girls. You have the foundation your father gave you. You have the lessons Pop-Pop taught you." Ava put her plate down and took Caila's hand. "You've been searching for security, but, sweetie, you've had it all along."

Caila waited for the familiar agony to engulf her at the mention of her grandfather. For the first time in months, it didn't come. Oh, there was sadness; a tightness in her chest at the thought that she'd never see or talk to him again. But it would ease in time and she'd be okay. In fact, she'd be better than okay. She could finally accept what Wyatt had been trying to tell her. Pop-Pop had already forgiven her. She just needed to forgive herself.

But Ava, Mother Nurturer, wasn't done.

"Now can you see that what you were doing for yourself, Wyatt was doing for his town? Thousands of people were going to lose their jobs. What kind of man would he be if he sat around and let that happen?"

Not one she would've come to love.

"I'm not saying that what he did was right, or that it didn't have an effect on you, but he had the best of intentions. And along the way, you fell in love with him."

She did. It had been fast, but that didn't make it any less real.

She loved Wyatt.

But how did he feel about her?

He'd been interested in pursuing something more with her, but that had been before he'd learned that she'd lied about her reason for being in Bradleton.

"What if he doesn't feel the same way?"

"The man who was willing to risk all of those jobs so that you could get what you wanted?" Ava smirked.

"But we had an awful argument."

Just like with Pop-Pop. She couldn't let that stand.

"Then apologize. He said horrible things to you. Did that stop you from loving him?"

"No."

"So, what are you going to do about it?"

Caila had a pretty good idea of where she would start.

She got up and gave Ava a hug. "I love you. Thank you for giving me a much-needed kick in the ass. I'll be happy to return the favor."

Ava waved a hand. "Oh please, I'll never need it. I have my shit together."

"Uh-huh. I have a lot to do, or else we'd get into it about that statement."

"Bring it," Ava said, lifting her glass of wine. "I'll be ready."

THREE DAYS LATER, Caila exited the elevator and pushed through the large etched-glass door that led into Endurance's main marketing department. Shoving her hands into the pockets of her black high-waisted, wide-legged dress pants, she strode past curious stares, whispered asides, and the boxes sitting atop Diane's desk, to enter her old office.

When Kendra had finally called her in to discuss Bradleton, Caila hadn't known what to expect, but she hadn't anticipated facing the entire board, sitting across from her in the conference room like an executive firing squad. They'd spent several minutes running through the events of the past few months that had landed her before them.

"Frankly," one of them had concluded, "with all of these issues, why should we give you the promotion?"

She'd stared him in the eye. "With all due respect, sir, you're not *giving* me anything. I've worked my ass off for this company. And, as my report shows, I'm continuing to do so. You could close the plant in Bradleton and save some money, but that's short-term thinking. I believe I've laid out a plan that's better for Endurance long-term and situates us exactly where we should be in this new global marketplace."

Shaking off the recollection, Caila sat at her desk and turned on the computer. Then she pulled her phone from her pocket and placed a quick call.

"Any reason you're not FaceTiming me?" Ava's curious voice blared out of the speaker.

"I only have a minute and I'm multitasking."

"How'd it go?"

"Great!" The excitement at the unexpected outcome still sparkled in her chest. "You're talking to the new director of marketing for the entire cosmetics division!"

Ava squealed. "Oh my God! Congratulations!"

"Thanks!" Caila logged on to Endurance's travel portal and began requesting the accommodations she needed.

"Are you going to call Nic and Lacey or do you want me to do it?"

"Do you mind?" Caila asked, typing in some last-minute instructions before logging off. "I'll send out a group text in the next week or so, but I have something to take care of first."

"Wyatt?" Ava guessed.

"Yeah. I can't believe this is happening." Caila sat back in her chair and shook her head as the beautiful irony of it all washed over her. "For the second time, I'm leaving behind my life in the big city to go to a small town."

Ava laughed knowingly. "Because of a man."

Caila smiled, having finally understood the real reason behind the move all those years ago . . . and this one now.

"No. For love."

Chapter Twenty

Exhausted, Wyatt ran a hand through his hair. In the days following the Harvest Ball, he'd gotten little to no sleep as he'd worked to extinguish one fire after another.

Once he'd known the truth about Caila and the plant's future, he'd met with Nate and Joe to discuss their options.

It wasn't good.

For the time being, Chro-Make still had a contract with Flair that needed to be fulfilled. They didn't know when the deal with Endurance would go through, but it was only a matter of time. Until they had confirmation, it was business as usual.

Wyatt had called a town council meeting and informed them they probably had six months to a year until Chro-Make no longer had the Flair contract. Without it, roughly a third of Bradleton's citizens would lose their jobs. If they didn't want to be another small town sacrificed on the altar of big business, they needed to find a way to replace the lost revenue.

The council had worked for hours. They'd discussed how to draw new businesses to town and the types of business they should target. They looked at how to put forth the most attractive offer, including their prime location—being close to D.C. and Richmond, but with less expensive property prices—and their willingness to offer incentives.

It was going to be hard, but Bradleton was worth saving. Wyatt had taken his eye off the ball for a while and had gotten caught up in what he wanted instead of what the town needed, and now the town was paying the price.

His doorbell rang and he frowned. It was almost midnight. Who'd be visiting him now?

For a second, he thought it might be Caila and his heart leaped in his chest, before he tamped it down with a firm hand. She wouldn't come here. Not after everything they'd said to each other.

Being without her was even worse than he'd ever imagined. He'd gone his whole life not knowing her. And in the span of a few weeks, she'd turned his world upside down. Memories of her were everywhere. In his house, at the diner, around town. It drove him crazy.

He answered the door, surprised to see Dan standing on the porch.

"Is everything okay? Is my mother or grandfather—"

"No, no. Everyone's fine," Dan reassured him, holding his palm out. "This isn't a professional visit. Can I come in?"

Wyatt sighed in relief and loosened his death grip on the door. "Of course. You want something to drink?"

He turned and headed into the kitchen, knowing his friend would follow.

"It's late and I shouldn't . . . hell, you twisted my arm. I'll take a beer."

Wyatt laughed. "Yeah, make sure you put some ice on that in the morning."

He pulled out two bottles, popped the caps off, and handed one to Dan.

"Thanks." Dan leaned against the counter and took a long swallow. "How are you?"

Wyatt scrubbed a hand over his face. "Tired."

Dan nodded. "It's been a long month since the Harvest Ball. You've been working yourself ragged trying to calm everyone down."

Wyatt shrugged. "I have to. It's my fault."

Dan paused in the act of lifting his bottle for another drink. "What's your fault?"

"What the town is going through. I let everyone down. I have to fix it."

"Blame advancing technology, the change in the economy, Nate being complacent with his business. But this isn't your fault. Caila—"

His lungs constricted, making it hard to breathe. "I don't want to talk about her."

"Why not?"

"Because I don't need to rehash it. It's done. She came here, she lied, she used me. It's over."

"I thought giving you some time to get past the hurt and think about everything would be helpful. Instead, you've settled deeper into your resentment. Laura told me I should've talked to you immediately, but I gave her the men-need-time-to-process-their-emotions speech. Thanks for making me look like an ass."

"That's all you." Wyatt sighed. "Look, I don't know why you're here, Dan. Go home. Be with Laura. I'm fine."

"You're the least fine that I've ever seen you. Caila didn't come here to use you. She didn't even know you. She came to do her job. And as much as I don't like what that job was, it had nothing to do with you."

He flinched. "How can you say that?"

"It was your idea to pay Joe to stay out of town longer, so she'd be forced to remain here and get to know the town. And you could've delegated that job. Any number of people could've shown her around. But you did it. Because you wanted to. I was there the first time you guys met. I saw the way you looked at her. You wanted her from the jump."

"I did. And look where it got me. I put what I wanted above the needs of others and almost ruined everything."

Just like his father.

"You're conflating the two issues. Yes, the factory losing the contract sucks. But it was going to happen. If they hadn't sent Caila, they would've sent someone else. They'd already made up their minds. In fact, because it was Caila and because of the connection the two of you had, you probably had a better chance of getting them to reconsider. Do you think that Gerald Thorpe would've given you the benefit of the doubt?"

He scuffed the toe of his shoe against the bare floor. "No."

"And all of that is separate from the issue of Caila and how you feel about her. You deserve to be happy. And when you were with her, you were happy. Happier than I've ever seen you. Do you love her?"

Did lumber turn into furniture in his hands? "Yes."

Dan punched Wyatt's arm. "Then tell her that."

"What if she doesn't feel the same way?"

"I was there, remember? At Turk's when you met, at the football game, at the bonfire, and at the Harvest Ball. She loves you."

The Harvest Ball.

Wyatt replayed their conversation and the things he'd said to her.

"She'll never forgive me."

Dan smiled. "Yes, she will. Because you've already forgiven her. And if you get desperate, just remember, you're Mayor McHottie. Try turning on that devastating charm you're known for."

THERE!

With a flourish, Wyatt signed the last document in the folder. He didn't think he would ever be done. He'd stopped by the office to tie up a few loose ends and return some phone calls before he left for the airport.

He was heading to Chicago. To Caila. Granted, he didn't know where she lived, but he knew where she worked, and he intended to go there and get her to listen to him. He loved her. And he needed to see if there was any chance for them to be together.

"Wyatt Asher Bradley IV, I want to talk to you. Now!"

Wyatt's head jerked back as his grandfather strode into his office, brackets carved on either side of his mouth. He didn't know the last time his grandfather had visited him at city hall. In fact, Wyatt couldn't remember the last time his grandfather had visited him anywhere. When Asher wanted to see him, he usually summoned Wyatt to the house.

"Grandfather. What are you doing here?"

"Is that all you have to say to me? Your mother and I haven't seen you in weeks!"

He hadn't been back since the night of their disastrous dinner with Caila.

Wyatt sighed. "I've been busy. As you know, a lot has happened."

"It has. But that woman is gone and this sulking is beneath you. We need to get back to focusing on your future."

Wyatt stared at his grandfather. He'd never considered how tough it must've been for Asher. The heaviness of his burden. He'd spent his entire life carrying on the Bradley legacy, and when the time came to pass it on, his son had bailed.

But instead of learning from what had happened with Tripp, Asher had doubled down with Wyatt and firmed his grip, thinking that would keep him in line.

And Wyatt had allowed it.

Because Caila had been right. He'd been afraid. Tripp's selfishness and failures had been drilled into Wyatt since he was a little boy. He didn't want to risk alienating the only family he had with the notion that he might be exactly like the man they seemed to despise.

But Wyatt wasn't like Tripp. And he wasn't like Asher. He was his own man. And he had to live his life in the way that was best for him.

He looked at Asher. "I love you and I'm grateful for everything you've done for me. It couldn't have been easy, but you did it and you instilled some wonderful values in me. But"—he reinforced his words and his spine with titanium; he didn't want there to be any misunderstanding between them in the future—"I'm not a little boy and I won't tolerate or accept being spoken to as such. Do you understand?"

Asher's jaw worked and his hand flexed on the table. They stared at each other for a long moment before Asher gave a brisk nod.

"As for my future, I will always welcome any advice you offer, but that's all it'll be. Advice. Not dictates."

"Dammit, Wyatt—"

Wyatt shook his head. He would've gotten around to this later, but since Asher was here, he didn't want to waste the opportunity. He glanced at his phone. Even with the possibility of missing his flight if he didn't leave soon.

"I'm not done. Despite myself, I think the idea of being governor is intriguing. There's a lot of good I can do at that level, but right now, I'm the mayor of Bradleton and I intend to focus on that job. And if my constituents see fit to reelect me next year, then I'll continue to hold the office and fulfill my duties to the best of my capabilities. This is my town and I'm not ready to let it go without a fight. Now"—he stood—"I really do have to go. I'll come by and see you both when I get back."

"Where are you going?"

"To Chicago."

"For that woman," Asher said, his disapproval obvious.

"Yes. For Caila, and I'd advise you not to speak about her—"

His cell phone rang and Vince's name flashed across the screen.

Fuck! Wyatt didn't have the time or patience to deal with Vince. He declined the call, only to have it ring two seconds later, Vince's name flashing again.

"Dammit!" He accepted the call. "This had better be go—"

"You need to get down here," Vince said, his voice frantic.

Wyatt frowned. "I'm on my way to the airport."

"I don't care where you're going. You need to get down to Chro-Make right away. There's some trucks and town cars parked in front of the building. I thought you said we had time—"

Wyatt disconnected the call.

"I have to go," he told Asher, as he rounded his desk.

"We're not done here."

"I'll talk to you when I get back."

Ignoring Asher's sputtering and exaggerated outrage, Wyatt hurried to his car and headed over to the plant. On the way, he tried calling Nate several times, only to have his calls go straight to voice mail.

What the fuck was going on?

He pulled into the parking lot and found that for once, Vince was right. In addition to the cars of the employees working their shifts, there were a few construction trucks and a couple of luxury vehicles he didn't recognize.

Vince ran up to him as he exited his car. "Do you know what's going on?"

"No, but I intend to find out."

He strode up to the front of the building, but the door opened before he could get there and Nate strode out, talking to a man Wyatt didn't recognize.

"—not using that space, so there's plenty . . . Mayor, hey . . . hold on," he said to the guy, before rushing over to Wyatt.

Wyatt jammed his hands on his hips. "Nate, what's going on?"

"Great news. In fact, I was just getting ready to call you." His smile stretched ear to ear on his thin face. "We won't have to close down the plant!"

"What are you talking about?"

"We're not going to lose the Flair contract. In fact, in addition to producing Flair products, we're going to start manufacturing more of Endurance's products."

Wyatt looked at Nate. "I don't understand. When did you find this out?"

Nate jerked his thumb over his shoulder. "Just now. Caila told me."

Wyatt looked up and saw Caila step out of the building and stand just beside the door, her hands clasped in front of her. Just like the first time, she took his breath away. His legs ate up the distance between them until he was standing before her.

"Wyatt, I'm so sorry."

He gathered her into his arms and held her tight, shuddering as he realized how close he'd come to never holding her again.

"Aren't you mad at me?" she asked against his chest.

"No." He pressed a kiss to her hair, wishing they were somewhere private, so he could kiss her the way he wanted. "It doesn't matter. You're here. We can deal with everything else."

"I'm so glad you said that. That's why I came." She pulled away from him. "Did Nate tell you?"

"The main point," he said, his eyes skimming over her features, drinking them in. Was it possible she was even more beautiful than he remembered? "You tell me the rest."

"Endurance has decided to continue its acquisition of Flair Cosmetics and honor the contracts Flair had with its co-packers."

That sounded promising, but—"Nate mentioned something about manufacturing more products?"

She nodded. "Endurance doesn't manufacture its own products. We use several co-packers around the world. I convinced them that in the interest of streamlining our process and strengthening our brand, it might be better to bring as many products in-house as possible, to cut down on costs and to present uniformity. Once they saw the benefits of that idea, I told them I knew of a plant that had good bones but needed a little overhaul."

"A partnership," Nate said, coming up to stand next to them. "They're going to invest money in the business, which I'll use to overhaul our machines and get up to date with the latest advancements in the field. For that, they'll own thirty percent of the company. Then we'll both have a stake in this relationship working."

Caila continued. "As our other co-packing contracts end, Endurance will be able to begin fulfilling them in-house, here, instead."

"So that's what all these trucks are here for."

"Yes. Just looking at the building and the property. Getting some initial measurements and an inventory of what they have on-site right now," Caila said.

Wyatt's heart still hadn't settled from his mad dash here and seeing her again. "I thought they were closing the plant down now."

"No."

Nate was so happy, he could barely stand still. "That means no one is going to lose their job. In fact, we're going to have to hire more people as we start running shifts twenty-four seven. Excuse me."

He headed back to the man he'd been talking to.

"It should also mean better paying jobs," Caila added. "Some of this new equipment is specialized and will require additional training. Hopefully, you'll be able to attract a younger, more upwardly mobile workforce, who will buy houses and pay taxes. Stimulate the local economy."

"How did you convince them to do this?"

She waved a hand. "It was easy. I pointed out it wouldn't look good to have to deal with the PR backlash when they were on the verge of announcing the merger and rolling out a new product."

"What backlash?"

"Oh, you know the media can be relentless when they get a whiff of stories about another small-town plant closing, and corporations favoring profits over investing in the country. Add to that the lure of Southern royalty and this story would've led morning talk shows for weeks to come. Even spawned some documentaries. Or maybe a movie, starring Christian Bale or Tom Hanks, depending on the tone."

He laughed. "We weren't planning to do any of that."

She shrugged. "They didn't know that. And to them, I'm the expert on Bradleton. They seem to think I may have an in with the mayor."

Damn, her intelligence and shrewdness were a complete turn-on.

"But it only worked because it made financial sense, too. In the long term, it's a win for everyone."

He cupped her cheeks in his hands. "You are amazing. Why did you do all of this?"

"Because it was the right thing to do. And because I know how important this town is to you. Wyatt"—she gripped his wrist—"I'm so sorry for what I said. You're not a coward. You're strong and brave and—"

"No, you were right. I wasn't being truthful with my family, for the exact reason you said. But I've taken steps in the right direction. They'll always be my family, but I don't need to feel smothered by their expectations any longer."

"All of this made me rethink my issues with my mother. We've had some good conversations, some much-needed conversations, and I'm heading up to visit her when I'm done here."

Done here . . .

"Caila, I love you. In fact, I was on my way to Chicago when Vince called me in a panic and told me to come here."

"You were?" Confusion clouded her expression. "But you didn't know about this. As far as you knew, the plant was going to lose the contract."

"You were doing your job. And whether it was you or someone else, Endurance would've still wanted to get out of their contract with Chro-Make. But only you could've done what you did." He exhaled. "So if we need to be in a long-distance relationship, then that's what we'll do. I can't leave; this town is going to need me, especially with what's going to be happening in the future."

Her dark eyes sparkled. "That's the best part. It doesn't have to be. This is a massive project and Endurance is going to need someone to oversee it and the brand. And that someone is me! I got the promotion!"

"That's wonderful," he said. And he meant it. Even though it likely implied one of them would have to make a difficult decision down the road.

She raised a brow. "You don't sound very enthusiastic."

"No, I am, I just don't see how that makes a long-distance relationship any better."

"I wasn't finished," she said, a smile teasing her lips. "We're looking at a two- to three-year initial time frame, and for that period I'll need to be on-site, which means living here."

To hell with an audience. He captured her lips and felt his world shift back into focus and settle back onto its axis.

"I'm glad you approve," she murmured when they drew apart. "I'll still have to fly back to Chicago a couple times a month—"

"I don't care. I'll take it. I love you."

"I love you, too. Which is good, because this could've been extremely awkward if it didn't work out."

He laughed and kissed her again. "I have something for you."

He raced over to his car, where he'd put the bag he'd packed for his trip, and grabbed the parcel from inside.

She smiled. "A gift?"

She opened the package and gasped at the wooden box, about the size of a hardback novel, nestled within the tissue paper.

"You made this?"

He nodded.

"And you used the Olivia Pope wood?"

He had. Just for her.

"It's your new dream box, like the one your father gave you that you had to leave behind."

"Oh, Wyatt. This is beautiful."

She lifted the latch and opened it to reveal a red velvet-lined interior . . .

And a small black jewelry box.

She stilled. "Uh, Wyatt, I love you, but we've only known each other a short time."

"Just open it."

She did. A necklace with two entwined hearts encased in diamonds winked up at them.

"So that no matter where you are, our hearts will always be together."

Chapter Twenty-One

Three Months Later

To: Ava Taylor <ATay@gmail.com>; Nicole Allen
   <NicAl@gmail.com>; Lacey Scott <Lasc@gmail.com>
From: Caila Harris <CAHarris@us.Endurance.com>
Date: February 20, 2020
Subject: The Ladies of Lefevre Annual Vacay

Ladies—

Last year was extremely difficult for me,
between losing Pop-Pop and almost losing my job.
But in the midst of all of that darkness, I met the
love of my life. At the time, I wondered why these
things were happening, but—like that fateful day
we all met back in college—I know things happen
for a reason.

I can't wait for all of you to meet Wyatt, but us
being together will not change anything. My time
with you is sacred and I'm never giving that up.

Which brings me to the point of this email. It's
that time of the year again, y'all: vacay!

Since it's my turn to plan, we're going to do this in a methodical fashion. (Shut up, Nic!) Unlike checking the safest places in the past year (Ava), suggesting the place she last heard about (Nic), or consulting a Tarot reader (Lacey), I've made a list of three destinations. Rank 1–3 in order of your preference. The place with the lowest total ranking score wins. Let's not take forever to send these back, please. A week is plenty of time. (Looking at you, Lacey.) Once we've chosen the destination, I'll begin looking at accommodations.

I don't know what I'd do without you, ladies. You all are my lodestars, my inspirations, and the people who keep me grounded. You have my back and you know I will always have yours. Any time you need me, anywhere you are. Can't wait until we're all together again, talking, laughing, and sipping on one of Lacey's potent concoctions.

Here's to best friends who ride or die and our next vacay!

Love,
Caila

Don't miss the next outrageously fun
Girls Trip novel from Tracey Livesay,

LIKE LOVERS DO

Available from Avon Books
Summer 2020

Next month, don't miss these exciting new love stories only from Avon Books

A Hero Comes Home by Sandra Hill

After being held prisoner for three years in an Afghan prison, Jake Dawson is finally going home—except everyone, including his wife Sally and young sons, believed he was dead. As summer winds down, all the folks in Bell Cove are pulling out all the stops to get Jake and Sally together again for a Labor Day Love Re-Connection . . .

Wicked Bite by Jeaniene Frost

Veritas spent most of her life as a vampire Law Guardian. Now, she's about to break every rule by secretly hunting down the dark souls that were freed in order to save Ian. But the risks are high. For if she gets caught, she could lose her job. And catching the sinister creatures might cost Veritas her own life.

Never Kiss a Duke by Megan Frampton

Sebastian, Duke of Hasford, has discovered the only thing that truly belongs to him is his charm. An accident of birth has turned him into plain Mr. de Silva. Now, Sebastian is flummoxed as to what to do with his life—until he stumbles into a gambling den owned by Miss Ivy, a most fascinating young lady, who hires him on the spot. Working with a boss has never seemed so enticing.

REL 0120

At Avon Books, we know your passion for romance—once you finish one of our novels, you find yourself wanting more.

May we tempt you with ...

- **Excerpts** from our upcoming releases.

- Entertaining **extras**, including authors' personal photo albums and book lists.

- Behind-the-scenes **scoop** on your favorite characters and series.

- **Sweepstakes** for the chance to win free books, romantic getaways, and other fun prizes.

- Writing **tips** from our authors and editors.

- **Blog** with our authors and find out why they love to write romance.

- **Exclusive content** that's not contained within the pages of our novels.

Join us at
www.avonbooks.com